RIVER

When, like Ruth and Roger Mallard, you inherit a large house but no money to keep it up, one thing you can do is turn it into a guest house. And having made up their minds, the Mallards decided that River Lodge was to be a guest house of the very best kind.

The first week's guests were specially chosen—or self-invited: a rich aunt; a theatrical producer and the lovely Felicity; Felicity's sister and her twins; a famous artist and the amiable 'Goosey'; the fattest dog in fiction; and a not-so-rich but very comic uncle and aunt; these make up the list of guests at River Lodge's inauguration. With them comes an element of discord in the person of Roger's brother Paul, who casts an uneasy shadow over the forthcoming engagement between Felicity and her producer. Oddly enough, the well-meaning interference of the other guests does not seem to help matters. In fact, there is trouble. But it is not disastrous, and by the time the first guests have left River Lodge several matters have worked out to the entire satisfaction of the Mallard family, whatever anyone else might think.

Once again Elizabeth Cadell reveals her flair for elegant comedy. Her intensely individual characters, with all their foibles acutely observed, and the wit and charms with which she guides them through their summer storms, are in the true tradition of the English humorous novel.

RIVER LODGE

By
ELIZABETH CADELL

ROBERT HALE · LONDON

© Elizabeth Cadell 1948 and 1978
First published 1948
This edition 1978
Reprinted 1979
Reprinted 1982

ISBN 0 7091 6677 x

Robert Hale Limited
Clerkenwell House
Clerkenwell Green
London EC1R 0HT

Printed and bound in Great Britain by
The Garden City Press Limited, Letchworth, Hertfordshire SG6 1JS.

CHAPTER I

RUTH MALLARD came out of the house into the pleasant September sunshine and stood hesitating at the top of the three circular steps which led to the drive. She glanced dubiously at her feet, clad in the lightest of sandals, and then stepped down on to the gravel and walked until the drive curved and hid the house from view.

She stopped and, turning, went slowly back until the building was in sight once more. She approached it deliberately, her eyes taking in its charm and graciousness and the beauty of its setting, while her mind attempted to accustom itself to the idea of ownership. She walked round the house and stood on the terrace, her head back, her hands clasped loosely behind her, and studied the line of windows overlooking the lawn.

Her husband, on his way into the house with an armful of tools, passed her with an absorbed air. At the door leading into the library he paused and frowned, looking backward over his shoulder, as if to assure himself that he had seen his wife standing staring aimlessly at the bedroom windows. He watched her for a few moments and then spoke with a touch of irritation.

" Something wrong? " he asked.

Ruth continued to stare intently at the house, and answered without taking her eyes from it.

" I'm trying to see it with a stranger's eye," she said. " I walked down the drive as far as the bend and then came back with a blank mind trying to imagine how the first glance would affect all those people when they come to-morrow. I think it's lovely."

" I see," said Roger Mallard. " Well, you're wasting your time. You own the place—or I do, which comes to the same thing, so you can't study it with the necessary

5

jaundiced outlook. You haven't got to pay anything for staying here, and they have, so it's no use walking up and down a stony drive in those silly shoes saying it's lovely. You've got to come up to it, as they will, saying, ' Am I going to get my money's worth? '"

" Well, they are," said Ruth. " Have you ever stayed in a guest-house where there was practically a bathroom apiece? "

" No—and I've never stayed in a guest-house which is going to charge as much as this one is," said her husband. " I don't want to spoil your simple pleasures," he went on, " but may I point out that this is the last day and we're expecting a houseful of clients to-morrow, and there's a hell of a lot to get through."

" This," pointed out his wife, " is the first time I've stopped for weeks, and my department is practically running already. If you want any help——"

" I do," said Roger unhesitatingly. " You can come in and help me to fix these blasted rods on the back staircase."

Ruth followed him and sat on a stair below him holding rods and passing tools, her eyes on him as he worked. Nothing in the world gave her greater pleasure than looking at her husband.

Roger Mallard was thirty-two, seven years older than his wife. After five years of marriage she still thought him incomparably the best-looking and most attractive man she had ever seen. She liked almost everything about him—his great height and breadth and his quiet manner. She pitied with all her heart women who owned, ordinary humdrum husbands whose physical shortcomings were embarrassingly obvious when they stood beside hers, and she admired the brave way in which the wives concealed their chagrin.

She liked Roger's disposition. He was not, she admitted, an easy man to live with; he was quick-tempered and irritable and often wore a scowling, almost sullen expression. She saw nothing in his frowns, however, but a justifiable impatience at the foolishness of others, and was content to ignore them and remember only his lighter moods.

Above all, she liked his acumen, which had made him aware, at the first moment of their meeting, that here was the perfect wife for him. They had met at a dance and he had been, it seemed to her, surrounded by women with far more beauty and charm than herself. Across their heads he had seen her—slim, small, brown-eyed and shy. He had detached himself from the beauties around and had walked across the room and into her life. . . . Five perfect years of marriage, and many more to come. . . .

There was, she admitted with a pang, one small cloud —there were, so far, no little Mallards. Ruth was aware of Roger's deep disappointment. Lately he had not mentioned children, but she noticed that he frowned more often and more deeply and was frequently irritable without apparent cause. She understood his despondency, but thought it far too early to lose hope. There would be babies in good time. . . .

She handed up the last stair-rod absently, her expression dreamy, and her thoughts busy with the changing fashions in bringing up children. Nowadays parents were beginning to——

"What," enquired Roger, "are you looking so earnest about?"

Ruth found that he had finished and was seated on the stair by her side.

"Nothing in particular," she answered. She looked at him with a frown for a few moments and then spoke again.

"Roger," she asked, "you don't feel—now that it's actually here, I mean—you're not sorry you're doing it, are you?"

"No," said Roger promptly. "It isn't a profession I'd have chosen, exactly—guest-house-keeping—but I'm not at all sorry and I'm going to make a hell of a lot of money out of it—I hope. After all," he pointed out, "the idea isn't new. Ever since I was twenty and Uncle

Jake first asked me here, I said to myself, 'Well, if he ever leaves it to me, I'll turn it into a kind of hotel.' It was so obviously suitable for that sort of thing—all those bathrooms and all those bedrooms—not too large and not too small—and all those rooms downstairs. It would take an income of God knows what to live in it by ourselves." He turned and looked at her curiously. " Why did you start this? " he asked. " Are you worrying about money? "

" Not exactly," said Ruth. ." It would have been nicer if he'd left you a bit of money as well, but it's no use thinking about that. I don't think I'd have felt so—so safe about it if you hadn't brought Brenda in."

At the mention of his cousin, Roger's frown reappeared. " She's a damned annoying woman at times," he said irritably. " Sometimes I wonder how I'll stand seeing so much of her—but we're lucky to have someone to run the money side of it efficiently. By the way," he went on, rising, " she's coming back on the six whatever it is—she rang up—and she wants someone to take the van down to the station—she's got a whole train-load of parcels."

" I'll go," promised Ruth. " She'll be tired—she left the house before I was up."

" You look tired yourself," commented her husband. " You're not overdoing it, are you? There's a hell of a lot of work . . ."

" There was," corrected Ruth. " I'm through most of mine. I'll fetch Brenda, have a large dinner and then go to bed."

At a little after six, Ruth drove the small van into the station yard and found that the train was in. She saw a tall, thin figure at the door of a carriage pulling out parcels and handing them backwards to a waiting porter. Ruth went to the carriage door and watched the pile increasing steadily.

" I think that's the lot," said Miss Mallard, addressing the occupants of the carriage. " Oh—thank you—yes, those two are mine—up on the rack—and that—no, that isn't mine—or is it?—Oh! It's yours? I'm so sorry. Well, that must be the lot. Thank you so much. Good-bye."

She withdrew her head, closed the door, and turned, seeing Ruth for the first time and giving her a smile of welcome.

"Here you are," she said. "Look at that collection of stuff. I went without lunch and tea and shopped steadily for seven hours and I never want to see a shop again. Did you bring the van?"

"I did," said Ruth, walking out to it. "Roger told me you'd rung up."

"He said he'd come himself," said Brenda, "but I suppose the lazy hog is sitting in a warm bath and pretending he's exhausted."

"He isn't sitting anywhere," said Ruth. "He's fixing the pelmet in the dining-room and looking awfully tired."

"You're looking pretty done, yourself," said Miss Mallard. "We'll all have to go to bed early or the reception committee'll scare the guests away in the morning. Any news about any of them?" she asked.

"Yes. My uncle rang up—he and my aunt can't come until the day after to-morrow," said Ruth. "Neither can Paul."

"Who's coming first?" enquired Brenda.

"First?" repeated Ruth, steering the van through the little town. "Oh! I think Aunt Ella."

Brenda groaned. "What a start to a hopeful venture!" she exclaimed. "Throw open the doors with a flourish and admit Lady Warne—Aunt Ella."

"It wasn't Roger's idea," began Ruth. "It——"

"Oh, I know," said Brenda. "Nothing could have kept her out. She wouldn't come to my christening—or to Roger's or to Paul's—and she wouldn't come to Roger's wedding. And never, from the time we were born, has one of us ever received a single penny from her, but now—because we've turned her late brother's house into a guest-house, we find that curiosity is stronger than affection. She can't wait to find out how we've arranged everything. It would have been difficult, I suppose," she ended, " but I do think that Roger ought to have made a stronger effort to ward her off."

" Is she really so frightful? " asked Ruth. " I've never seen her, of course, but I could never understand why Roger's father and your father were so nice and the other brother and sister such—such——"

" Stinkers is the word," said Brenda. " I don't see," she went on, " that there's anything odd about it. Families often do differ in that way. It's quite certain that Uncle Jake Mallard, God rest his soul, and Ella Warne, *née* Mallard, can go down to posterity as the world's meanest man and woman. I don't think either of them, rolling in the stuff as they were, ever gave away a penny. I'm ashamed of being related to them, but when you come to look at it in cold blood—which is the way they look at it—you can see their point of view. You see, they all started off equal. Jake and Ella went on piling up money, and my father and Roger's simply spent all theirs and never made any more. Perhaps it isn't quite fair to call the other two mean just because they wouldn't support their brothers' orphans. But it's a bit of a record, all the same—Roger didn't even get a cheque when you were married, did he? "

" Well, Aunt Ella sent those two chairs," said Ruth, turning into the drive and drawing up before the house.

" So she did," acknowledged Brenda. " What a good thing you've still got them. I must make a point of leading her round by that entrance and pointing them out to her."

The two women, helped by a neat maiden in a pretty pink overall, carried the parcels into the hall and arranged them on the table. Brenda looked after the pink overall with a doubtful expression as the maiden, her task over, tripped away.

" It's a pretty pink," she said, " but I think the over-alls are a mistake."

" I know," acknowledged Ruth. " Roger loathes them

—he says it makes us look like a hairdresser's. But it wasn't worth losing two maids over. When I went to see Mrs. Hyde she said, ' Yes, you can both come, but, No Uniform—only overalls.' I pictured something white."

" No, that would have looked a bit clinical," said Brenda. " We're lucky to have two good girls living on the place, with a gardener father and an occasional-help mother. Is the grocer's daughter in pale pink, too? "

" No—she's in pale green," said Ruth. " But the question of her transport is solved—her gentleman-friend drives the grocer's van and is going to deliver her every morning and take her home at night."

" I doubt it," commented Miss Mallard. " She doesn't look the sort that goes home at night." She went up the stairs and glanced at the clock in the hall. " Twenty minutes for a bath and a change," she said. " I'll do it. Pour me out a sherry, Ruth darling, will you? "

Ruth poured the sherry and had it ready for her cousin when, changed and refreshed, she came into the room which had been chosen as a private dining-room for the family. Brenda went to the small mirror over the mantelpiece and smoothed her greying hair.

" I meant to go into the hairdresser's," she said, " but there wasn't time. I want to have one of those bleaches that turns you an instant grey and saves all this slowly-silvering stage."

" You're too young to go grey," protested Ruth.

" Forty-one isn't too young to go anything," said Brenda. " I passed myself in one of those shop mirrors to-day, and thought ' My word, that woman's like my grandmother.' Where's Roger? " she asked.

" Here he is," said Ruth, as her husband entered. " Drink, Roger? "

" I'll get it," said Roger, going to the sideboard.

" That's because I'm here," said his cousin. " If I weren't, you'd sink into a chair and let Ruth bring it to you. If you ask me, I think your wife's looking washed out."

" I didn't ask you," said Roger from the sideboard.

"Don't start quarrelling, you two," said Ruth lazily. "Let's all relax."

"Relax?—I don't feel like relaxing," said Brenda. "I feel I'm on the edge of a long, slippery slope, and I'm not quite sure whether I'm going to enjoy sliding down it or not. After eleven years in this house while it was being run as a mausoleum, it's going to be a change to see it full of noisy strangers."

"Was it as long as eleven years?" asked Roger curiously.

"Almost to the day," said his cousin, leaning back in a deep chair and closing her eyes. "I was about thirty—I'd just given up hope of getting married and was feeling strangely relieved about it. But I'd never got used to life in a London office—after three years of it I was beginning to choke."

"Then what?" asked Ruth.

"Then I got home one evening to find Uncle Jake waiting for me," said Brenda. "He looked terribly old—I don't think I could have taken it on if I'd known how long he was going to live. He said he wanted me to come to River Lodge and take all his business affairs off his shoulders—resident-secretary post. He wanted to spend most of his time abroad and didn't want a stranger left in the house. He asked me what I was getting and I doubled it and he said he'd double that, and gave me twenty-four hours to think it over."

"And so you came," said Roger.

"Who's telling this story?" enquired his cousin. "I didn't come at all—I mean I didn't jump at the offer, though if you'd seen the pig-in-a-poke way I was living, you'd have wondered how I could have held out. But I said, 'Oh, no!' I knew that with a man as mean as Uncle Jake there was no question of a nice little codicil and a nest egg, and I wasn't going to live in a luxurious home for four or five years and then—when he died—get thrown back into my tenement, all that much older, and no more efficient. So I stipulated for a moderate fixed salary—the one I'd first thought of, doubled—and an absolutely legal, binding agreement by which I was to get a nice round sum if I worked for him for ten years. So it was his turn to take twenty-four hours chewing it over. He came back the next day and it was all done in a proper way. I suppose he thought he could easily get rid of me before the ten years were up, but later, I think he found me too useful. I liked the life, and I loved the house," she went on. "I was pretty certain he'd leave it to Roger—without any money, of course —but I didn't think you'd ask me to stay on and help to run a guest-house. I wish," she ended regretfully, "that you could have got Paul into it too."

"Paul?" echoed Roger. "What the hell could Paul have done? Put on a play for the residents once a week? Paul's an actor, not a worker."

"What's an actor without parts?" asked Brenda gloomily. "He hasn't had a part worth calling a part since he left Martin West. And that reminds me, Roger," she went on, sitting upright and looking at him. "It's too late to do anything, of course, but I don't like the list of guests at all. You've got a whole collection of misfits."

"I haven't got anything of the sort," replied Roger. "I couldn't help Aunt Ella."

"No," admitted Brenda. "But you've got Martin West and Felicity Grant and——"

"What's the matter with them?" asked Roger. "West is the biggest producer in London, and Felicity Grant is his leading lady——"

"Don't they call them stars nowadays?" put in Ruth.

"All right—star," said Roger, "and what's more, they're practically engaged. What's wrong with opening with a big producer and a star?"

"If you weren't a cold-blooded money-grabber," said his cousin, "you wouldn't, in the first place, have Martin West because Paul——"

"Because my brother happens to be in love with his fiancée," said Roger. "What's that got to do with it?"

"She isn't his fiancée yet," pointed out Brenda, "and

if you hadn't agreed to have them here together for a week, she probably never would have been. You've given him seven whole days to—to press his suit, and on top of that you invite Paul to watch him doing it. You must be out of your mind."

" I didn't," said Roger, speaking slowly and distinctly, " invite Martin West. I did ask Felicity to come, because Ruth wanted to see her again. When West heard Felicity was coming, he got hold of me one day in town and asked if he could come too. I said he could. Paul knew they were both going to be here, because you took care to tell him, and if there's any awkwardness about his being here too, it isn't my fault."

" No, I suppose not," acknowledged Brenda with un-wonted humility, " but the thought of Martin West do-ing a whole week of uninterrupted wooing was too much for me—and besides, I thought that if Paul could see Felicity again they could—well, make it up . . ."

" Well, you can have a nice busy week straightening it all out," said Roger. " I hope you'll have some time over for the General."

" Have you heard what time he's coming? " asked Ruth.

" No—perhaps he'll ring up to-night," said Roger. " Be funny to see the old boy again."

" I hope he won't talk about his regiment all the time," said Brenda. " Last time we met, his entire con-versation started off, ' Do you remember So-and-So who was Adjutant in '88, and old Whatnot, who commanded the Salukis.' I suppose he'll feel a bit upset when he sees you reduced from soldiering to hotel-keeping. Where exactly," she asked, " does it come in the social scale? "

" Oh, pretty low," said Roger. " Somewhere between the Pharisees and the skinners."

" Not bad, not bad," said Brenda, opening her eyes at this unusual attempt at a joke. " I must remember to bring that out some time. But first I'd like this time-table straight. To-morrow, Aunt Ella and possibly the General before lunch."

"And Martin West," said Roger. "He's going down to meet Felicity at three-ten, and then they're both going down after tea to meet the five o'clock and fetch Felicity's sister, Mrs. Hellier, and the twins."

"I think that's another mistake," said Brenda. "Nobody wants to come and stay anywhere where there are three-year-old twins popping in and out."

"Then they needn't come at all," said Roger. "If people want to bring children here, they can. The sort of people who want to avoid children are poor fish, anyhow, and we can do without them. And the children won't be popping about—they've got their own room on the ground floor and a nice bit of garden. Nobody but their parents need ever see them."

"No children ever stayed where they were meant to," said Brenda. "They can't read the notices for one thing. And I'm on the side of the poor fish—I don't see why you call them poor fish because they don't want to be annoyed by other people's children. But, of course," she added, "there's another side to it—I once travelled on one of those ships that won't let children on the upper deck, so the upper deck was a veritable haven of rest—lines of long chairs with be-whiskered occupants one end and pretty girls in shorts playing deck tennis the other. But downstairs there were forty-four children on what they called the nursery deck. When I went down the first time, I thought I'd be deafened for life. It was appalling—and those poor mothers had to stay down there the whole voyage and endure that inferno."

"It's tough on mothers," admitted Roger. "But Mrs. Hellier ought to be all right with only one pair of twins, and Felicity can give her a hand. If the mother's anything like what she was the last time I met her," he ended, "Felicity'll have to give both hands."

"Do you know her well?" asked Brenda, turning to Ruth.

"Not awfully," said Ruth. "She's a year younger than Felicity, which means she's three years younger than I am. Three years is a lot of difference at school—she was coming in as I was going out, and I didn't see much of her later, in London."

"Well, Aunt Ella, the General, Martin West, Felicity, her sister and the twins," summed up Brenda. "It's going to be quite a day." She stretched luxuriously, looked at her watch, and rose, glass in hand.

"I'm hungry," she said. "Dinner time." She raised her glass and looked at the others. "We ought to drink to the memory of Jake Mallard," she said. "He wouldn't have left it if he could have taken it, of course, but I suppose we do owe it to him—Uncle Jake."

"Uncle Jake," said Ruth and Roger, with glasses upraised.

CHAPTER II

THE following day, which everybody had hoped would be fine, with sunshine showing the house to the best advantage, began in a series of heavy showers which settled into steady and unceasing rain. Ruth, looking out after breakfast at the numerous little trickles on the drive, remarked that it would be obvious to the guests why the house was named River Lodge.

"Don't stand looking at the rain—come upstairs and tell me what you think of the General's rooms," said Brenda. "I'm rather sorry the old fellow's having a private sitting-room—he's not bad company on the whole. Any message from him yet?"

"None," replied Ruth. "I'll be working upstairs most of the morning," she went on. "Do I have to come down to greet Aunt Ella?"

"I shouldn't think so," said Brenda. "You can go and say 'How d'you do' when she's settled. I'm sorry she's such a nasty specimen of an aunt. What's yours like?" she enquired "—the one who's coming to-morrow."

"Oh, sweet," said Ruth. "Timid and a bit mousey."

"I see," said Brenda. "Well, Aunt Ella's bold and hippopotamousey—they ought to get on. I don't think I'm going to like this guest business," she went on with a serious note in her voice. Seriousness in Brenda was so unusual that Ruth looked at her curiously.

"You're worried," she said after a few moments. "You're worrying about Paul, aren't you?"

Brenda walked to the table on which the breakfast things still lay, and, picking up a fork, drew a series of rectangular diagrams on the table-cloth.

"Yes, I am," she said at last. "I know it's silly, but I can't help it. I think Roger worries too, although he won't admit it. When I met Paul a fortnight ago in Town, I thought he looked frightful—sort of drawn and peaked. I know he's behaving like a madman, but I suppose he's doing it out of his honest convictions and I can't see where it's all going to lead. I think the idea of having him in the same house with Martin West for a week, with things as they are between them, is pure lunacy." She put down the fork and faced Ruth. "Tell me," she asked, "is Paul right? Is Felicity really such a —such a rotten actress?"

Ruth was silent for some time, frowning thoughtfully. "I honestly don't know," she said at last. "In the first place I don't know anything about acting, and then I've known Felicity so long that I can't see her as anything but herself, if you see what I mean. When Roger and I saw her in that first play she was in, I remember asking him what he thought of her and he said he hadn't noticed her acting, but he thought she was the loveliest girl he'd ever seen. Everybody seemed to talk more about her looks than about her performance, but until Paul said she couldn't act, I don't think I ever heard anyone say anything, actually—what's the word? —derogatory."

"What made her take up acting if she can't act?" demanded Brenda.

"I don't know," said Ruth. "Her family have a great deal of money—she needn't have done anything. She

was the star diction pupil at school and she always took
the lead in all school plays—then when she left, I think
everybody said, ' Oh of course you'll go on the stage.'
I wasn't there—I left before she did, and I married
Roger and didn't see her until we were on leave and
took a flat in Town. Felicity was in the same block,
sharing a flat with her sister—Nan Hellier. Nan's husband had just gone to sea, and Felicity was studying at
that school of drama place." Ruth paused and gazed
dreamily out of the window. " It was a happy time,"
she went on musingly. " Martin West had just put on
his first production—it was Paul's first big part, and his
first success. Paul used to come round a lot—then he
met Felicity and of course after that he practically never
left the place."

" Who met her first—Paul or Martin? " asked Brenda.

" Oh—Paul," said Ruth. " Ages before. She and Paul
and Roger and I used to go everywhere together—Nan
used to do her best to make a fifth and Paul would ring
Martin up and say could he take a troublesome grass
widow off his hands, and get rid of her that way. I think
that if Paul had had the least bit of money then, he'd
have married Felicity, and then everything would have
been all right and none of this beastly business would
ever have happened."

" Well—go on," said Brenda. " I want to get the
details right before I take sides in the forthcoming
shambles."

Ruth gave a derisive grin at the thought of Brenda
being on any side but Paul's.

" There isn't much more," she said. " Martin came
in one night and met Felicity and he simply fell in love
—just like that—straight away. It was an extraordinary
thing—for a week or two he lost all his assurance—all
his usual ease of manner—and seemed quite lost. Then
he recovered—at least, he got his poise back, but not
his heart. And from that time the whole happy band
cracked up. You couldn't really see it happening, but
before we gave up the flat at the end of our leave, Martin

had offered Felicity a part in his next play and she'd
accepted and was seeing more and more of Martin and
less and less of Paul."

" Then what? " asked Brenda.

" Then nothing," said Ruth. " Things just got to the
point they're at now. Felicity didn't do too badly the
first time—she just had to be a lovely young girl and
she was, and everybody called her Martin West's dis-
covery or some drivel like that, and then Martin gave
her the lead in that play with Paul. Paul says—and I
believe him—that everything was magnificent—his part,
the play, Felicity's part. But she couldn't play it—he
said—and so instead of being a serious play well performed, it became just another show with an audience
content to let the acting go and—it's Paul's phrase, not
mine—and look at Felicity's lines instead of listening
to them. So Paul told her—very nicely, he said—to stop
trying to act and take up cooking and marry him. And
she didn't like that very much and neither did Martin
West and so Paul—got out."

" And the play went on very nicely without him,"
said Brenda bitterly, " and now everybody thinks that
he did it because he was jealous——"

" That's the worst part of it," said Ruth. " They think
he was jealous of Martin and of Felicity too—and I get
frightened sometimes because I think he won't ever get
back where—where he was."

" Martin West isn't the only producer in London,"
pointed out Brenda.

" No—o," said Ruth. " But Roger says these things
get about, and most people think Paul behaved rottenly."
She stopped, and, picking up a pile of letters, walked
to the door. " Don't let's talk any more about it," she
said. " Let's wait and see what happens when they come."

" I can tell you now," said Brenda. " I'm going to
pick a dark night and carve Martin West into pieces..."

Nothing of this sinister intent was visible on her
countenance, however, when she stood in the hall three
hours later and watched Martin West open the door of

his beautiful long car and step on to the gravel. He took out two suit-cases and, entering the house, glanced appreciatively round the charming hall and shook Brenda's hand.

"How d'you do, Miss Mallard?" he said. "It's a long time since we met—Roger's wedding, wasn't it? How is Roger?" he asked.

"He's very well indeed, thank you," said Brenda. "It's nice to see you—you're not wet, are you? It's poured here all the morning. Come in here, will you?" she went on, leading the way into the room which she used as an office.

Martin followed her, and throughout the brief formalities, Brenda, studying him with guarded interest, found herself with the same faint dislike of him that she had felt at their previous meeting. He was, she conceded, good-looking, well-mannered and extremely well groomed, but something in his air irritated her. She sought for a word to sum up her impressions, and decided that he was what her father would have called cock-a-hoop. There was a smoothness and assurance about him which antagonized her. She admired confidence, but thought it a quality which needed a little disguise or a little overlay of modesty. This man, she decided, was too superior by half, and she hoped she would see him brought down.

"I'll take you to your room," she said. "You're in Zambesi. The rooms are all named after rivers," she explained, as Martin raised his eyebrows enquiringly. "It wasn't Roger's idea—his uncle put in all those little name plates you'll see on the doors, and we felt it wasn't worth while having them taken out."

"Zambesi," said Martin thoughtfully. "It sounds a little warm. What's Miss Grant in?" he asked.

"Felicity? Oh, she's in Danube—blue, of course," said Brenda. "You're going down to fetch her after lunch, aren't you?"

"She'll be on the three-ten," said Martin, following her upstairs. "Am I the first arrival?"

"You are—but I think General Horder ought to be here before lunch," said Brenda. " Do you know him? "

" I know his son," said Martin. " The one they call Goosey—wasn't he in Roger's regiment? "

" He still is, though of course it isn't Roger's any more," said Brenda. " Goosey isn't coming, thank heaven—we've been spared that."

" Hello, Martin," called Roger from below. He came to the bottom of the stairs and waved a welcoming hand. " Glad to see you—come down and have a drink when you're ready."

Martin gave a cheerful reply and followed Brenda into his room. Roger turned from the stairs and paused at the sound of an approaching car. Going to the door, he opened it and looked out. Martin West's car still stood outside, and behind it another, and far less presentable vehicle had come to a standstill. It gave a series of machine-gun explosions, coughed and was silent. Two figures alighted and turned towards the front door, and at the sight of the foremost, Roger's brows came together in a black frown and he gave an exclamation of amazement and annoyance.

" Goosey! " he exclaimed. " What the hell are you doing here? "

Guy de Courcey Horder—known from earliest youth merely as Goosey—turned to his companion.

" There's a welcome for you," he remarked. " Together, man and boy, through innumerable campaigns, and look at his face. Put it there, Roger, old boy," he went on, extending a hand. " It's good to see that horrible scowl again. How's Ruth, and where? "

" Where's the General? " enquired Roger grimly.

" Papa? " said Goosey. " He's out. Gout." He raised a foot stiffly and indicated by a wave of his hands that it was swathed in imaginary bandages. " He can't come," he went on, " and as he'd got two rooms and I only sleep in one, I brought Felix along. You won't mind him, will you?—he's a harmless chap. Felix, this is Roger Mallard—fine chap, foul disposition." He paused and looked about him. " Where's Miss Mallard?" he asked. " She's here too, isn't she? "

Roger looked at the familiar face before him and found some of his anger evaporating. It was, he knew, impossible to make any impression on Goosey's bland good humour. Nobody, moreover, could be angry with a man who looked like an amiable seal. The likeness was ludicrous and was considerably heightened by the extraordinary moustache which sprouted, rather than grew, from Goosey's lip. His friends endured the growth only because he assured them that he looked much worse without it.

" Oh, I forgot to mention," said Goosey, " that Felix here is Felix Lenner—the fellow who does those Lenner mermaids—you know them."

" Of course I do," said Roger, looking with new interest at the gloomy-faced artist.

The Lenner mermaids were, indeed, well known. Everyone was familiar with the drawings depicting enchanting little figures playing everywhere but in the sea. They made disturbing appearances in the everyday affairs of prominent men. Impudent mermaids tickled the ears of a popular male vocalist, murmuring invitations to run down the scales. They posed prettily in a peer's dressing-room, enquiring whether his preference was a dinner jacket or tails. Nobody could be offended at the gambols of the pretty creatures—they provided a great deal of amusement for the public and much money for Mr. Lenner.

" Don't you have a reception desk or anything of that sort? " asked Goosey, looking round the hall.

" No. There's an office here," said Roger. " This way."

He led the newcomers towards the office and they followed, Goosey pausing to watch the passage of a trim maiden in a pink overall who was on her way to the dining-room.

" That's a nice little piece," he remarked admiringly. " Who thought of the pink——"

He stopped. A second maiden followed the first, and

Goosey's eyes opened to their widest extent with honest admiration and delight.

"Another one! " he exclaimed. " Did you see that? " He turned to Roger with a hopeful air. " I suppose," he said, " this is an hotel? "

"You'll know," said Roger grimly, " at the end of the week, when you get your bill."

"You can't frighten me," said Goosey, unmoved. " The old man's going to do this. I didn't fix the thing up, so I don't have to pay. I've got a lot of news for you, Roger," he went on. " Old faces, old places. D'you remember——"

" No," said Roger, " I don't. Do you want someone to take your car round? It oughtn't to stay there—it's in the way."

Goosey regarded him with concern.

" You've still got that nasty, short-tempered way of chewing a chap up, I see," he remarked without rancour. " He's got a hell of a temper," he explained to Felix, who looked more melancholy than ever at the news. " He had it as a boy, and——"

"Your car," repeated Roger.

" Oh, my car," said Goosey. " Well, if you've got a henchman who can push it round to the stables, then let it be pushed. It's the only way it'll go. And it isn't in the way at all—it's that other opulent-looking cabriolet that's choking up the gangway. Who runs that one? "

"Fellow called Martin West," said Roger.

" Martin West? You mean that big, good-looking chap that ushed with me at your wedding? " asked Goosey. " I remember him. I saw him recently coming out of one of those swell joints with that actress—what's her name?—the one in that show we went to," he said, turning to Felix.

Felix merely shook his head sadly.

" Felicity Grant—that's the one," said Goosey. " How does he meet people like that? " he enquired enviously. " D'you think he'll introduce me some time? "

"I'll do it myself," promised Roger. "She's coming this afternoon."

Goosey's face expressed a hope he scarcely dared to put into words. "Coming?" he said incredulously. "You mean coming, or coming to stay?"

"Coming to stay," said Roger. "Don't look like a performing fish. I'll take you up to your rooms and send your things up. There's no bed in the second room —I'll have one put in. Your father was going to use it as a sitting-room."

"Imagine—a private sitting-room with all those attractions downstairs," said Goosey incredulously. "The old man oughtn't to run away from life like that. I feel kind of warmed up," he told Roger gratefully. "Two pink overalls and Felicity Grant. Anything more to tell me?"

"Yes. You behave decently," warned Roger, "or I'll throw you out. It won't be the first time."

"No," said Goosey, with relish. "D'you remember——"

"No," said Roger. "I don't. You'll find a name on your door—the rooms are all named after rivers."

"That's a rum idea," said Goosey. "Oh—River Lodge—I see. What am I in? I can't write and tell my friends I'm in Seine—ha, ha, ha."

"That's not funny," said Roger. "It's been overworked, too."

"Well, I can't help that," said Goosey. "I thought of it all by myself. Is there a Mizzizzipi?"

"There's a St. Lawrence, and you're in it," Roger informed him. "You," he went on, turning to the silent Mr. Lenner, "are in Hudson, next door."

"Well, they both sound damn cold," commented Goosey. "Do the pink overalls bring my morning tea?"

"A man brings your morning tea," said Roger. "If you'd like him in a pink overall, just mention it to him. Lunch at one-fifteen," he ended, going to the door. "Drinks on the house to-day. Unless," he added, opening the door, "I catch you looking at the pink overalls."

"You won't catch me," promised Goosey.

Roger went downstairs and found that Goosey's car had been removed, while Martin West's stood a short distance from the front door. Brenda came into the hall and nodded towards the drive.

"I've had the decks cleared," she explained. "If my psychic reactions are working properly, dear Aunt Ella isn't far away. I think you'd better be here to receive her—she'll expect it."

Twenty minutes later, Roger heard the note of a car horn and went into the hall to greet his aunt. He nodded to the old chauffeur, and, opening the car door, offered his hand to the stout figure within. The process of alighting was a slow and difficult one—Lady Warne was not young, had never been of an active disposition and was now of a bulk which made swift or supple movement out of the question. She clambered out with her nephew's assistance and achieved the short ascent to the hall, where she stood looking about her. Roger waited beside her until she regained her breath, studying with a feeling of detachment the numerous chains and jewels adorning her stout person. There must, he calculated, be many hundreds of pounds twinkling on her ample bosom.

"You haven't changed anything, I see," remarked Lady Warne. "That was very wise. Have you given me Ganges, as I asked?"

"Yes, Aunt Ella," said Roger. "Brenda is in the office—will you come in?"

Lady Warne entered the office and greeted her niece without enthusiasm.

"I've brought Rameses with me," she said, taking the chair Roger offered her. "You'll make all the necessary arrangements for him, won't you?"

Brenda sent Roger a glance expressing clearly her opinion of her aunt's pet dog, and promised that the animal should have proper attention.

Roger answered the question his aunt had omitted to ask.

"Ruth's very well," he said. "She's looking forward

to meeting you—she'll come and see you when you're settled."

Lady Warne nodded with little interest. " Is Paul here? " she asked.

"He comes to-morrow," said Roger. " Shall I take you up, Aunt Ella? "

Lady Warne rose and, after looking at him for a moment, spoke in a slow and thoughtful tone.

" I think that as this is a purely business arrangement," she said, "we ought not to be too informal. I don't think that addressing me as Aunt Ella sounds very well under the circumstances. I should prefer to be on the same footing, shall we say, as the other guests."

There was a second's pause. Roger carefully avoided his cousin's glance.

"Yes, Lady Warne," he said. " Won't you come to your room? "

His aunt frowned.

" Don't be silly," she said irritably. " Of course you can call me Aunt Ella when we're by ourselves."

" Yes, Aunt Ella," said Roger. " I'll take you up."

He opened the door for her and she went through and waited for Rameses, who, having got comfortable on the hearthrug, was having difficulty in getting up again. Brenda watched his waddling gait, so like his mistress's, and, waiting until the party had mounted the stairs, went in search of Ruth.

" They're coming in nicely," she announced on finding her. " What," she went on irritably, " does Felicity Grant see in that man? I think he's a snake and I wish he really was in the Zambesi."

" Has Aunt Ella arrived? " asked Ruth.

" Yes, with pet dog," said Brenda. " One's got a black fur coat and the other's got a white fur coat. Aunt Ella's the two-legged one. We're not—she says—to call her Aunt Ella in public, so that saves us a certain amount of humiliation. And another thing," she went on, " the General isn't coming and he's sent Goosey instead."

Ruth laid down the linen she was counting and stared in amazement.

"Goosey—here!" she exclaimed. "Oh, I'm so glad. I must go and see him. Darling Goosey."

"That isn't what Roger said," Brenda told her. "He's brought a friend—that Lenner man—the artist who does the mermaids—you know."

"I know the one," said Ruth. "What's he like?"

"You should see him," said Brenda. "He must be earning thousands a year, and he's got a long face and a dreary expression, and he doesn't look as if he had any what they call intelligence quota at all. Just think," she went on, on a higher note. "Just think of all that work we did at school, adding up and taking it away again and trying to be intelligent—and look where we are. Now, if we'd only practised drawing mermaids all over our exercise books, we'd have been making our fortunes."

Ruth smiled. "We'll have to get him to make us a mermaid frieze in one of the bathrooms," she suggested.

"Mermaid freeze?—oh, I see what you mean," said Brenda. "That kind of frieze. No, I don't think it would be good for Roger. Well," she said, on her way to the door, "I'm feeling rather excited. We're soon going to be like one of those cinema plots, where——"

"I know," said Ruth. "Where unsuspecting guests come in at the front door while——"

"While unsuspecting corpses go out at the back," finished Brenda. "Well, I don't mind, as long as one of the corpses is Aunt Ella and the other——"

"I can guess," said Ruth. "Can't you see the head-lines?"

"I can," said Brenda grimly. "West goes West."

CHAPTER III

BRENDA'S dislike of Martin West took more definite shape when he knocked on her office door shortly before tea and ushered in Felicity Grant. The sight of the girl, fresh and smiling, and undeniably lovely, brought home to Brenda for the first time the knowledge of what Paul was losing, and made her heart ache.

She had seen little of the girl and, while prepared for her beauty, had not expected so delightfully natural and unaffected a manner. She had a vague idea that most actresses looked like actresses, and she had, therefore, expected something groomed to the last degree, with clothes of the type she sometimes studied with awe in the more expensive fashion magazines. Felicity Grant, in a simple tweed suit and loose coat, had a fresh and healthy appeal that surprised Brenda and made her dislike of Martin West rise almost to utterance point.

Nor was his attitude calculated to appease her. He spoke little, but his manner towards Felicity hovered between the protective and the proprietary. Brenda looked at her as often as she could do so unobserved, and noticed nothing in the girl's air beyond a quiet friendliness. She confessed to herself that she knew little about girls in love, but this certainly didn't look like one. Her spirits rose a little.

It was, she decided, upon reflection, going to be a gloomy week. Nothing could prevent Martin West from seeing all he wanted to of Felicity—he had ordered tea for two in the library, to the fury and disgust of Goosey Horder, who, with Felix, had been waiting in a fever of anticipation in the drawing-room. It was a neat beginning, indicating an expectation that the other guests would respect his rights. Meals, Brenda decided, were going to be difficult. A succession of intimate tête-à-têtes. Ruth was the only person who could have claimed

Felicity's attention, and she had her meals elsewhere.
Nan Hellier, the only other hope, would of course have
meals with her children in the large, pleasant room set
apart for them. She could join her sister at dinner,
Brenda reflected with more pleasure—that would make
an awkward party of three and cramp Martin West a
little.

She forgot her gloom in the excitement of greeting
the twins. They were both boys, so much alike as to
be indistinguishable—a pair of small, chubby, adorable
creatures, silent—almost stolid—with large eyes, brown
and serious and enquiring. They stood in the hall and
gazed earnestly at Brenda, and she knelt down and
greeted them with delight.

" They're sweet, aren't they? " said Felicity, who, with
Martin West, had led them into the house. " They
never talk much—they just stare, but they don't miss
much."

It was obvious that they missed nothing. Their
solemn gaze travelled slowly from Brenda's hair down
to her knees, and rose once more to her face to take in
any details left out in the first survey.

A childish, affected voice behind her made Brenda
turn. At the sight which met her eyes she rose, purely
for the purpose of getting a better view.

She had heard a good deal from Ruth and Roger
about Nan Hellier, and Paul had spoken of her once
or twice. From these comments Brenda had gathered
some details of Mrs. Hellier's peculiarities, but she was
quite unprepared for the combination of youthfulness
and sophistication standing looking up at her.

Nan Hellier was twenty-two and had been married
four years. In spite of these facts, and the two figures
standing solemnly in the middle of the hall, she looked
like an immature school-girl. Everything about her
heightened the illusion; she was very small and slight,
with short, curly hair, and large, rather staring blue eyes.
Her features were small and regular and her face totally
expressionless, with the hard and vacant look of a china

doll. Brenda found it impossible to believe that she was the mother of two children.

" I've heard about you," announced the newcomer in a high, confident tone. " You're Miss Mallard."

" I am," acknowledged Brenda. " How d'you do."

" I'm crushed. I'm finely powdered," stated Mrs. Hellier. " It was an *ag*-onizing journey. Ever since half-past two. And three e-*nor*-mous suit-cases and a rug, and the children's trunk which some porter told me was in the back van when it was in the front van, and a carriage full of imponderables and nobody to help me with the twins . . ."

" Who was the man holding Robert? " enquired Felicity.

" Oh—that? That was a peculiar old party who did sort of tricks with pieces of paper," said Mrs. Hellier. " The children liked it."

" I thought the old lady with the feather was going to get out," said Martin West. " I began to get her luggage out for her."

" Oh, no—she only got out to carry Jeremy," explained Mrs. Hellier. " She read them stories nearly the whole way—Piggy this and Piggy that, until we all nearly went mad. I couldn't *bear* it, but there wasn't any way of stopping it, so when the man in the corner offered to change seats with me I got comfortable and read my book. Do we have to stand here? " she went on without a pause, " or are there bedrooms and things? "

Brenda pulled herself together, sent Felicity upstairs with the twins, disposed of the luggage, and took charge of Mrs. Hellier.

" I'll take you up to your room in a moment," she said. " This "—she opened a door and stood aside—" is the downstairs playroom for the children."

" Is there anyone staying here with a Nannie? " enquired Mrs. Hellier hopefully.

" Nobody, I'm afraid," said Brenda.

" They're difficult to keep," commented Mrs. Hellier. " Mother prefers to manage without one. Mother adores the twins—I do think grandmothers are awfully useful nowadays, don't you? " she asked. " They used to be just old girls, and now they're simply marvellous—Mother absolutely runs the twins, but she had to have a rest for a week and so I came here."

" Do you like the room? " asked Brenda.

Mrs. Hellier studied it briefly and without interest.

" I don't have to like this one particularly, do I? " she enquired.

" Well, the twins won't be allowed into the drawing-room or the library," said Brenda, " and Roger thought they could have a lot of freedom here and in the garden."

" Oh, did Roger arrange it? " asked Mrs. Hellier. " Well, I must tell him that the idea was all right, but children don't always stay where you put them. At least, mine don't. You wait and see. If I leave them in here for a time they'll be all over the house exploring."

" Perhaps you could curb their enthusiasm for exploring while they're here? " suggested Brenda pleasantly.

Mrs. Hellier gave her a long, expressionless stare.

" Do you really mean," she asked finally, " that Roger thinks I'm going to shut myself in here with two babies so's nobody else need be bothered with them? "

" That wasn't——" began Brenda.

" I sit here," continued Mrs. Hellier, " reading about Piggy Piggy while everybody else enjoys themselves— is that it? "

" We thought——" tried Brenda again.

" You thought wrong," said Mrs. Hellier. " I always imagined Roger was stupid—but this is even stupider than that. If I'd wanted to sit and read Piggy Piggy to the twins, I could have stopped at home and done it, couldn't I? "

" Why didn't you? " asked Brenda with interest.

" Because Felicity said it would be fun here and I like being in places where there's fun, and if there's any fun, then I like to be in it," came the reply. " Do you think," asked Mrs. Hellier plaintively, " that twenty-two is too old to have fun? "

"I would have thought the twins——" began Brenda.

"Don't finish it," said Mrs. Hellier, holding up a small hand. "I know that one by heart. You would have thought that the twins would be all the fun I wanted. Everybody's got the same idea. Well, I had the twins when I was nineteen and it was all a frightful mistake and I simply refuse to sit in here like a stuffed turtle while Felicity—who's older than I am—has all the fun and no twins."

"It sounds hard," said Brenda, "but mothers——"

"I know that one, too," said Mrs. Hellier. "Don't think I'm not fond of the twins," she went on. "I like them all right, but nobody ought to expect a girl to stop living at nineteen. I didn't know that getting married at eighteen would mean getting twins at nineteen. I think it's grossly unfair. It's—well, as I told my husband at the time, it's a sort of confidence trick. So if Roger wants this room for any sensible purpose, tell him he can have it. I'm not going to be segregated as though I'd got beri-beri as well as babies." She stopped and pointed at a figure moving slowly in the garden. "Who's that fat woman out there?" she enquired.

"That's my—that's Lady Warne," said Brenda.

"Well, why can't she look after the twins?" asked Mrs. Hellier.

"She's got her hands rather full with a dog called Rameses," said Brenda, "but you could ask her."

"Is she allowed to take her dog into all the rooms?" demanded Mrs. Hellier.

"As long as she keeps his feet off the chairs," said Brenda.

"Well, I'll keep the twins off the chairs," promised their mother. "And you can tell Roger they're house-trained, too."

"Shall we go upstairs?" said Brenda, who was beginning to feel out of her depth.

"There's no need," replied Mrs. Hellier. "Felicity knows where all the things are—I couldn't put the twins to bed the first night when I'm still feeling train-sick, coulud I? Is it true," she asked suddenly, "that Paul's coming down to-morrow?"

"Quite true," said Brenda.

"Good—that makes at least one extra man," said Mrs. Hellier. "I'm not proud—I'll have the one Liss— Felicity—isn't using. She can't manage both of them at once—she hasn't got the technique. You have to have pretty steady nerves to stop them just this side of bloodshed."

Brenda, to her joy and relief, heard Ruth's footsteps on the stairs and went to meet her.

"If you're looking for Mrs. Hellier," said she, "she's here."

"Hello, Nan," said Ruth. "Liss sent me to fetch you—she's put the twins into their bath and she says they're not going to get out until you come up and take them out."

Mrs. Hellier's blue eyes became more vacant than ever and her mouth drooped petulantly.

"Would you like to come and watch?" she asked Brenda, a note of hope in her voice.

"Some other time," said Brenda.

"Perhaps you could do one, and I'll do the other," suggested Nan, turning to Ruth.

"Liss is waiting," said Ruth firmly. "You'd better hurry. First door up there on the left—Brahmaputra."

"What was that last?" asked Mrs. Hellier with a stare of amazement.

"Brahmaputra. Your room's called Brahmaputra," said Ruth.

"Why?" enquired Mrs. Hellier blankly.

"Because this is River Lodge and all the rooms are named after rivers," explained Ruth.

"Ah, I see," said Mrs. Hellier. "And this Bra-some-thing—that's a river, I suppose. Whereabouts?"

"When I was at school it was in India," said Brenda, "but that's a long time ago. It may be anywhere now."

"My God," murmured Mrs. Hellier, going disconso-lately upstairs. "What an existence. Taking twins out

B

of a bath and putting them to bed in a room called Bra-brahma—what was it? " she asked, pausing and looking down at the two women below.

" Putra," said Brenda and Ruth together.

" Putrid. Brahmaputrid," groaned the visitor, as she disappeared round the corner of the landing.

Brenda drew a deep breath.

" You might have warned me," she said reproachfully.

" To tell you the truth, I'd forgotten what she was like," said Ruth. " She's so vacant that she really doesn't make much impression—after the first shock, I mean."

" I can see that if I'm not careful," said Brenda, " she's going to have me on a string looking after the twins."

" She won't ask you—that's the danger," said Ruth. " Liss has just been warning me—she says Nan just goes off and leaves the rest to Nature—other people's good nature. It always comes off, too, Liss says."

" Well, thanks for the warning," said Brenda. " Every time I see her coming I'll lock myself in the office. Look —here's Goosey," she added, as Goosey, accompanied by Mr. Lenner, came down the stairs. " Do you think we ought to warn him too? "

Goosey was looking happier than he had done since tea. He reached the hall and came close to Ruth.

" Tell me," he asked in guarded tones, " did I see a pretty girl upstairs just now or was I just imagining things? "

" She was real," Ruth told him. " She's Felicity's sister—Mrs. Hellier."

" Mrs.? " echoed Goosey in despair.

" And she's got the most adorable pair of twins," said Brenda.

" Oh, no—that can't be the one," said Goosey, hope rising once more. " This girl was awfully young."

" The twins are awfully young, too," pointed out Brenda. " Do you like looking after young children? "

" I've never tried it," said Goosey, " but I've no doubt I'd do it to perfection. After all, all you do is hand them your necklaces or watches, or whatever you're wearing, and——"

He stopped, his eyes on the staircase and his moustache standing out more stiffly than ever. The others followed his glance and saw Felicity Grant descending. Ruth presented the two men and prepared to go up to her room, only to be stopped by Felicity and Goosey, who, each holding one of her arms, protested forcibly against her leaving them.

"Don't let her go, Major Horder," said Felicity. "I've been here ages and I've only had three words with her."

"She keeps popping off to her private wing," complained Goosey. "I can't follow her—I tried it after lunch and ran into Roger and he said if he ever caught me trespassing again he'd break my b—he'd break my neck."

"He would, too," said Brenda. She opened the door of her office and ushered the party in. "If anybody wants a drink——" she said.

Goosey went in first to prevent, he explained, any unseemly rush that might follow Brenda's provocative words. Everybody being comfortably settled, she poured drinks and Goosey handed them round.

"Before I leave this place," said Felicity, looking at Felix Lenner, "I'm going to demand one little mermaid all to myself. Will you do one for me, Mr. Lenner?" she asked.

Felix, looking as though he were about to cry, nodded his head with an unintelligible murmur which Goosey assured her meant that he would be most happy.

"I hope you won't be jealous, Miss Grant," he added, "but Felix is going off to Hollywood next week."

"I'm not a bit jealous," declared Felicity. "Are the mermaids going to be signed up?"

"He doesn't know yet," said Goosey. "But it's a paying game, drawing mermaids. Fancy all those other chaps writing poems about them and songs about them and never realizing that the big money came from merely sketching them. A firm in America has offered him a whole dishful of dough—they want to use them in advertisements."

"What could a mermaid advertise?" asked Ruth.

"I hadn't really thought of that," said Goosey. "Come to Sportem-on-Sea.   Then all the hopeful males all over the Americas would rush there to get their mermaids. That right, Felix?"

Felix shook his head mournfully.

"Combs?" hazarded Ruth.

Mr. Lenner's head went from side to side once more.

"Aren't you guessing, Brenda?" asked Ruth.

"I don't have to guess—I know," said Brenda. "The only thing a mermaid could possibly advertise is hair tonic."

There was a burst of applause, and Mr. Lenner's nod of confirmation was scarcely noticed. In the midst of the congratulations the door opened and Roger appeared. He stood looking at the company with eyebrows raised.

"What," he enquired, "do we keep public rooms for?"

"Come in and shut the door," invited Brenda.

"And take that frown off your face," commanded Goosey. "Ever since I saw you this morning you've looked like a man loaded with trouble."

"Doesn't the coincidence strike you?" asked Roger, pulling up a chair next to his wife.

"Roger, you're a pig," protested Ruth.

"I warned him—years ago," said Goosey solemnly. "I said, 'Look here, Roger old boy, if you don't try and look pleasant sometimes your face'll set that way.'"

"Which way?" enquired Roger, taking a drink from Brenda with a nod of thanks.

"The way it is," said Goosey. "And this money-grubbing," he went on, turning to Ruth, "is deplorable. Almost the first words he greeted me with to-day were in connection with hotel bills."

"Don't mention it to anybody," said Roger, "but we're running this place on a profit basis."

"You are?" said Goosey, on a pained note. "What a sordid outlook. Do you really mean that, having enjoyed Miss Grant's incomparable company for a week, you actually reduce it to pounds, shillings and pence——"

"Just pounds," said Roger. "And then we sit on her suit-case until she pays. By the way," he went on, "I came in to say that Lady Warne asks me to tell everybody that Rameses can't——"

"Can we have that again?" asked Goosey.

"Rameses. Name of a dog," said Roger. "Short though his walks are, they're longer than Lady Warne cares to take, so she'll be delighted if anybody . . ." His voice died away and there was a long silence, which was broken by Goosey.

"First they make you pay," he said, "and then they make you take the dogs out."

"While we are on the subject of hobbies," said Felicity slowly, "I would like to say that my sister, who is in other ways a charming person, has a habit of leaving two delightful children about in places which she knows to be frequented by tender-hearted people. You have been warned."

Goosey rose to his feet and placed two glasses on one side of the mantelpiece and one on the other. He pointed a finger from one side to the other, closed his eyes and counted under his breath.

"Eeny, meeny, miney, mo," he chanted. His finger stopped at the single glass and he opened his eyes and heaved a sigh of relief. "The dog," he said. "What did you say his name was again?"

"Robert and Jeremy," said Felicity instantly. "It's too sweet of you, and I hope they won't tire you."

Roger set down his empty glass and rose.

"Milk and biscuits are extras," he pointed out. "I'll include them on your bill. . . ."

CHAPTER IV

SOON after breakfast on the following morning, Brenda, after a prolonged search for Ruth, came upon her in the little sewing-room upstairs, and spoke in a puzzled tone.

"A telegram's just been 'phoned through," she said, "signed Beddington—that's your uncle, isn't it?"

"Yes," said Ruth. "What does it say?"

"It's a bit cryptic," said Brenda. "It just says 'Have you seen Lena?' Have you?"

Ruth, on her knees before a low drawer, turned her face up to her cousin with an exclamation of dismay.

"Oh—no!" she exclaimed.

"What do you mean by 'Oh, no'?" demanded Brenda. "Do you mean 'Oh, no, you haven't seen Lena' or 'Oh, no, the telegram can't be that'? And who," she went on, "is Lena?"

"Lena's my aunt," explained Ruth. "His wife."

"How can Lena be his wife?" asked Brenda. "You said his wife was Aunt Emmie. Has he got two wives?"

"Aunt Emmie's Lena," said Ruth. "Emmelina—we call her Emmie and my uncle calls her Lena."

"Well then, obviously you've seen Lena," said Brenda. "Silly sort of thing for the old boy to telegraph."

"It isn't silly at all," said Ruth, rising and going to the door with a worried air. "He simply wants to know where she is."

"Where she is?" repeated Brenda in astonishment. "Well, didn't you tell me that they stayed the night in Town and are coming on here together sometime this morning?"

"Oh, yes, yes," said Ruth, hurrying downstairs, "that was the plan. But obviously she's gone and got lost again."

"Again!" echoed Brenda, keeping close behind Ruth as the latter hastened out of doors and went in the direction of the garage. "How often does she get lost?"

"Every time they travel," said Ruth, hurrying down the flagged path. "She practically never leaves home, and he's not the best of travellers either, and this is rather a long journey for them."

"Long journey?" squeaked Brenda, breathless from astonishment and haste. "What—from York to King's Cross, then a night's rest to get over the strain, and then from Paddington to here—long journey?"

"Oh, I know it sounds absurd," said Ruth, "but once she gets into a train she gets terrified, and gets fussed and everything goes wrong. If I'd had any sense I'd have gone up and fetched them from Town this morning. That's why I wanted Paul to meet them—he could have looked after them on the way down." She reached the garage door and looked inside. Roger paused in his task of wrenching open a wooden crate and looked up expectantly.

"A telegram from Uncle George about Aunt Emmie," said Ruth.

"Oh, my God!" said Roger. "She hasn't gone and got lost again, has she? What does he say?"

"The telegram says 'Have you seen Lena,'" put in Brenda. "Reply paid, so the poor old fellow'll be waiting for a yes or a no."

"What'll we do, Roger?" asked Ruth.

Roger considered.

"Get hold of Paul," he decided after a few moments. "Then he can glue Uncle George on the spot where Aunt Emmie's most likely to look for him, while he goes round and searches. Where was the telegram from?" he asked.

"I forgot to ask," said Brenda. "Perhaps she's fallen off one of the platforms."

"Not necessarily," said Roger. "I doubt whether they even got as far as the station together."

"Why couldn't he telephone?" asked Brenda. "Then we could have got hold of some details."

"He gets fussed in a telephone box," explained Ruth.

All that getting out the money with one hand and pressing buttons——"

"Well, couldn't we ring up Paddington Station and ask them to make a loud-speaker appeal?" suggested Brenda. "You know—helloo, helloo, will Aunt Lena please come to the station-master's office and pick up Uncle George——"

"Oh, don't joke," begged Ruth. "She might be run over or something frightful—oh, Roger, isn't there something we can do?"

"Yes—ring up Paul," said Roger, wiping his hands on a duster and taking his coat off the peg on which he had hung it. He strode along the path, followed by Ruth and Brenda in procession.

As they neared the hall telephone, however, they heard it ringing. Roger nodded to the pink overall who had come out to answer it, and picked up the receiver.

"Petsham three four," he said. "Roger Mallard speaking." He paused to listen, and a frown appeared suddenly on his face.

"Who?" whispered Ruth at his side.

"Police," answered Roger in an undertone.

Ruth's face turned white and her eyes became fixed on her husband's face as if to read the news there. Roger was speaking again.

"Yes," he said. "Yes . . . I see . . . Yes, she does get frightened—I'm afraid she's really a very bad traveller . . . Yes . . . thank you very much."

Ruth's colour came back. The present tense was reassuring.

"Half a moment," said Roger into the receiver. He turned to his wife.

"They've got Aunt Emmie," he said. "Safe but quite petrified. They think the best thing to do is to get her straight down here, but the question is, how?" He spoke into the receiver once more. "If you wouldn't mind looking after her for a short while," he said, "I'll get hold of my brother—he's in London and he's coming down here to-day."

After some further details about time and place, Roger put down the receiver.

"Get Paul, will you?" he asked his wife, "and then wire to Uncle George and tell him to come on by himself."

He left the house and walked in the direction of the garage and his interrupted task. Half-way there, however, he saw something which caused him to halt abruptly, his face darkening with fury.

Major Horder was standing near one of the ground floor windows, watching with pleasure and interest the movements of a fresh-cheeked, pink-clad maiden with dimpled arms who, seated on a window-sill, was engaged in cleaning the panes. She worked busily while Goosey addressed remarks to her on the charming effect of gleaming windows and gleaming hair, both reflecting the sun's rays. Behind Goosey, thrust through the rhododendron bushes close by, was the face of an old man wearing an expression even more furious than Roger's. Goosey glanced round at the malevolent apparition once or twice with a puzzled air, and was about to resume his conversation when he caught sight of Roger, and gloom overspread his countenance.

"Hello, Roger," he said, with an attempt to sound welcoming.

Roger swept by him, with a gritted "Going my way?" so pointed and so threatening that Goosey found himself falling into step beside him. At the garage door Roger stopped and turned in fury.

"Look here," he said. "I told you that if I caught you anywhere near one of those girls I'd throw you out. Didn't you believe me?"

"No, I didn't," said Goosey warmly. "If a fellow can't say a word to a pretty girl without being suspected of Nellie-in-the-snow motives, it's a pity. What d'you take me for—a ruddy Casanova?"

"Not yet," Roger informed him. "And you can't practise here. The next time you——"

"All right, all right, I know," said Goosey. "But

will you tell me," he went on, " why I can't address a word to a girl without being threatened with eviction and having faces popping out of rhododendron bushes? Who was the face? " he asked. " Looked like a gardener. Isn't there any work for the old prowler to do in the garden? He was sticking his neck out of those bushes as if he wanted to hear what was going on."

" He did want to hear what was going on," said Roger.

" Well, instead of accusing me of things I don't do," said Goosey, " you ought to go and tell him to mind his own damn business."

" He was minding his own business," said Roger.

" Rot," said Goosey. " He was watching me talking to the girl. She's not his business."

" No—she's his daughter," said Roger.

Goosey's face assumed a look of horror.

" My God! " he ejaculated. " So that's why he was boring holes in my back——"

" You're lucky he didn't bore another kind of hole in your back," said Roger. " Why can't you keep your eyes off women? "

" I don't do any harm," pleaded Goosey. " I don't know why you go on as though I were a sort of lustful Lothario. Good Lord! " he continued, a certain surprise in his voice, " I don't suppose I ever harmed a girl in my life. I like to look at them—who doesn't?—but the only harm I do is to rouse your foul suspicions. You always used to suspect the worst. Don't you remember——"

" No," said Roger. " I don't. Where's that Lenner fellow? "

" Felix? Don't tell me you're going to follow him round, too," said Goosey. " You're wasting your time. Why, poor old Felix doesn't see girls as girls at all, poor devil—he only sees them as mermaids. No wonder the poor chap's got a permanently soured expression. Just shows you how odd all these artist chaps must be—all they want to do with a young and lovely is get her on a sheet of paper."

Goosey gave a sigh of pity and, choosing a clean place on the running-board of the nearest car, sat down to watch Roger as the latter resumed his task.

" Don't sit there," ordered Roger. " Come and hold this."

Goosey glanced hastily at his watch.

" Holy Moses! " he exclaimed, leaping to his feet, " look at the time! Sorry, Roger old boy—any other morning . . ."

He walked rapidly in the direction of the house, slowing down as he left the garage and the risk of work behind him. He caught a distant glimpse of Mrs. Hellier coming out of the house with her children and, scenting more danger, made a wide detour and entered the house by the side door. Going inside, he met Ruth on her way upstairs with two vases full of flowers. Goosey, pleased to assist in a task within his powers, took them from her and accompanied her.

" One's for my aunt's room," said Ruth, " and the other's for Paul. It's really Brenda's job, but the thought of seeing Paul seems to have deranged her temporarily, so I've taken over."

" Is Paul her special pet? " asked Goosey, drawing in his chin as the prickly branches from the vase brushed his face.

" Yes," said Ruth. " She likes Roger, but she thinks he's moody and cross and they're always having arguments and she says Paul's by far the nicer brother."

" I don't suppose you agree with that," commented Goosey, relinquishing one vase at the door of Aunt Emmie's room. He followed Ruth into Paul's room, put down the vase in the place she indicated and stood looking at her thoughtfully.

" It's not my business," he said after a few moments, " but is Paul all right? I mean how's the acting and all that? "

" Why do you ask? " returned Ruth.

" Well "—Goosey hesitated—" I'm not often in London, of course, but last time I saw him he didn't seem—

I don't know quite how to describe it—he didn't seem quite on his feet, as it were.   He always used to be fit and in good form, and good for a party. And lately——" He stopped.

" And lately what? " asked Ruth.

" Well, lately he's been—not exactly hiding," said Goosey uncertainly, " but you don't see much of him and when you do he seems to want to get away.   And he's left the decent flat he was living in and gone to a mouse-hole. As I said, it isn't my business, but I thought I'd ask you about it if I got a chance.   I don't like to mention it to Roger—he goes off at a tangent and chews you into pieces if you tread on one of his innumerable corns—and I wasn't sure whether Paul was a corn or not."

Ruth walked to the bed, smoothed the counterpane carefully and then sat absently upon it, staring in front of her.

" It's money, chiefly," she said at last.   " You know, of course, that we had just about the richest uncle and aunt in the country? "

Goosey nodded.

" Well," continued Ruth, " the uncle died.   He left this house to Roger, but no money with it, and he left Paul nothing whatsoever."

" Well, where did all his packet go? " enquired Goosey.

" It went to his sister—Aunt Ella," said Ruth.   " She was already nauseatingly well off—she was well off to begin with, and then she married a wealthy baronet and he died and she got his money."

" No children? " asked Goosey.

" None," said Ruth.   " But no hope of anything for us, now or in the future."

" Acting's a chancey profession," said Goosey thoughtfully.   " Paul doesn't seem to be up on the electric signs any more."

" Not at the moment," admitted Ruth.

" That's what I mean," said Goosey, " about not see-

ing him about so much. I don't know much about it,
but it seemed to me that he wasn't going about things
the right way—I mean if he wants jobs, he can't live
in that out-of-the-way hole he's got hold of and emerge
from it at intervals looking pensive. Are you sure it's
only money? " he enquired. " I thought he had a look
in his eye that denoted girl-trouble. Are you sure there's
no girl? "

" There's a girl, but that isn't the trouble," said Ruth.
She got off the bed and smoothed the counterpane once
more. " It's only a passing phase, we hope, Goosey," she
said. " He'll get on his feet soon and then everything
will be all right."

Goosey followed her out in thoughtful silence.
" Money's the devil," he said sadly, " if you haven't
got it. I wish I had a nice round sum to hand over
to Paul."

" I know, Goosey darling," said Ruth warmly. " But
Roger says if we wring the utmost out of all our visitors
we'll soon be able to hand him something ourselves."

" Well, pile it on to my old man's bill," said Goosey.
" He can stand it. So can Felix. Just add up the totals
and multiply them by four."

Warmed by this generous gesture, he went in search
of his friend. Felix, he found, was not in the house,
but a glance from an upper window showed him the
pretty spectacle of Mr. Lenner seated on a wooden
bench, by a little fountain, drawing something on a
piece of paper, while the twins, close beside him, looked
on with interest. Goosey made his way downstairs and
joined the little party.

" Hallo, twins," he said in a Children's Hour voice.
" What's the funny man doing—drawing pictures? "

There was no reply. Felix continued to draw and the
twins remained motionless, watching. Goosey sat on the
bench and treated the children to a running commentary
on the sketches.

" There's a pretty lady," he said, " with nice long hair.
And now look—she's got a pretty tail, too—you watch

her pretty tail coming. You know what she is?—she's a fish lady."

Two pairs of large brown eyes were raised to his for a moment and then lowered again in silence.

"They don't say much, do they?" commented Goosey.

Mr. Lenner shook his head sadly.

"And you don't say much either," said Goosey, rising from the bench. "In fact," he went on, "this party's too quiet for me. I'm going to see what's going on inside—perhaps I can give the lovely Felicity a drink. You coming?" he asked the artist.

Mr. Lenner rose from the bench, tore the sketch from his pad and handed it to the twins. They took it carefully and studied it with close interest.

"Not that way," said Goosey, stooping and turning the paper round. "You've got the fish-lady upside down. You have to have her tail down, or she won't be able to swim—you see?"

The twins made no response, and the two men turned to the house, Goosey pausing to look over his shoulder at the children.

"Who's in charge?" he asked, a trace of uneasiness in his voice. "Is their mother coming out?"

Mr. Lenner lifted his shoulders in a shrug.

"That's all right, then," said Goosey in a relieved tone. "Come on and let's find the refreshment booth."

They walked round the garden and entered the house by the front door. The dilapidated station taxi was just driving away, and on the steps stood Ruth in the act of embracing a white-haired, worried-looking man.

"But, Uncle darling," she was exclaiming as Goosey and Felix came up, "I can't think how you missed them —Roger's cousin Brenda took the car to the station——" She broke off and took the old man gently by the arm. "Let's go inside," she said. "Uncle, this is a very old friend, Major Horder—and this is Mr. Lenner. Goosey, this is my uncle, Mr. Beddington," she went on. "He came down on the same train as Paul and my aunt, but he was in the front and he didn't see the others

—he just came away in the station taxi and missed them."

" I didn't know they were going to be on that train," pointed out Mr. Beddington. " If you'd met us I should have seen you waiting, but as I've never seen Roger's cousin, of course I didn't recognize her."

" She insisted on going to meet Paul," said Ruth. " There they are now," she said, as a car drew up outside.

Goosey opened the door. Outside, Paul Mallard was assisting a thin, timid old lady out of the car, while Brenda took suit-cases from the front and placed them on the drive. Ruth went down to greet her aunt, and led her up the stairs and into the hall.

" Lena!" exclaimed Mr. Beddington, hurrying forward and relieving his wife of a light handbag. " Oh, Lena—you didn't listen—you left the luggage, my dear —you——"

" No, no, no, no," denied his wife in an agitated twitter. " You said I was to wait just there with the porter and I——"

" No, dear," corrected Mr. Beddington. " I said, ' Whatever you do don't leave the luggage,' and——"

" That's just it," said Aunt Emmie breathlessly. " It went away. The man put it all on to a little trolley and he drove it off."

" But you should have followed him," said Mr. Beddington. " You should have come with the trolley."

" Oh, Ruth dear," said Aunt Emmie, turning appealingly to her niece, " how could I? So fast—so winding —in and out, in and out. And so many people, and such a shocking noise—and then the policeman— and——"

" Policeman!" exclaimed Goosey, who had been following the dialogue with unconcealed interest. " Where does the policeman come in? "

" I was lost," said Aunt Emmie, clasping her hands together. " I asked a policeman if he had seen my husband—he was very helpful indeed, but we couldn't find him, so the policeman took me with him and——"

"I say, you have had a time," said Goosey.

"Come upstairs, darling," said Ruth soothingly, "and have a nice rest. You must be awfully tired."

"Of course she must be," said Mr. Beddington, "but I made it quite plain—I said 'Don't leave the luggage,' and——"

"Those trolleys go awfully fast," put in Goosey. "I've often wanted to drive one."

"They're dangerous, my dear Major Goosey," said Mr. Beddington. "Positively dangerous——"

Brenda flashed an optical signal to Ruth, indicating her willingness to help in the task of clearing the hall of the agitated old couple. "Let me take something up for you," she said, addressing Mr. Beddington.

"Not at all, thank you," said Mr. Beddington. "I'm so sorry I missed you at the station. I was worried, of course, or I might have stopped to make enquiries. Such a terrible morning——"

"But much worse—much, much worse for me," said his wife, gently reproachful.

"Awful, darling," said Ruth. "Do come up."

"The policeman said——" began Mrs. Beddington once more. She stopped as her eyes fell on some figures which had just appeared from the garden.

Martin West stood at the other side of the hall. Dangling in his arms were two small figures, mud-soaked from head to foot. Mrs. Hellier stood beside them, her wide blue stare fixed on Felix Lenner.

"There he is," she said, pointing accusingly at him. "Miles away while the twins drown. Why," she demanded of the bewildered artist, "did you go away and leave them in the fountain?"

"Who left them in the fountain?" asked Goosey indignantly. "Felix and I left them safe and dry in the garden and we haven't been near them since."

"You left them out there absolutely alone—absolutely unprotected," said Mrs. Hellier, "and if Martin hadn't seen them lying there, they'd have been drowned."

"Lying where?" asked Brenda.

"On their fronts, hanging over the side of the fountain," explained Martin West. "Trying to sail boats or something."

"No, they weren't sailing boats at all," said Mrs. Hellier. "Nothing of the sort. They don't like boats. They hate boats. They were trying to make the paper swim—they said there was a fish-lady on it."

"I say, that was jolly intelligent!" said Goosey admiringly. "I think that's really bright, I must say. I told them it was a fish-lady."

"There you are," said Mrs. Hellier. "I told you. They drew mermaids for them, told them to make them swim and then left them—just left them—to drown."

"Oh, I say," protested Goosey. "That's a bit——"

"You're entirely to blame," said Mrs. Hellier, "and you might both have been murderers."

"Oh dear," said Mrs. Beddington. "Such a——"

"Upstairs, darling," said Ruth firmly.

"Take the twins up," said Brenda to Martin West. "You go with them," she ordered, turning to Mrs. Hellier.

"And take off all that mud?" said Mrs. Hellier. "Don't you believe it. I didn't come here to scrape mud off just because——"

"Upstairs," said Brenda, sweeping her up with Martin and the twins. Ruth followed with her bewildered and chattering aunt and uncle, in whose minds the amazing adventures of the morning mingled with the shockingly narrow margin by which a pair of innocent babies had escaped drowning. Mr. Beddington paused at the head of the stairs to give a suspicious glance at the two figures still standing in the hall wearing what the old gentleman considered a guilty and sheepish air.

Goosey's air of sheepishness was entirely due, however, to his having caught sight of Felicity Grant peering cautiously round the door of the library.

"Have they all gone?" she asked, emerging.

"They've gone," confirmed Goosey. "Did you hear your sister accusing us of murder?"

"I warned you," said Felicity, with no trace of sympathy in her tones. "I've been trying to get out of that door for the last fifteen minutes," she went on, "but there's been pandemonium——" She stopped and looked round enquiringly. "Did Paul go up with them?" she asked.

"Paul?" said Goosey, following her gaze and examining the hall as though the missing man might be concealed in one of the alcoves. "I didn't see Paul—he——"

Goosey stopped. Felicity, looking through the open front door, had seen the figure she was looking for. On the steps outside, Paul Mallard sat, his suit-case by his side and his elbows resting on his knees. In one hand he held a half-smoked cigarette. His attitude was one of patient waiting.

Felicity stepped out and stood looking down at him with a little smile. He glanced up at her with no other greeting than a quizzical raising of his eyebrows.

"Hello, Paul," she said quietly. "The panic's over —you can come in."

"Ah," said Paul.

He got to his feet with a slow, lazy movement and stood looking at her for a moment, his eyes level with hers as she stood on the step above him. He studied her with a long expressionless look before greeting her.

"Hello, Liss," he said. "How's the cooking?"

CHAPTER V

PAUL MALLARD was twenty-eight. A description of the two brothers, Ruth had found, could lead the listener to the erroneous conclusion that they were very much alike; both were tall and dark, both were good-looking, attractive and liable to outbursts of ill-humour.

If the mould, however, was the same, the mixture was not. Roger was the taller, but gave the impression of breadth rather than height, while Paul's slenderness made him appear the taller of the two. The colouring of both, though dark, differed a good deal, and though there was a certain similarity of movement, Roger was active and energetic while Paul was slow and, on the surface, lazy.

Nor were their tempers alike. Roger's irritation rose swiftly and died soon. Paul, on the other hand, had when angry a deceptive calmness of manner which had led many an unwary attacker beyond the bounds of discretion and left them bewildered by the suddenness and violence of the counter-attack.

Paul Mallard was regarded as one of the most promising young actors of his day. The reasons for his sudden break with Martin West in the middle of a successful run were not generally known, but it was assumed that the two men had quarrelled over Felicity Grant. Paul, unsuccessfully seeking engagements during the following months, had realized that the sympathies of the majority lay with Martin.

Brenda continued to hold the opinion that the inclusion of Paul in the same list of guests as Felicity Grant and Martin West was unwise, but the sight of him gave her so much pleasure that she put her misgivings resolutely aside.

On his first night, Paul joined the family in their own dining-room. It was a quiet party, only Brenda being in her usual spirits. Roger was silent, watching Paul when he thought he was unobserved, and Paul, inwardly amused, watched his brother watching him.

" Did you tell Paul about Aunt Ella not being Aunt Ella? " asked Ruth, turning to Brenda.

" Oh, no! " exclaimed Brenda. " I hadn't thought about her at all. She's Lady Warne to you," she went on, turning to Paul. " She's here incognito, like the prince in whichever pantomime it is. When we're alone with her—and you know how often we'll seek that pleasure—we can call her Aunt Ella for a treat."

"God!" said Paul lazily. "What is it?—shrewishness or snobbishness?"

"Can't say," replied Brenda. "I've only caught glimpses of her since her arrival. She emerges for food and then lumbers back to her own fireside."

"She's been twice round the garden with Rameses," said Ruth. "I saw her."

"So did I," said Roger. "A most peculiar feeling came over me as I watched her negotiating the bend near the lupins."

"Nausea," suggested Brenda.

"Nothing of the sort," said Roger. "I didn't recognize the sensation for some time."

"Well, come on," said Brenda impatiently. "I can't bear guessing competitions—what was it?"

"Pity," said Roger.

There was a silence. Then Brenda shook her head.

"No," she said decisively. "You must send it up for a further analysis. Distaste, a natural recoil, a feeling of——"

"Pity," said Roger again. "She looked like a sow on the eve of the great event."

"But she's looked like that ever since you've known her," pointed out Brenda. "Why the sudden surge—the unexpected uprush of——"

"That's all I can tell you," said Roger. "She looked like a——"

"All right, all right," said Brenda hastily. "Don't let's have the poetry again. But remember you're pitying a woman who could buy up half the hotels in England and put you in charge of them all."

"I feel sorry for her, too," said Ruth. "Nothing but that long antiquated limousine and that poor old chauffeur and that shocking dog——"

"And half a million pounds sterling," finished Brenda. "Poor woman!—I'm beginning to feel chokey myself."

"You're an ass," said Ruth, rising from the table. "Don't get up, Paul," she went on. "Stay here and chat to Roger. Brenda and I have got all sorts of jobs to do. Come in and have a drink with us before you go to bed, won't you?"

Paul, opening the door for the two women, nodded and, closing the door behind them, pulled out a chair and settled himself near his brother. He took out a cigarette and Roger held a light for him.

"Brenda asked me—in her professional capacity," began Paul in his slow voice, "whether I was paying for this visit."

"What did you tell her?" asked Roger in an interested tone.

"I told her," said Paul, "that she could keep my luggage."

"I see," said Roger.

"There isn't much," went on Paul, "but the case used to be a good one."

There was a pause, during which Roger looked at his brother speculatively.

"Is it as bad as that?" he asked quietly after a time.

"By and large," said Paul.

"Aren't you," said Roger, speaking in a reflective tone and looking at the table, "making rather a bloody fool of yourself?"

A gleam of amusement appeared in Paul's eyes.

"I wouldn't be surprised," he said lightly. "Wouldn't be the first time, would it?"

"Have you," said Roger, persevering, "really had a row with West?"

"Good Lord, no," said Paul. "What makes you think that? I merely told him that he was making bloody monkeys out of all his company for the sake of a girl who didn't know the alphabet of acting. Was there anything wrong about that?"

Roger suppressed an impulse to go back to his youthful days and punch his brother on the nose. He controlled himself and spoke calmly.

" Nothing at all that I can see," he said. " What did Martin say? "

" He said that if I thought I was the whole show, I could put the matter to the test by going to hell and staying there until he went out of the show business," replied Paul. " What could be more reasonable than that? "

Roger's jaw worked as he made strenuous efforts to keep down his rising anger. He knew if he lost his temper, Paul would entrench himself behind a wall of contemptuous silence and refuse to discuss anything at all. Roger thought quietly for some moments and then looked up.

" I don't know much about it," he said, " but I like being on one side or the other. I've known Martin a good many years—he isn't everyone's man, but I find him all right. And he did you a good turn when he put you into that first big thing you did. I——"

" Half a moment," said Paul. " If you're assembling facts, then get them correct. Don't run away with the idea that West put me on my feet. He didn't—not by a devil of a long chalk. When he made his offer, I was pretty well there. His wasn't the only offer, or the only good offer. But he seemed the best bet—he *was* the best bet, as it turned out—and so I joined him. Now go on from there."

" Well, it's no good talking round the damned situation," said Roger irritably. " What makes you think you can choose all the players, or whatever you call them, in somebody else's show? It's your business, isn't it, to do your part as well as you know how and leave it at that? "

" Correct," said Paul.

" Well, for God's sake tell me what it was all about," said Roger, exploding at last. " I haven't time to sit here and screw the thing out of you piece by piece. And don't go into one of your schoolboy sulks," he added, his fury and his voice rising. " If you must know," he went on savagely, " I'm worried about you.

Ruth's worried about you. Brenda's worried about you. We're all worried about you. But I'm only worried about your mental condition. If I've got to have a raving lunatic for a brother, then just let me know. I'll get used to the idea, and it isn't such a new idea, either. Now will you tell me the only thing I want to know: did you chuck over a big part just because you were jealous of Martin West for breaking into your— your affair with Felicity Grant. Yes or no? "

Paul's face was white.

" No," he said.

Roger looked at him for a moment and drew a deep breath.

" That's all right," he said slowly. " I'm sorry I thought you did."

" That's all right," said Paul. " You're not the only one."

" What was it? " asked Roger, after a time. " Did it really matter whether the girl could act or not? "

" I don't suppose so," said Paul slowly. " You get all sorts in the profession. You get the real, bred-in-the-bone theatrical families and the old troupers and you get poor devils who hang on for years doing small parts and doing them perfectly. And then again "— his voice became bitter—" you get the other kind. I needn't enumerate them. Liss wasn't the first wooden woman I'd worked with—not by a long way. A living's a living, and girls like to go on the stage. But Liss was different. She didn't need the job. She didn't even particularly want the job—she'd have been quite happy playing around thinking she was studying dramatic art —she'd have done another year or two, perhaps walked on once or twice and then walked off again and settled down, married to—married to someone or other. Martin West," he went on, " had four first-class, top-notch, experienced actresses after the part he handed Liss. And he didn't give it to her because he thought she could play it. He wanted to see her, to have her there all the time—even to order her about. As his principal he could be with her whenever he wanted to. So he talked her into accepting."

He stopped. Roger waited, but Paul appeared to have finished.

"But—well, she did the part pretty well, didn't she? " he asked after a pause.

"That's what you think," said Paul.

"What I mean is," went on Roger, with unusual patience, "that Martin took a chance with a new performer. If she didn't let him down and the play went well—didn't that justify his choice? "

"Only in a cinema plot," said Paul. "Martin West doesn't produce revues—he's supposed to be putting on first-class plays with first-class players. No actor who has to work with Liss gets a dog's chance. But I wouldn't have cut the whole thing if—if it had been any other girl but Liss. I couldn't stand there and watch her reciting all those tremendous lines like a—like—a——" His voice died away.

There was silence once more, and this time Roger made no attempt to break it. The two men sat for a few minutes and then Roger pushed back his chair and rose.

"I'll see you before you turn in," he said. "I think you'd better go up and look in on Aunt Ella."

"Couldn't I wait till the morning? " asked Paul.

"It doesn't get any easier—I've tried it," said Roger. "The thing is to get it over."

"Well, if I have to, I have to," said Paul resignedly. "Where does she live? "

"In Ganges," said Roger. "Half a moment," he went on, as Paul went towards the door. Paul turned expectantly, and Roger hesitated, choosing his words carefully.

"About Liss and Martin West," he began. "You won't forget they're here on an even sounder footing than you are, will you? "

"Meaning they're paying and I'm not? No, I won't forget," said Paul. "I'd thought of that already, as a

matter of fact, and decided that as an honorary member
I ought to keep my hands off his throat."

"That's all right," said Roger. "I thought you'd
see it my way. Thanks."

Paul made his way to the door marked Ganges, and
knocked upon it. He heard a voice from inside the
room.

"Who is it?" called his aunt.

Paul gave a swift, mischievous grin.

"Paul Mallard here, Lady Warne," he replied in
polite tones.

"Oh—come in," came the reply.

Paul, composing his features, opened the door and
entered. His aunt was seated in a comfortable chair
before the fire. On her knee was a book, and at her
feet lay Rameses, sleeping noisily. She gave Paul her
hand and nodded to a chair opposite. Paul drew it away
from the excessive heat and sat down, studying his aunt.

She was, he thought, an extraordinary figure. He
wondered what she weighed, and thought with wonder
of the amazing strength and elasticity of the human skin.

"How are you?" enquired Lady Warne.

"I'm very well indeed, thank you," said Paul politely.
"How are you?"

His aunt gave a slight inclination of her head to
indicate that she, too, was in good health. There was
a long pause.

"London," said Lady Warne presently, "must be
very empty."

"Oh—very," said Paul, reflecting that there were
after all, only seven million or so in the capital at that
moment.

"Your Uncle Jake," resumed Lady Warne after a
pause, "wouldn't have liked this."

Paul followed the direction of the speaker's eyes, and
found them fixed on the leaping fire.

"A large fire in September? No, rather not," he
agreed heartily. "I believe he always——"

"Your Uncle Jake," repeated Lady Warne, turning

with a slight frown, "wouldn't have liked to see his house turned into this." She raised a podgy hand and waved it in the air for a moment.

"You don't think so?" enquired Paul respectfully.

"I know so," replied Lady Warne. "He would have objected very strongly."

Paul thought the subject of his late uncle's feelings scarcely worth discussing, and remained silent.

"What do you think?" asked his aunt.

"Well," said Paul, thus pressed, "he didn't seem to express any opinion on the subject during his lifetime, and now, of course, he isn't in a position to—well—state his views. He left the house to Roger without any strings, I gather. He couldn't have expected him to live in it just by himself, or he'd have left him the means to do it. After all, when anyone dies——"

He stopped, brought to a halt by a peremptory movement of his aunt's hands. She gave a little shudder and spoke sharply.

"Please don't speak about—about dying," she said. "It's a subject I particularly dislike."

Paul said nothing, and watched Rameses rise painfully to his feet and waddle to a cooler spot near the door. His mistress watched his progress anxiously until he was settled once more.

"He's very intelligent," she remarked when his grunts had subsided. "The moment he gets too warm, he moves."

Paul, reflecting that there were other reasons for moving, rose to his feet and, with a feeling of deep relief, said good night to his aunt. He moved to the door, almost stumbling over the dog as he went. He paused and looked down at the swollen, unlovely creature, finding it difficult to hide his aversion. As he looked, however, he experienced a feeling akin to that which had swept over Roger as he watched his aunt in the garden. It wasn't, Paul reflected, the poor animal's fault if some frightful woman overfed him and ruined him and destroyed his doghood. In somebody else's hands he might have been an active, happy, bounding creature, instead of a waddling mountain of flesh. Almost unconsciously, Paul stooped and laid a hand on the dog's head.

"Poor old fellow, then," he said softly and with genuine feeling. He opened the door and went out, and Lady Warne, after staring at the door for some time with a peculiar expression, turned her gaze slowly on the sleeping dog.

Paul, reaching the end of the corridor, saw Major Horder coming to meet him. A disappearing flash of pale pink caught his eye.

"Did I see a bit of pink?" he asked the innocent-looking Goosey.

"Liver," said Goosey promptly. "Spots-before-the-eyes. It's nothing to worry about, but you ought to take something for it."

"If I told Roger I saw a——" began Paul.

"Great Scott, no!" exclaimed Goosey, turning and proceeding in Paul's direction, "don't do that. He thinks I want to ravish all his maidens."

"And don't you?" enquired Paul.

"Of course not. What's the matter with your minds?" returned Goosey indignantly. "Seriously, Paul, I'm only like the fellow in the aquarium, leaning over and watching the pretty little things darting here and there. Another thing," he went on without bitterness, "girls don't always take to me. Roger ought to know that. When we were subalterns he used to wait until a girl had got over the first shock and was beginning to see my finer points, and then he'd simply step in and break it up. In two seconds he'd ruin the work of months. He said he did it to protect me. I say," he added, as Paul went past the main staircase towards his brother's room, "are you going in to see Ruth?"

"Yes," said Paul. "You coming?"

"Well, I'd like to," said Goosey, "but strictly speaking, I'm not allowed past those three stairs. If you said you'd brought me along with you——"

"Come on," said Paul, leading the way and knocking on a door at the end of the corridor. "Nobody's come up yet," he went on, as no reply came. "We'll go in and wait."

He entered the comfortable sitting-room and, taking the best chair, kindly allocated the second best to his companion. Goosey sank into it thankfully and leaned back with a sigh.

"I like it up here," he said. "You meet the best people. Miss Grant, for example, frequently comes up and pays long visits to Ruth, and it's the only chance one gets of meeting her without that big, conceited-looking West fellow poking in his nose. Girls are funny things," he went on gloomily. "You'd think she'd see he wasn't half good enough for her. You seem to know her fairly well," he went on enviously. "I suppose you meet her on the stage and so on?"

"Not so much on as off," said Paul.

"Do you like this West chap?" enquired Goosey.

"Yes and no," said Paul.

"What the hell does that mean?" enquired Goosey.

"It means," said Paul in his slow, lazy way, "yes, I did once, and no, I don't now."

Goosey took some time to digest this piece of information.

"Roger must be fond of him," he said after a thoughtful pause, "to invite him here and give him a clear field like this. I think it's a rotten idea, myself."

"What," enquired Paul, "is your interest in the affair?"

"I see—you mean what the hell's it got to do with me," said Goosey. "Well, nothing except that that chap gets on my nerves. Every time I try to say a civil word to Miss Grant—and she's a nice friendly girl—this whoever he is comes up and makes me look no end of a damn fool—oh, it isn't difficult, I know—but if they're not engaged—and she isn't wearing a ring, so they can't be—then I've got as much right to address the girl as he has. Do you," he enquired hopefully, "know her well enough to ask her to detach herself now and again?"

"Yes," said Paul.

"Then will you?" asked Goosey eagerly.

"No," said Paul.

The entrance of Ruth and Brenda brought both men to their feet. Brenda looked at Goosey's disconsolate expression curiously.

"What have you done with your friend?" she asked. "You're wearing his expression."

"His exp—oh, I see," said Goosey. "Well, Felix is drawing mermaids for Mr. Beddington. I was just asking Paul to help me to get Miss Grant away from her shadow, and he said no."

"He's a wise man," said Ruth. "And you'll find yourself in trouble if you do anything so foolish as to——"

"Oh, I know what you're going to say," broke in Goosey, holding up a hand. "But I'm not such a fool as I look. Nobody could be, I gather. If I thought Miss Grant liked this fellow particularly, I'd simply put her down as a bad chooser and leave it at that. But there's a hitch—I know there's a hitch."

There was a silence. Goosey looked round and saw three pairs of eyes regarding him with a curious intentness. He went a little red.

"I'm not fooling," he said. "I saw her drop her bag and I rushed forward, of course—it was just outside the house, on that bit of grass, with a bird bath on it—and I helped her to pick everything up and shove it back again and instead of saying thank you, she gave a sort of whinnying noise and started going round and round like a—like a—oh, just round and round, awfully worried, looking on the ground. I never saw a girl in such a state. I looked too, and I spotted a lighter, a small gold one, and I picked it up and she fairly snatched it from me, but I got a look at it and I swear it's got what people who lose things call sentimental value."

He paused. The three pairs of eyes were still on him, but for a few moments nobody asked the question which

Goosey, as an experienced raconteur, was waiting for. At last Ruth spoke slowly and hesitatingly.

" What makes you think——" she began.

" There was a time engraved on it," said Goosey triumphantly. " Probably the time the other fellow met her, or proposed to her—or left her, though I can't imagine anyone——"

Brenda interrupted him.

" What time was it? " she asked.

" It was one p.m.," said Goosey.

" Ah," said Brenda.

" Ah," murmured Ruth.

There was, however, no comment whatsoever from Ian Paul Mallard.

CHAPTER VI

By the following day the guests, like the passengers on a liner, had finished the brief arrangement of their personal effects and emerged to take stock of their surroundings and their fellow passengers. Strangers ceased to be strangers and became, in Goosey's words, stranger still.

Certain mutual peculiarities were noted and respected. It became known that Lady Warne preferred the drawing-room to the library, and liked the big, wide chair between the fire-place and the piano. Rameses liked the big white hearthrug. Mr. Beddington was pleased when people talked to his wife, and Mrs. Beddington always liked a small chair left vacant by her side so that she could place upon it her innumerable bags and coats. It was learned that if Mr. Beddington was away from the room for any length of time, his wife became nervous and fluttered, and could only be soothed by others in the room inventing a number of convincing reasons for his absence. It became a pleasant pastime for some of the members of the party, and Mr. Beddington would have been astonished to hear of some of the places in which he had lately been seen.

It was also learned that no amount of patience or effort could win a smile or a syllable from Mr. Lenner, and the efforts of the entire company were needed to find constant and convincing excuses for refusing Mrs. Hellier's pleas that somebody should watch the twins for a " tiny moment."

Meals were quiet, with no sign of the irritation or torment simmering in the breasts of some of those present. It was torture to Goosey to sit through lunch and watch Martin West, at a table for two by the window, leaning across and speaking in familiar and confidential tones to Felicity Grant. It was fortunate that the tête-à-tête took place at only one meal. Felicity had taken upon herself the task of getting the twins up and giving them breakfast in the children's room, and at dinner, Mrs. Hellier, having put the children to bed with her sister's help, made, in Goosey's opinion, a welcome third at the table.

Paul enjoyed a unique position as half passenger, half crew, and spent a good deal of time in his brother's rooms. On the afternoon following his arrival, he joined Goosey and Felix at their table for lunch. Goosey greeted him with pleasure and Mr. Lenner waved him sadly to a seat at his side.

" Thanks," said Paul. " Had a nice morning? "

" Splendid," said Goosey. " I went up to talk to Ruth, and Roger kicked me downstairs. I went into the garden and the old gardener followed me around like a bloodhound."

" What for? " asked Paul.

" He's the sire of two of the pink overalls," explained Goosey.

" Ah," said Paul.

" Then," proceeded Goosey in lowered tones, " I tried to talk to—that pretty girl sitting behind you only don't turn round yet, and the piece of cheese sitting opposite her brought round a thousand-quid car and

said, ' How about some fresher air '—not to me, of course
—and so that was over. Then the dog-owner led out
the dog and said as I was doing nothing could I waltz
Matilda round, and the mother of the twins said as I
was obviously going for a walk perhaps I could just
take them a tiny way. Yes—on the whole," he ended,
" a delightful morning. What were you doing? " he
asked.

" Meditating," said Paul lightly.

It was not, indeed, far from the truth. Paul was uncertain as to the exact reasons which had brought him
down to his brother's house to watch Felicity spending
her time with another man. He had not yet encoun-
tered Martin West, and much of his morning had been
spent in bringing himself to a state of mind in which
he could face him without betraying his smouldering
jealousy. He was now feeling more sure of himself
and even looked forward to the inevitable meeting.

It was not, after all, difficult. He reached the door of
the dining-room with Goosey and Felix at the same
moment as Felicity and Martin West. He opened the
door and stepped aside to allow Felicity to pass.

" Hello, Liss," he said lightly. " Settling down
nicely? "

" Beautifully, thank you," said Felicity with a smile.

" That's grand. Hello, Martin," went on Paul, turning to her companion. " Which of the rivers have you
been thrown into? "

" Hello, Paul," replied Martin. " I'm in Zambesi,
and liking it."

" I asked Roger to keep a complaint book," said Paul.
" He said he wouldn't because the complaints would all
be on his side." He cut Goosey off neatly and imper-
ceptibly just as the latter was preparing to enter the
library, and led him, with Felix, towards the drawing-
room, leaving Felicity and Martin to have coffee by
themselves in the library. Goosey restrained his indignation until he reached the drawing-room, and then
turned on Paul.

"What did you want to do that for?" he demanded angrily. "Now you've let that feller go in there for a nice lonely coffee with Miss Grant."

"You mustn't," said Paul, "poke your nose in where it isn't wanted. When two people come down to a place like this together for a week, it's obvious," he went on, "that they want to see a good deal of each other. And so——" He paused.

"And so?" said Goosey.

"—and so I'm going to see that they do," ended Paul.

To this resolution he adhered, becoming a self-appointed bodyguard to protect Felicity and Martin from annoyance or intrusion. He behaved, the infuriated Goosey informed him, like a ruddy A.D.C. to a pink-eyed Governor. The methods were, indeed, not dissimilar; Paul allowed a brief exchange of courtesies and then with effortless skill, detached the intruder and left the pair in seclusion once more.

Brenda watched him for some time and then brought the matter up at dinner with Ruth and Roger.

"It seems odd," she said, "to think that we sat solemnly and worried ourselves into a fever over the possibility of having all the new carpets covered with blood. I was brushing up my First Aid and reading how to separate dogs when they fight—and now look at them! Paul's behaving like a mother pushing her eldest unmarried daughter down the throat of the first suitor."

"I don't like it," said Roger morosely. "And I'll tell you something else—Martin West doesn't like it either."

"Doesn't like it?" echoed Ruth in astonishment.

"What doesn't he like about it?" enquired Brenda. "I suppose you mean he likes the biscuit but longs to bite the hand that holds it out—is that it?"

"How do you know he doesn't like it?" asked Ruth.

"Perhaps I don't know quite that," admitted Roger, "but I know Martin. He prefers to do things his own way. And Paul knows it. I wish to the devil," he went

C

on savagely, " I'd told Paul to stay out of here until it
was too late to do any harm."

" The biggest mistake you made," remarked Brenda
bitterly, " wasn't Paul or Martin—it was letting in that
poisonous Hellier product. That woman is going to
upset my mental balance."

" I wouldn't have thought you'd have seen anything
of her at all," said Ruth in surprise. " She can't take
the twins into the office, can she? "

" My office," pointed out Brenda, " overlooks that nice
little lawn that Roger so generously roped off as the
children's playground. So what does their mother do?
—she puts the children there and leaves them and puts
her head inside the office and says—and how I hate that
voice of hers—half whining and half insolent—she says
' Oh, Miss Mallard, I'm just going off for a tiny minute
—you'll peep out occasionally, won't you? ' "

Roger grinned.

" And do you peep out? " he asked.

" Well," said Brenda, " I thought we'd better have it
out once and for all, so I said, ' Look, Mrs. Hellier '—
firmly, like that—' Look, Mrs. Hellier, I'm a busy
woman and I haven't time to peep at anything but my
own work—I'm frightfully sorry.' "

" Well, that's pretty conclusive," said Ruth.

" You'd think it would convey the idea that I wasn't
exactly in tune," said Brenda. " But what did she do?
She threw me a flashing smile full of gratitude, said
' You're a darling—I thought you would '—and
vanished."

" You should have sent for me," said Roger. " I've
had two short scraps with her up to date. Once when
I found her taking the twins into the drawing-room and
the other when I heard her trying to persuade the green
overall to drop what she was doing and take over the
twins. I gave her both barrels both times—I quite
enjoyed it. Did you amuse the twins? " he enquired.

" I sat still for a long time," said Brenda, " saying
to myself I-will-not-look-out-of-that-window. I almost

didn't, but of course I took a look finally, and saw the
two children playing happily, so I started on some work.
I forgot them for a bit, and suddenly I looked out again
and felt frozen with horror—they'd just disappeared. I
rushed outside and searched and called and at last I
found them standing on the gravel poking their fingers
into Rameses in the entirely correct assumption that he
was a stuffed dog. By that time I was a jellied wreck.
Can't one," she asked peevishly, " have a woman of
that sort locked up? "

"I don't know what you could charge her with,"
replied Roger. " Odd, isn't it," he went on, " to think
of a dimwit like that being the sister of a nice girl like
Felicity? "

Brenda rose.

"It's ludicrous," she said on her way out. " Now, if
Martin West were wooing a woman like the Hellier,
I'd adopt Paul's tactics and foster the romance for all
I was worth."

She closed the door behind her and Roger and Ruth
sat for a few moments in silence. At last Ruth looked
across the table with a smile.

"Well, do you like running hotels? " she asked.

Roger frowned, his eyes fixed on her face.

"Look," he said abruptly, ignoring her question.
" I'm worried about you."

"About me? " said Ruth in astonishment. " Why? "

"Because you're looking—oh, sort of peaked," said
Roger. " If you're going to find this too much for
you——"

"Oh—don't be silly," protested Ruth.

"There's nothing silly about it," said Roger, his
irritation rising as it did in any kind of argument. " If
one's wife suddenly begins to look pinched and tired,
then one's justified in assuming she's doing too much.
And if you happen to be fond of her, it begins to get
on your nerves and you decide that if the thing's going
to get her down you might as well burn the ruddy place
at once and start on something easier."

He came to an end and sat staring moodily across at his wife. She looked back at him and gave a little laugh.

"Dear Mr. Mallard," she said gently, "I am perfectly well."

"I see," said Roger. "Well, you don't look it and I believe you're lying just to try and put me off. Honestly, Ruth," he ended earnestly, "are you really feeling all right?"

Ruth hesitated, but at the sudden look of fear in Roger's eyes, spoke hurriedly.

"I'm absolutely all right," she said. "Honestly, Roger. I did feel a bit upset when we were working hard, but I feel quite nice again now."

Roger rose slowly from his chair and, going round the table, pulled his wife to her feet and took her face between his hands. He studied the gentle little mouth for a few moments and then stooped and laid his lips lingeringly upon it. He released her, and Ruth leaned her head for a moment on his coat sleeve.

"It's ages since you did that," she said. "The last time was last Friday night at ten past eleven."

"Did you have the stop watch out?" asked Roger with a grin.

"No," said Ruth. "Don't you remember?—I was just doing my face and you said how can you put that muck on and then you kissed me nicely like that and you said 'Well anyhow, it tastes nice!'"

Roger gave one of his rare, attractive laughs.

"Funny things, women," he remarked as he went out. "All I remember about last Friday night is the leak in that bally pipe . . ."

Ruth stood still after the door closed, staring straight before her, a thoughtful frown on her face. She turned after a while and walked slowly across the room, studying herself in the glass above the mantelpiece.

She was, she decided, looking a little done. Roger would be angry when she told him . . . but perhaps, after all, there would be nothing to tell. Angry or not, she was going to be sure before she spoke. Next time she would tell him her suspicion, as other wives told their husbands, and they would wait together, as other couples did—with joy or apprehension—to see whether it would be a baby or merely a rumour of one.

Next time . . . but not this time. It went too deep to risk the possibility of disappointing him. She would not even confide in Brenda.

Ruth turned from the mirror with her decision unaltered. She would say nothing for another day or two. She would wait, and pray earnestly . . . and go in and see Doctor Mills . . .

She was, she told herself exultantly, almost sure . . . almost sure . . .

CHAPTER VII

GOOSEY, turning over in the middle of the night and punching the pillow to accommodate his right ear instead of his left, was seized with an idea so brilliant that he could scarcely restrain himself from getting out of bed, going into the next room and rousing Felix to tell him about it.

He awoke in the morning, recalled details of his scheme and put them before Paul at breakfast.

" What do you think of it? " he asked finally.

Paul buttered his toast with an air of indifference.

" Not much," he said briefly.

" But it's good," said Goosey eagerly, " it's really good. And look at the day—I couldn't have chosen a better day for it."

Paul looked out at the sparkling sunshine.

" How did you know—in the middle of the night— that it was going to be sunny this morning? " he asked.

" Oh, I guessed," said Goosey. " I say, Paul," he went on, " you'll help me, won't you? "

"Help you?" said Paul in astonishment. "What do you want help for? You're going to ask Felicity Grant to go on a picnic—do you want help when you ask a girl out?"

"Don't be a fool, Paul," entreated Goosey. "You know jolly well it isn't as simple as that. And besides, I can't ask her out with me alone—even if she'd come, which I doubt. I want to organize a small, select party," he went on, "leaving out all the——" he glanced over to the window table where Martin West was eating a solitary breakfast "—all the superfluities."

"Well, go ahead and organize it," invited Paul. "I'll watch you."

"That's no use," said Goosey. "In the first place, I want to borrow Roger's car. He wouldn't lend it to me, but he'd let you have it—so you see, you've got to do a bit of—of co-operating. You go to Roger when you've finished eating, and I'll get hold of Miss Grant and see what she thinks of it."

He took the last piece of toast to prevent, he explained, Paul or Felix getting it and so prolonging their breakfast unduly. He ate it hurriedly, keeping an anxious eye on Martin West to make sure that the latter did not leave the dining-room first.

Paul secured Roger's permission to borrow his car, with the stipulation that Goosey was not to drive it, and then went in search of Goosey to see how he was progressing. He found him standing by the large window in the children's playroom, pointing out to Felicity the warmth and perfection of the day.

"It is lovely," agreed Felicity, "and I'd simply love to go. Where's it going to be?"

"Roger was talking about a place last night," said Goosey. "That's really what made me think of it. It's a sort of pub right on the river—it's got a garden with a sort of pavilion, and a little sandy bit of beach. They put up coloured umbrellas and you can sit out under them, or in the pavilion place. It's the local swimming place—only I don't know whether you think it's a bit late in the year to swim—cold——"

"Nothing could be cold on a day like this," declared Felicity. She turned to Paul. "Are you coming too, Paul?" she asked.

"I've got to," said Paul briefly. "Roger says that if Goosey drives the car he'll sue him for a new one. Well, you're organizing this," he continued, looking at Goosey. "What time do we start?"

"About eleven, I think," said Goosey. "I'm going to see Ruth about the food. I didn't bring any bathing things," he went on. "I suppose Roger would throw them in with the car. Well, then," he ended, as the door opened to admit Mrs. Hellier. "Eleven at the front door."

"Eleven at the front door, what for?" enquired Mrs. Hellier, looking from one to the other.

"Oh, nothing," said Goosey airily.

"You're not going to stand at the front door at eleven just for nothing," stated Mrs. Hellier contemptuously. "Anyhow, I shall come and stand there, too."

"Oh, no—I mean, there won't be room," said Goosey hurriedly, noting with a feeling of panic that Martin West had just come into the room. "Well, I'm just going," he continued, edging to the door.

"Wait a minute," said Mrs. Hellier peremptorily. "If there's no room in your car then I can go in Martin's, can't I, Martin?"

"Oh—he isn't coming," said Goosey hastily. "Are you, West?" he asked, turning to Martin.

Martin West walked across the room without any sign of haste and stood beside Felicity. He took out a cigarette-case, offered it with a single gesture to everybody present and, being refused, took out a cigarette and lit it unhurriedly.

"Not going where?" he enquired.

"I don't know," said Mrs. Hellier. "Major Horder won't tell me."

"Paul and Felix and I," said Goosey, "are just going for a little run with Miss Grant."

"Sounds good," commented Martin lightly.

"And I can't fit in their car, so can't I go in yours?" asked Mrs. Hellier.

"By all means," said Martin.

"Look, Nan——" began Felicity.

"Oh, I know what you're going to say," said Mrs. Hellier. "Who's going to look after the twins? Well, I haven't left their side for seventy-two hours and I think I need a break. I'll go and ask that Mrs. Beddington—she sits and knits all day so she can just as easily sit and knit near the twins."

"Nan," said Felicity in a firmer tone. "This isn't a party—it's just a drive and——"

"Oh, no!" said Mrs. Hellier on a sing-song note. "Oh, no, it isn't. You're taking food—I heard him say so. I'm not butting in—I'm going with Martin—aren't I, Martin?" she asked.

"I've said so," said Martin with a smile.

Mrs. Hellier, with a joyful exclamation, took Goosey's arm and pulled him out of the room.

"Come on," she said. "You get the food and I'll get that old——" She came to a sudden halt as she saw Mrs. Beddington, followed by her husband, coming down the stairs.

"Oh, I was looking for you," she said.

Mrs. Beddington looked flustered. "Oh, good morning," she said nervously. "Good morning. George," she said as her husband came down. "Mrs. Hellier was just looking for us."

"Ah," said Mr. Beddington. "Good morning."

"Major Horder wants to take me for a tiny drive," said Mrs. Hellier, "and I wondered—couldn't you bring your knitting, or whatever it is you're doing, and do it near the twins for a tiny moment? It's the most marvellous day and the sun's absolutely boiling. It's just the day for getting out."

"That's just what I told her a few moments ago,"

said Mr. Beddington, on a note of triumph. " I said
' Lena, dear, wouldn't you take a little drive this morning? ' Didn't I, Lena? "

"Yes, dear," said Mrs. Beddington. " That's true.
But I thought—so much to ask Roger—nobody to drive—
but it would," she ended wistfully, " be very, very nice."

" Capital, capital," said Mr. Beddington gleefully.
" Now I must find Roger and see what he can arrange
in the way of a car and a chauffeur."

He took a few steps and was brought up by a little
cry from his wife.

" Oh, but, George," she said. " Mrs. Hellier—she
asked us—the twins——"

Mr. Beddington looked distressed.

" Tck, tck, tck," he said remorsefully. " How thought-
less of me. You must forgive me," he went on, addressing Mrs. Hellier. " I have such difficulty in persuading
my wife to go out anywhere . . . But the twins—if you
think a drive would do them good," he said, " we should
love to take them—we should look after them very
well . . ."

" Oh, that's marvellous! " said Mrs. Hellier. " We're
taking some food so we may be out a bit longer than
you."

" As a matter of fact," began Goosey, " I'd just—as
it were—borrowed Roger's car myself——"

" What for? " asked Mrs. Hellier. " You've got your
own, haven't you? "

" Yes," said Goosey miserably, " but——"

" Well, that's all right," said Mrs. Hellier. " Your
car and Martin's car and Roger's car—that's all settled.
You go," she ordered, "and see about the food."

Goosey took a deep breath.

" Look here——" he began indignantly.

" Oh, don't stand and argue," said Mrs. Hellier impatiently. " Go on and don't let's stand talking—it's
almost eleven now."

Goosey, furious but helpless, went in search of Ruth
and saw Paul a little way ahead of him.

" How's the organizing going? " asked Paul, as Goosey caught him up.

Goosey opened his mouth and gave vent to a short summary of his opinion of Mrs. Hellier.

" I entirely agree," said Paul, " but it's a bit beside the point. How's the picnic? "

" It's a—a mushroom growth," said Goosey bitterly. " It started as a small, tender plant and now the entire boatload is going to assemble in the hall and climb into fleets of cars. What's more," he went on, " we haven't even got Roger's car any more—that's gone. We're left with mine."

" Well, that won't go," said Paul comfortingly.

" Don't start being funny," begged Goosey. " If you'd been a bit helpful in the first place you could have nipped that Hellier woman in the bud."

" How could I do that? " asked Paul. " There's only one method with a woman like that, and it isn't one which nice fellows like ourselves can adopt."

" You could have kept West out of it," said Goosey. " After all, you know him pretty well."

" Too well to try and keep him out of it," said Paul. " Well, don't let's get involved in an argument—it's time you got on with a bit more organizing."

The expedition which set out at a quarter to twelve was scarcely the delightful, intimate little affair which Goosey had planned.

Three cars stood in the drive—Martin West's, opulent and shining, Roger's, solid and serviceable, and Goosey's—long, lean and a veritable museum piece.

Goosey surveyed the passengers with distaste. Matters had, he thought, gone sadly astray. The last knell had sounded when Lady Warne, passing through the hall, asked the reason for the gathering.

" It's a picnic," Paul told her, packing parcels of food into Goosey's car. " Major Horder's organizing it."

" Where are you all going? " enquired Lady Warne.

" Oh—a sort of place on the river," said Goosey, whose enthusiasm for the scheme had long since died.

" I don't care for outdoor affairs," stated Lady Warne.
" Is there any shelter? "

" Well, yes, there's a sort of pavilion or something,"
said Goosey vaguely and without interest.

" Ah," said Lady Warne. " Then I may as well join
you." She studied the three cars for a moment. " I'll
go in that one," she said, pointing to Martin West's.

Goosey felt that he cared little where anybody went.
At least, he told himself, Felicity Grant was going in
his car, with Felix as a third. Paul was to drive the
Beddingtons in Roger's car, taking the twins, and Martin was to take Mrs. Hellier and Lady Warne.

Goosey's cup of misery, however, was not yet full.
Having settled Felicity and Felix in his car, he got into
it and prepared to drive away. The car, however, remained motionless. No efforts could make it move, and
the unfortunate Goosey, who from the corner of his eye
had seen Martin West looking on with barely concealed
amusement, now had the humiliation of seeing him
approach to suggest the obvious way out of the difficulty.

" You'd better get out and come with me, Felicity,"
he said over Goosey's head, bowed over the engine in
shame and rage. " I'll take Miss Grant, Horder," he
went on. " You can follow when you—er—get going."

A general reshuffling of passengers now took place.
Paul offered to stay behind to help Goosey to start his
car, and Felix took his place at the wheel of Roger's
car, with Mrs. Hellier beside him and Mr. Beddington
and the twins at the back: Martin West drove his own
car, Felicity beside him and Lady Warne, Rameses
and Mrs. Beddington behind. Martin leaned out and
called a question to Goosey.

" Where are we headed for? " he asked.

Goosey looked up. " Oh—yes," he said vaguely.
" Well, Roger says turn right when you get out of the
drive, and go on to where the road forks and then stick
to the river the whole time and about eleven miles out
you get to the ' Nag's Head ' and that's it."

Martin nodded and leaned back, and the beautiful

car moved soundlessly away. Goosey looked after it bitterly.

" If I had a gun," he muttered desperately to Paul, " I'm damned if I'd know whether to shoot that fellow or his two back tyres."

" Keep calm," said Paul soothingly. " This was your idea."

" If you say that again," said Goosey fiercely, " I'll forget myself."

Felix halted for instructions, and Goosey repeated his directions. Felix, about to set off, was stopped by Mrs. Hellier.

" Half a minute," she said, and leaning across him, addressed Paul.

" Paul, the twins are going to ruin poor Mr. Beddington's enjoyment," she called. " Couldn't they go with you?—it's only a tiny way."

Goosey, his jaw dropping, stared at the speaker in utter astonishment. He attempted to speak, but no words came. Paul gave a glance at his face and fought down a desire to shout with laughter.

" I don't think——" he began.

Goosey recovered his voice.

" We'll take the twins," he said with a sort of savage calmness. " We'll take the twins and anything else you don't want. Just hand 'em over. You all go along and have a nice time till we get there with the children."

Paul lifted the children out of his brother's car and placed them on the drive to await the moment when Goosey's car would become mobile. The second party drove out of sight and Goosey, straightening his shoulders, looked at Paul.

" I tell you what," he said. " We'll just push the blasted car back into the garage, go in and get a drink and tell 'em we didn't get started."

" It wouldn't be a bad idea," said Paul, " but we've got the food."

" Well, when they get there and no food turns up, they'll come back, won't they? " said Goosey reasonably.

"I don't suppose Roger'd like that very much," said Paul. "They're all supposed to be having lunch out, and if they roll up here and demand food——"

There was a silence. Goosey bent resignedly over the engine once more and the twins looked on with stolid interest.

In twenty minutes, after strenuous efforts on the part of Goosey and Paul, the car sprang into life. The twins, with a certain instinct that this was the last bus, hurried to Paul's side and waited to be lifted in.

Goosey drove disconsolately, depressed and gloomy, and there was silence for some time. At a bend in the road, he brought the car to a standstill and looked about him.

"D'you suppose this is the fork in the road?" he asked.

"Are you sure Roger said the road forked?" asked Paul. "If my memory's accurate, it's the river that forks, and we keep along the right fork."

"Well, something forked," said Goosey, "the road or the river—what does it matter which it was?"

"Keep right," directed Paul, "and then along this road for seven or eight miles and then we're there."

They reached the "Nag's Head" and took a narrow lane along the side of the building. The track came to an end near a large, barn-like erection on the river's edge. The two men looked round the desolate-looking scene.

"This doesn't look much like anything," commented Goosey, without enthusiasm.

"Well, there's what you called a pavilion," said Paul, "and I can see the holes in the ground where the umbrellas are stuck when they stick them in, only it's a bit late in the season for striped umbrellas, I suppose."

As if to prove the truth of his words, the sun, which had been disappearing at intervals behind patches of cloud, now became lost behind a grey, ominous-looking cloud bank. Goosey looked up at the sky and spoke emotionlessly.

"Rain, and packets of it," he commented. "It only needed that. Where d'you imagine," he enquired, "the others have got to?"

The others had not, in fact, got far. Martin West drove for some miles, stopped the car and turned to Felicity.

"I don't think we're on the right track at all," he said. "What did that Horder fellow say? Right at this fork, didn't he?"

Felicity nodded.

"Well, if the place is on the river," went on Martin, "we're going a long way round to get at it. This is taking us miles off it."

He drove a few miles further and stopped abruptly.

"This is a pure waste of time," he said irritably. "We're heading straight away from it."

"There's a sign on that inn place straight ahead," said Felicity, "which looks awfully like a nag's head."

"You're right," said Martin, following the direction of her glance. "That's the third Nag's Head we've sighted. But not one of them is anywhere near the river."

He drove up to the building, got out and walked round the back, reappearing with a frown on his face.

"This isn't it, obviously," he said. "Pity I didn't ask Horder the name of the village we're supposed to be making for."

He looked round as if searching for something, and Felicity watched him.

"What are you going to do?" she asked.

"Find a telephone and ring Roger up and ask him where we're supposed to be going," said Martin. "No use going round in circles collecting Nags' Heads."

"Oughtn't we to—to go home again?" faltered Mrs. Beddington. "If we're lost, I mean."

Felicity turned to her and spoke in reassuring tones. "We're not lost," she said. "Major Horder didn't explain very well, that's all."

Martin walked into the inn and the three women

waited in silence for his return. Lady Warne was occupied with Rameses, who was getting restless; Mrs. Beddington was trying to subdue her nervousness, and Felicity was looking anxiously at the black skies. When Martin came back she indicated the threatening clouds and spoke anxiously.

" Do you think it's worth going on? " she asked.

Martin started the engine and turned the car in the direction from which they had come.

" It might pass off," he said, " and anyhow, I take it this place has a shelter of some sort. They've got the food," he pointed out.

They drove on in silence, gloom settling on the party. They had set out in sunshine and warmth to picnic by a pleasant river. There was now no sunshine, an unpleasantly cold wind had sprung up and the prospect of eating cold food beside cold water had lost its attraction. As they drove, a drizzle of rain fell, growing into a downpour as they reached their destination.

The sight that met their eyes on their arrival did nothing to dispel the gloom.

Goosey's car was parked close to the river and its owner was struggling to get the hood up. His hair clung damply to his head and raindrops coursed down his face and neck. Paul, seated on one of the long wooden benches which ran along the sides of the shelter, was using his handkerchief in an attempt to dry the children's heads and shoulders. After one glance, Felicity slipped out of the car and, unrolling the towel which was to have served to dry her after her swim, went across and began to rub the twins vigorously.

Mrs. Beddington, from her seat at the back of the car, looked round with an uneasiness and anxiety mounting almost to tearfulness.

" I don't see anything of—of the others," she said dismally. " Do you think perhaps they got—could they have got lost? "

" I don't suppose for a moment they're lost," said Martin West, forgetting the general agreement to allay the timid creature's fears. "If Nan Hellier gets at the wheel they'll be taking short cuts over hedges——"

Too late, he stopped. Mrs. Beddington leaned across Lady Warne and looked at him with tear-filled eyes.

"Oh, I think we ought to go home," she moaned. "I really do. If anything—if anything happens, they'll take them home, and I shan't be—be there!"

"Oh, come," said Martin in tones which he attempted to make hearty. "They'll be here any minute—why, we've only just got here ourselves."

"I don't propose," put in Lady Warne in decided tones, "to stay here. I shall not, in fact," she continued, "get out of this car. I can't think what Major Horder was thinking of to get us all out here in the pouring rain."

Goosey, from the open side of the shelter, stood and looked across at her with a cold stare, wondering whether he could point out that Major Horder had not asked her to come and had not, in fact, desired her presence in the least.

"I don't think we can go back now," said Martin in a tone of doubt. "We're supposed to be lunching out —we can't walk in at half-past two and demand hot meals for a large number of people."

"What," Lady Warne demanded of Goosey, "is there to eat here?"

Goosey opened one or two packages and peered inside.

"This one's sandwiches, I think," he said. "And this one's sandwiches with brown stuff inside, and this one's sandwiches with red stuff inside and——"

"Is there anything hot?" interrupted Lady Warne.

"There's a flask," said Goosey. "I don't know whether it's for us or whether it's hot milk for the twins . . ."

Lady Warne looked at Martin.

"I should like," she said in commanding tones, "to be taken home."

"Oh, and so should I," begged Mrs. Beddington. "Please, Mr. West!"

Martin hesitated, looking across at Felicity.

"We're going, Felicity," he said. "Lady Warne and Mrs. Beddington are anxious to get home."

Felicity looked round the dreary little spot, glanced briefly at Goosey's stricken countenance and shook her head.

"I'll stay here and give the twins lunch," she said, "and then come back with Major Horder."

Goosey turned upon her a look of dog-like devotion and gratitude.

"Oh, no, Miss Grant," he protested quickly. "It's awfully—it's awfully decent of you, but it's a frightful washout, the whole thing—I mean, a literal washout, and you ought to get back. The twins," he ended, "can go with you."

"The twins," answered Felicity firmly, "simply adore picnics, and I shouldn't dream of taking them away. Besides," she added, "think what a lot of extra food there's going to be."

Goosey's countenance lightened a little at this thought.

"Won't you be cold?" he asked, looking at her light dress. "You didn't bring a mack or anything, did you?"

Paul picked his mackintosh off the bench beside him and rolled it into a ball.

"Catch," he said, throwing it across at Felicity.

"Thanks, Paul," she said. "That makes that all right. I'm so sorry," she said to Lady Warne, "that you won't stay."

Martin West stood by the door of his car for a moment, his eyes going from Paul to Goosey, his face expressionless. At last he turned abruptly, got into the driving seat and started the engine. Leaning out, he called to Felicity as the large car moved backwards down the narrow lane.

"I'll come back for you," he said, "when I've taken Lady Warne and Mrs. Beddington home. You can't possibly all fit into"—his gaze turned contemptuously for a moment on Goosey's ancient model—"into that thing."

A little frown appeared on Felicity's face. " We can and we will," she said.

Goosey watched the car out of sight and turned to the girl beside him.

" That was a nice thing to do," he said, " but you're going to give the twins and yourself pneumonia. I'm sorry," he went on, " that it's such a fizzle."

" You can't help the weather," said Felicity. " It's a dreary place now, but think of it in the sunshine, with nice bright umbrellas and little tables and people having drinks in the shelter."

" Takes a lot of imagination," said Goosey. " Hey, Paul," as Paul moved in the direction of the inn, " it's no use asking them for anything. I tried that—they said they couldn't let us have anything at all—the season's over and all you can get is beer—if you want it."

" I'm going up," called Paul over his shoulder, " to ask if they'd mind our making a fire."

" Making a fire? " Goosey's face brightened. " Great Scott, that's a good idea," he said. " We'll be campers instead of picnickers."

Roused by Paul's example, he set about making the party a success. He took the car seats, carried them into the shelter and spread Paul's mackintosh beside them. Finding some comparatively dry sand in a sheltered hollow, he made a little sand-pit for the twins and, sitting happily beside them on the mackintosh, showed them how to make sand pies, using the top of Ruth's flask as a mould.

As if to congratulate them on this brave attempt to beat the elements, the sun came out—at first in brief flashes and then with increasing frequency. Paul appeared and went by without pausing.

" Fire O.K.," he called. " Woodpile somewhere up here—I'll go and collect a bit."

Felicity sat still and looked after him for some time, her expression puzzled. At last she roused herself and spoke to Goosey.

" I think the children ought to have something to

eat now," she said. "It's long past their lunch time."

"We'll all eat," said Goosey. "I'll unpack the stuff now."

"Do," said Felicity, "but let the twins have theirs— I'm going up to help Paul."

She got to her feet and walked up the little slope in the direction Paul had taken. He was in a little wood, breaking sticks and laying them in a little heap.

"Can I help?" she asked.

"No thanks," said Paul, looking up for a moment. "I think I've got about enough."

He picked up the pile and settled them on his arm, Felicity stooping to pick up stray pieces as they dropped. She looked round the pretty little spot, standing in a pattern of light and shade, the sun's rays touching her hair.

"It's nice here," she said.

"Not bad," said Paul, starting on his downward journey. "Won't be bad down there when we get the fire going."

Felicity, after a moment's hesitation, followed him, her eyes on his back and a puzzled frown on her face. At the edge of the wood she came to a sudden halt and opened her mouth once or twice without finding the courage to speak. The distance between them widened, and she called in a soft, urgent voice.

"Paul," she said. "Please—do stop a minute."

Paul halted and looked back over his shoulder.

"What for?" he asked.

"Oh—I don't know," said Felicity, coming to his side and looking up at him. "It's nice here, and it's the first time I've seen you—seen you properly, I mean, for ages—and you haven't said a word to me since you arrived at River Lodge. When I heard you were coming," she continued a little breathlessly. "I thought —I thought you——"

She stopped. Paul looked down at her with a cool air of patient waiting.

"You thought——" he said after a pause.

"I thought," began Felicity again, and stopped. "Oh, nothing," she ended desperately.

"You thought," said Paul, " that I was going to bother you. You thought I was going to be troublesome. Well," he went on in light, reassuring tones, " now you know I'm not."

He took a step forward to resume his journey. Felicity put out a hand and caught his arm.

"Paul—just a moment," she said quietly. She released him and he stood waiting. " Why," she asked, " didn't you answer the two letters I wrote you? "

Paul frowned as if attempting to recall the reasons for the omission.

"Well, as far as I can remember," he said at last, "there wasn't anything to answer."

"But I said——" began Felicity.

"You said that Martin was willing to overlook the whole thing and to forget everything I'd said," interrupted Paul. " Well, I didn't want him to overlook anything and I particularly wanted him to remember everything I'd said—especially," he ended, " what I'd said about your acting."

Felicity's face whitened. " You can be—awfully cruel," she said in a half-stifled tone. " How can you be so—so——"

She stopped, afraid that tears would overwhelm her. Paul raised his eyebrows and spoke with genuine astonishment.

"What's cruel about it? " he asked. " Think of it this way: if a girl sings a song in her mother's drawing-room and asks what you think of her top notes, you give a polite smile and say she was only a couple of semi-tones off. But if she gives up her amateur status and announces her intention of singing Gilda to your Rigoletto then you have to come out into the open and say what you really think. But why," he went on reasonably, " should you worry about what I really think? I'm not a member of the theatre-going public, I'm not a dramatic critic, and I'm not the fellow who has to pay your salary. If I were, you wouldn't be getting one—for more reasons than one," he ended with a wry grin. " Now come on and get the twins thawed out."

" Paul "—Felicity made a last appeal—" couldn't you stop being like this? Couldn't we be friends, as we used to be? "

Paul stared down at her for a moment and then gave a short laugh.

" My darling Liss," he said lightly, "what a short memory you've got! We were never friends. We were what the old songs call sweethearts, loving, tender, clinging sweethearts. We were mad with love and wild with longing. We were man and wife in everything but name—and deed. We were soul mates planning a splendid future—surely you remember? I was to act for a living and you were to live—and cook—for an actor. There was never anything friendly in the situation at all."

" If you really hate me," said Felicity, tears welling up at last, " then why did you come here? You knew I was going to be here, and you knew Martin was coming. Why," she repeated, " did you come? "

" Principally to kick his teeth out," said Paul quietly, " but I gave up the idea when I saw how much weight he'd put on—fourteen odd, I reckon, to my twelve odd. You'll have to watch him or he'll fill out like Rameses. And then, when I saw how nicely he squired you and what a splendid couple you looked and what a handsome chap he was, I thought I'd leave his teeth alone and let you have him the way you like him." He pulled out his handkerchief, felt it and shook his head. " I can't dry your tears on this," he said. " The twins had first go. And it's silly to cry because I said you couldn't act. You didn't cry the first time I told you, did you? "

Felicity shook her head and wiped her eyes resolutely.

" No, of course you didn't," went on Paul. " You simply told me to go away and stay away and never to go near you again because you were through with the whole thing and I was a conceited and dictatorial pig and it was a pity you'd ever set eyes on me. Wasn't that how it went? "

Felicity looked up at his set, unhappy face. Paul met her eyes with a cool, hard gaze.

" Paul," she whispered, " I——"

" Let's go," said Paul. He turned abruptly and strode down the slope and Felicity, clutching her little twigs desperately, followed him without another word.

CHAPTER VIII

Goosey drove his car into the garage two hours later, having left Paul, with Felicity and the twins, at the front door. He got out, banged the door behind him, and walked back to the house slowly, reviewing the events of the day.

It had started badly, of course—half the party pushing in unasked; the disgrace of watching Felicity leaving his car when it refused to start; the dreary picnic site and the rain . . .

But after a time, things had improved. On the whole, thought Goosey, he hadn't done too badly. There had been a delightful camp-fire scene with Felicity. It would have been better if Paul and the twins had not been there, and it had seemed to him that Felicity was a little tired and out of spirits, but . . .

A peculiar sound made Goosey pause. He stopped and looked about him. He had reached the little path near the kitchen—perhaps a little pink overall . . .

" Psst! " came the sound again.

Goosey turned towards it and saw, to his extreme astonishment, the face of Miss Mallard poking through a small window on the ground floor. A hand came out and signalled urgently. Goosey, his mouth open in wonder, approached the window slowly.

" Come round to the side door," hissed Brenda, when he was close enough to her. " Come quietly—and hurry!"

Her head was withdrawn, and Goosey, after a few moments' bewildered pause, went cautiously round the building. At the door to which he had been directed stood Brenda, her finger to her lips and her eyes glancing round. She put out a hand and seized Goosey by the sleeve.

"Come with me," she hissed.

Goosey, feeling more bewildered than ever, tried to match his long steps to his companion's short, swift, scurrying ones. He found himself being half led, half dragged along a passage, up an unfamiliar staircase and along a corridor.

" Where are you taking me? " he asked.

" Sh!" hissed Brenda fiercely.

" Where? " repeated Goosey in a whisper.

" To my bedroom," panted Brenda.

Goosey came to a dead stop, his eyes starting.

" B-bedroom," he faltered, on a high note. " B-bedroom? "

He lunged forward as the impatient Brenda, with a firmer grasp of his sleeve, pulled him forward once more. She reached a door, opened it and pushed Goosey inside. Following him, she shut the door behind her and stood against it for a moment, panting with exertion and relief.

" We did it," she said at last. " Why I bother about your wretched safety I don't know, but——"

" Safety? " echoed Goosey, his head whirling. " I don't know what you're talking about."

" You'll know soon," said Brenda, " but there was no time to talk downstairs. He's out for blood."

" Whose blood? " asked Goosey.

" Your blood," said Brenda.

" Who's out for my blood? "

" Roger," said Brenda.

" You mean Roger's angry about something and

he's looking for me?" said Goosey, his head clearing.

"I mean Roger's in a savage state about a great many things and if he sees you before he's calmer he'll tear you to pieces," said Brenda.

"But if he finds me in your b-bedroom," faltered Goosey, "he'll——"

"My dear Major Horder," said Brenda, "Roger owns this establishment, and he's entitled to walk into every room in it—except one. This one. While you're in here, you're safe. Safe from everyone," she added, as Goosey continued to regard her with a frightened countenance. "But I advise you not to move for some time. I'm perfectly serious. Roger is waiting for you—he heard your car and now he'll be looking for you, and if he finds you"—she paused dramatically—"neither your age nor your sex is going to protect you."

Goosey sank on to the bed and, seeing the look in Brenda's eye, got up again, smoothed the counterpane and seated himself on the little stool before her dressing-table.

"Would you mind telling me," he asked, "what I've done?"

"You haven't, strictly speaking, done anything," Brenda said. "Organizers don't, as a rule. They draw the scheme up and leave the other fellows to carry it through. I don't doubt," she went on kindly, "that your idea of a quiet picnic was quite a sound one, but you left a lot of ground uncovered. You took lunch for nine people and two children, and at half-past two, three people returned unfed and demanded a hot meal. Very upsetting for anyone who's trying to run an hotel."

"Well, yes," admitted Goosey, "but they wouldn't stay. But that isn't enough," he went on, "to put Roger into a tearing rage?"

"Correct," said Brenda. "Not nearly enough. But it started from there. The hot meals were prepared, but Mrs. Beddington wouldn't touch hers. Mr. Beddington hadn't come back, and she walked up and down the hall wringing her hands and weeping and begging

Roger to ring up the police. Ruth had a dreadful time trying to soothe her, and of course——"

"Yes, I know," said Goosey gloomily. "If Ruth got upset, then Roger would—but where," he enquired suddenly, "were the others? They didn't come to the Nag's Head."

"Not that Nag's Head," said Brenda. "I don't know how many heads a nag is entitled to have, but in the neighbourhood you chose there appears to be a large collection of them. Roger's car left here, you remember, with your artist friend at the wheel——"

Goosey nodded. "Yes, and Mrs. Hellier next to him and Mr. Beddington at the back," he said. "Where did they go?"

"They went to the Nag's Head," said Brenda. "To this Nag's Head and to that Nag's Head, but never, it seems, to the right Nag's Head."

"Well, what did they do?" enquired Goosey. "Just drive round and round?"

"Not exactly," said Brenda, leaning on the wooden rail of her bed and warming to her story. "At first, I gather, they made a serious effort to locate the place where the picnic was supposed to be. They had quite a routine—Felix drove until he saw a Nag's Head, stopped and turned off the engine and dismounted. Then he went inside to ask where they were and whether there was a river and if so, was there a picnic near it. Mrs. Hellier informed us that as Felix has never been known to utter a word, she advised Mr. Beddington to go in with him to do the talking. So Mr. Beddington went in each time and asked the questions and Felix, in the interval of waiting, ordered two beers."

"Two?" repeated Goosey, half curious and half envious.

"Two," repeated Brenda. "One for himself and the other for Mr. Beddington. Now perhaps you know," she went on, "that Mr. Beddington drinks one glass of beer every day with his lunch. *One* glass. And always *with* his lunch. So the first, and even the second Nag's Head didn't have much effect on him."

" He needn't have had any at all," pointed out Goosey. " Felix probably ordered them both for himself."

" Very likely," replied Brenda, " but Mr. Beddington didn't know that. He thought Mr. Lenner was being thoughtful and he didn't feel he ought to refuse."

" What did Mrs. Hellier do? " enquired Goosey.

" Well, she has her faults," said Brenda, " but she doesn't frequent Nag's Heads. She sat outside and waited—but when Felix came out of the fifth Nag's Head and mistook another car for Roger's and pushed the owner out of the driving seat, she thought she ought to drive, so she took over and on they went."

" Are they back now? " asked Goosey fearfully.

" They came back an hour ago," said Brenda. " By that time Ruth had got Mrs. Beddington to lie down, and she'd fallen asleep. Roger heard the car and went out to meet them. Your friend Felix was exactly as he always is—sad and speechless—the only difference was a sort of glassy look about the eye. But Mr. Beddington——" She stopped.

" Submerged? " whispered Goosey fearfully.

" That doesn't quite express it, but it gives you the general idea," replied Brenda. " Roger got him up to your room and put him in there. He's got to keep him away from his wife until he gets him into shape again."

Goosey groaned. " My God," he said. " I'll be in here for a week."

Brenda surveyed his stricken countenance and spoke drily.

" Well, it's flattering to see how the prospect excites you," she remarked, walking to the door. " Now I'm going. If I can get a tray of tea up to you, I will, but you can understand that if Roger sees me walking towards my bedroom bearing a man-size meal, he'll jump to dangerous conclusions."

She went out and, from the top of the stairs, saw Ruth

and Felicity disappearing into her office. She went down, entered the room and looked at them both critically.

" Felicity's looking tired," she remarked, " and so are you, Ruth. What are you creeping into my office for—shelter? "

" In a way," admitted Felicity. " I came in here to talk to Ruth—and to you, too, if you're staying."

" I can't," said Brenda. " I've got a man in my bedroom and he wants feeding."

" Goosey! " exclaimed Ruth and Felicity together.

Brenda looked offended.

" If I announce I've got a man," she said in injured tones, " why should you assume I won the booby prize? "

" It's very nice of you to hide him," said Ruth. " I haven't seen Roger so mad since——"

" Since the last time," said Brenda. " Don't try and make out he's a nice even-tempered man who only breaks out now and again. I never met a more active volcano."

" It's been an upsetting day," said Ruth. " I should have known—Goosey could always be trusted to make a hash of the most promising scheme."

Felicity leaned back in her chair and stretched out her lovely slender legs.

" It was my fault," she said. " If I'd said no in the first place——"

" That's true," said Brenda. " I don't know how a girl like you gets along at all without learning that golden rule."

" What golden rule? " asked Felicity.

" Saying no," said Brenda. " My father taught it to me, and I must say it's done more to simplify life than all the other hints massed together. ' Say, No,' he said. ' Don't stop to weigh up the proposition when it's put to you—just look regretful and say, No.' "

" But supposing you want to? " asked Felicity.

" That's easy," said Brenda. " When you've given a convincing refusal you think the thing over, and it's the easiest thing in the world to let the tucks out of your face, give a smile of relief and say, ' Oh, how marvellous, I've just remembered I can.' They're twice as pleased as they would have been if you'd accepted straight away. But the important thing is promptitude. If you hesitate for a mere second, or look uncertain, the ' No ' is offensive and anybody sees through it."

" I see the idea," said Felicity slowly. " It's worth practising."

" I'd have thought," said Brenda, " that you would have got it perfect long ago."

" Well, no," said Felicity. " I hate hurting people, and so——"

" That's just the beauty of this method," said Brenda. " Nobody is hurt because it's so spontaneous. While they're rolling out the invitation, your face is falling into creases of regret. You must try it. I must say, I got much too good at it," she went on. " It lost me at least one husband—I tried hard to keep my face muscles under control while he was getting the proposal out, but before he'd finished my face was all screwed up and I said—out of sheer habit—' Oh, my dear, I'm terribly, terribly sorry—I've too much on.' You can imagine how devastating that sort of thing can be to a shy young suitor. To think that by now I might have been a much-married woman, sitting here and giving you girls quite a different kind of advice. But I haven't time to sit here at all," she went on, rising. " Tell me, Ruth, will it be reasonably safe to go up with some tea to that half-wit secreted upstairs, or is Roger blood-hounding about still? "

" Roger's in the garage at the moment," said Ruth, " looking the car over to see whether Nan wrecked it or not."

" She's a troublesome girl, your sister," remarked Brenda to Felicity. " What were your parents doing—trying out separate systems on the two of you? "

Felicity laughed. " Oh, Nan's hopeless in some ways,"

she said, "but she really hasn't many of the—the major
failings. She doesn't smoke and she doesn't drink anything at all and she's got a kind heart. She just wasn't
ready to settle down, that's all. We all tried to put her
marriage off for a bit, but neither of them would hear
of it—he was very wild and gay and Nan adored him
and thought it was going to be one prolonged party.
She didn't dream of—of babies. In fact, she had no
idea the twins were coming. She went home to stay
with mother, and it was mother who found out. It
sounds incredible, but Nan and her husband had been
putting it down to curried prawns!"

There was a little shout of laughter from Ruth and
Brenda. "Poor Nan!" said Ruth. "It's a silly world
—I always think that storks must have a very poor
sense of direction——"

She broke off, and Brenda gave her a thoughtful little
glance. Then, going to the door, she looked into the
hall and, peering from side to side with an exaggerated
air of caution, went out.

Felicity looked after her with a smile.

"I like her," she said. "I'm glad I'm getting to
know her." She looked at Ruth and spoke with an air
of detachment. "She's very fond of Paul, isn't she?"
she asked.

Ruth laughed. "That's understating it," she said.
"She adores Paul—he's always been her pet. She'll
never give in to Roger, but Paul could walk over her
—if he wanted to."

Felicity drew her feet up, curled them under her and
rested her chin on one hand, gazing at Ruth with an
absent and dreamy expression.

"I wanted to ask you," she said slowly, "about Paul.
He's being——"

She stopped, and with a restless movement put her
feet to the ground and fidgeted herself into a more
comfortable position.

"Look, Ruth," she said, in a different and more
urgent tone, "don't you think he's behaving awfully—

oh! I don't know how to put it—he's so different, and I can't get him to talk to me."

Ruth was silent. She felt a little at a loss. She liked Felicity, but her love and her sympathies were entirely with Paul. The girl sitting before her had once, apparently, loved him, and had let him go. Ruth was unable to understand any girl letting Paul go . . .

"I know what you're thinking," said Felicity. "You're thinking that I came here with Martin and now I want to—to run after Paul and you think that's wrong and you're not going to have anything to do with it—isn't that it?"

Ruth turned slowly and looked at the younger woman.

"That's about it," she said.

"Well, listen," said Felicity, leaning forward and speaking with almost fierce urgency. "When I arranged to come here, I was coming alone. I was coming to see you and to stay quietly here with you and—and talk to you. I had nothing to do with Martin's coming—he arranged it with Roger and I didn't know it was done until—until it was done. I was going to write and say I wouldn't come, but then——"

She paused, and Ruth, after a few moments, prompted her.

"And then?" she asked.

"And then I heard that Paul was coming down," went on Felicity. "I thought it would be a good opportunity of seeing him and——"

"Liss darling," broke in Ruth, her voice a little cool, "you didn't have to come down here to see Paul—you could have seen him any time during the last few months merely by ringing him up."

"Yes," admitted Felicity, "I could. But——" She broke off once more and then continued impatiently. "Don't let's bring all that up, Ruth," she begged. "Let's talk about *now*. Can't you talk to Paul and try and make him behave more—more reasonably—more kindly, if you like."

"Why don't you talk to him yourself?" asked Ruth.

" I tried, to-day," answered Felicity. " I shan't try again. He's so cruel, Ruth—he says the most frightfully hurtful things without a—a qualm."

Ruth was silent. Roger, too, could say hurtful things when he was hurt himself . . .

" I'm sorry, Liss," she said at last. " It sounds unkind but—I can't do anything."

Felicity looked at her in silence, attempting to steady the quivering of her lips.

" You don't really mean you can't do anything," she said at last. " You mean you won't—because you're all angry with me for—for——"

" Nobody's angry with you, Liss," said Ruth gently. " At least, I'm not. But this matter you must settle with Paul—or with Martin, I wouldn't know which. I did suggest to Roger that I—or he—might say a word to Paul. We do realize that Paul's behaving in a rather silly way, but Roger made me promise to—to——"

" To keep out of it," finished Felicity. She rose to her feet and stood looking down at Ruth quietly. " I see," she said after a long silence. " Well, he's wrong. In theory, of course, he's right—it isn't his trouble, so he keeps out of it. But in this case he's wrong. I know Paul very well, you see," she went on steadily. " I can't get through this shell he's got into, but Roger could, and you could and you should . . . you honestly should, Ruth."

She opened the door and leaned against it for a moment, looking at Ruth.

" We're friends, aren't we? " she said with a little smile.

Ruth looked at her with affection, her eyes filling with tears suddenly.

" Oh—more than that, Liss," she said. " I promise that if I can make Roger do anything, I will."

" Thanks," said Felicity. " But it's no use—they're both exactly alike in some ways, and this is one of the ways. If you hurt them, they've got to hurt you back. I've seen Roger hurt you—just a little, but he isn't the

—the—artist at it that Paul is. Paul came down here
because it gave him a good chance of hurting me, and
—and if it's any satisfaction to him," she ended in even
tones, " you can tell him he's doing it very thoroughly."

The door closed behind her, leaving Ruth alone.

CHAPTER IX

DURING the two days following his attempt at organizing,
Goosey Horder did his best to behave in as self-effacing
a way as possible. He avoided Martin West, shrank
from Felicity's friendly overtures and only entered a
room after first casting a fearful glance round it to
assure himself that Roger was not inside.

Felix was seldom absent from his side, and the two
men found a certain pleasure in joining Lady Warne
on her leisurely perambulations round the garden. For
a man like Goosey, whose watch-word for many years
had been Fresh Air without Fatigue, there was something
satisfying in the slow, stately circumnavigation of the
fountain or, if Rameses showed a disposition to be
energetic, an entire circle of the house—along the terrace, past the shrubbery, round by the drive and back
into the garden, where Lady Warne would occupy one
half of the bench and Goosey and Mr. Lenner the
other.

The weather, content with having ruined one day's
outing, maintained a steady average of four hours' sunshine daily and greatly added to the pleasure of the
walks. Those within the house, chancing to glance out,
found a great deal of amusement in watching the melancholy little procession wending its way along the paths.

Towards the end of one of these periods of pleasant
exercise, Goosey, passing the window of the library,
looked in and saw Roger asprawl in one enormous chair
and Martin West in another. Between the two men

was a tray, and on the tray two large tankards . . .
Goosey withdrew his gaze reluctantly and walked on
with slow steps which became even slower and finally
dragged.

"I think," he said to his companions, "I'll go up and
get a book—it's a nice sort of day for reading outside."

His companions making no objection and, in fact,
no answer to this, Goosey went in by the front door,
crossed the hall and hesitated with his hand on the knob
of the library door. The thought of meeting Roger
face to face was a little alarming, but after a moment's
reflection, he decided that Martin West's presence
would act as a deterrent against violence. There had
been a reassuringly relaxed air over the little scene he
had observed, and he told himself that a man must risk
unpleasantness to gain access to so pleasant a party.

He opened the door and entered. Roger and Martin
West peered round the backs of their chairs and assumed
the expression most people wore at the sight of Goosey
—a mixture of resignation and restiveness.

"Time you came out of hiding," remarked Roger.

"I wasn't hiding at all," denied Goosey. "I was
merely keeping out of your way to spare onlookers the
disgusting spectacle you present in one of your nasty
tempers. Where," he continued, going on to essentials,
"do I find the third drink?"

"If you ring that bell behind you," said Roger,
"someone'll bring you one and charge it to your
account."

"I see," said Goosey, pressing the bell. "It's as well
I came in for a long one and not a free one." He selec-
ted a chair and hovered by it until the business of order-
ing drinks was completed, and then settled himself with
a deep sigh of content.

"This is the life," he said. "Nice bit of exercise
and then——"

"Was that what you call that funeral march you were
doing out there?" enquired Martin West.

"Old ladies," answered Goosey, "aren't as nippy on

D

their pins as they used to be—if ever they were. And when you're with them you have to—to accustom your gait to—well, you have to trundle along at their pace. The speed of the march," he ended, "is the pace of the slowest—or something of the sort."

"That friend of yours—Lenner," asked Martin after a pause. "Does he ever open his mouth? To talk, I mean."

"If he does, I've never heard him," put in Roger, "but after a long spell with Goosey, most people lose their tongues. Kind of disuse."

"He doesn't talk much, certainly," admitted Goosey, ignoring the interpolation. "It isn't a bad idea, really —he lets other people put all his wants into words and just nods or shakes his head, according to which. You get used to him after a bit. At first you keep stopping to hear what he has to say, but he doesn't say anything, so you go on again and after a bit you give up the habit and just make up the answers for him. Since I've been about with him I've been astounded at how well you can get on without saying a single word."

"I suppose he has to ask for what he wants at meals?" said Martin.

"That's where you're wrong," said Goosey. "He hands the card back to the waiter, looks expectant and the fellow reads it down and old Felix nods when and how."

"What is it—laziness?" enquired Roger.

"No," said Goosey. "He's been—in a way—inoculated against speech. He took me over to his home one evening, and, my God! I didn't say a word for a whole week afterwards."

"You ought to visit them more often," commented Roger. "What dried up the flow?"

"I'll tell you," said Goosey, putting down his drink and leaning forward. "You see, his father's English, but his mother's Hungarian or one of those races. She speaks English, but her brother stays with them—he's a Hungarian, naturally——"

" Why naturally? " asked Martin.

" Because his sister is, of course," said Goosey. " Well, *he* doesn't speak a word of English, and he's got a wife who's a Bulgar or a Bulgarian or one of those, and *she*——"

" Do we have to have it all? " asked Roger.

" Yes," said Goosey. " It's an interesting case, and anyway, you started it. Where did I get to? " he mused. " Oh, yes, the wife. Well, *she* doesn't speak a word of anything except her own language, whatever it is—Bulg or Bulgar—she can't even talk her husband's lingo, so what happens? "

" God knows," said Martin wearily.

" Well, the wife," proceeded Goosey, undaunted, " I mean the wife of Felix's father, not the wife of his mother's brother—well, she makes a remark—quite a simple, reasonable remark like ' What stinking weather.' And then it starts."

" I know it starts," said Roger. " What I never found out was how to stop it once it got started."

" Well, she's made the remark," went on Goosey, " and the first thing is that father looks up and says he hasn't quite heard it, being a bit deaf. So she shouts it in a loud voice and that attracts the attention of the other wife—the one who doesn't speak anything much. She turns to her husband and says—in Bulg—'What's she shouting? ' and he replies—also in Bulg—' What stinking weather.' Then his sister, who doesn't know any Bulg, says—in Hungar—' What's she on about? ' and the brother replies—in the same language—' Nothing.' And then father says—in English—' What's he saying? ' and mother says—also in English—' Nothing,' and father says—still in English, ' Well, I know damn well he's saying something because I heard him.' So naturally he gets mad, and his wife translates to the brother and the brother——"

He stopped. Both his hearers were lying back in their chairs, their eyes closed and their breathing deep and regular.

" I say——" protested Goosey.

Roger opened his eyes cautiously.

" Is that the lot? " he asked.

" Well, it wasn't quite," said Goosey, " but if you don't want to listen——"

" We don't," said Roger.

" Well, anyway, now you see why Felix doesn't talk," said Goosey. " If you'd been brought up in that tri-lingual monkey-house, you'd keep your mouth shut too, in case everything you said had to be repeated in a yell or a couple of cheesy languages. The only thing I'm afraid of," he went on, " is that the poor chap'll get hold of some frightful woman who never stops talk-ing——"

" How can he? " asked Martin. " He'll never get the proposal out."

" Who'll wait for that? " asked Goosey. " I'm sur-prised he hasn't got roped in already, with all that pile he makes. Every mermaid a money-maker. He keeps drawing them for the twins," he went on, " and I found Ruth's aunt—Mrs. Beddington—using them to make paper boats. She was quite fluttered when I told her she might just as well make boats out of bank-notes. Nice old girl she is," he added reflectively. " Sort of gentle—the genuine timid type." He turned to Roger. " Reminds me of the time we all fell in love with that little shy blue-eyed Lucy—you remember——? "

" No," said Roger, " I don't. Anyway, her eyes were brown."

" So they were," said Goosey. " And she wouldn't come out and so we all had to do our wooing at her house. My God! " he went on, " what evenings those were! We came for the maiden, and all we got was music."

" What's the matter with music? " asked Martin.

" You'd know," said Goosey, " if you'd known Lucy's mother and father. They sang. He sang and she sang. Lucy used to enjoy it, so of course we all had to pretend we enjoyed it too. Shall I ever forget," he asked, " trying to whisper to Lucy with father and mother giving out 'Oh, that we two-hoo were May-hing'?"

"That was better," commented Roger, "than the solos."

"Ah, the solos!" said Goosey with relish. "The best one was when father drew himself up to his full five feet two, and bellowed the one about 'Be-hold, be-hold, a giant am I.' And for years afterwards I used to wake up out of nightmares hearing 'Drink to me on-ly wi-hith thine eye-hies.'"

"Mother's best effort," said Roger reminiscently, "used to be the 'Ooh, noo, John, noo John, noo,' one."

"Lucy," said Martin, "must have been an outstanding charmer."

"Oh—she was," Goosey assured him earnestly. "She——"

He came to an abrupt stop as the door opened and Felicity Grant appeared, hovering uncertainly in the opening. The three men rose to their feet and she spoke hesitatingly.

"This looks like an all-boys sitting," she began.

There was a general protest, and Roger pulled a chair forward.

"Come and join us," he invited.

"No, thanks, Roger," she said. "I've been playing with the twins and I'm looking for Nan. Of course she knows I'm after her, and she's gone into hiding."

"How about that walk?" asked Martin.

"Oh, no!" protested Felicity. "I'm absolutely exhausted. I'll go on looking for Nan until I run her to ground, and then I'll hand the babes over."

Goosey went forward eagerly.

"I'll come and help you," he said. "I've been in hiding myself so I know all the spots and all the sliding panels——"

"Come on," said Felicity, holding out a hand. "We'll comb the entire establishment——"

The door closed behind them and Roger and Martin

resumed their comfortable poses. After a short silence, Martin spoke in a ruminative tone.

"Rum chap, that Horder," he remarked. "Only just short of certifiable, wouldn't you say?"

"No, I wouldn't," returned Roger. "He's a prize ass in the normal way, but get him in a tight corner—and we've been in some together—he becomes a different person altogether. He stops talking, for one thing, and he dries up—he becomes one of those fellows you see on the screen—all swift, strong action. He's a fighter," he ended. "He really likes fighting—he enjoys it."

"Most fellows of that type do," commented Martin. "Too crazy to see anything to be frightened of." He knocked his pipe out and looked across at Roger with a speculative glance.

"I've got something," he said slowly, "that I'd like to talk to you about."

Roger made no reply, merely leaning back further in the deep chair.

"D'you mind," went on Martin, "if I discuss Paul for a bit?"

"It depends," said Roger after a pause. "If you feel you want to, I can't stop you, but I've no say at all in anything Paul chooses to do and I'm not at all up in stage matters. It's all a bit outside my sphere."

"It oughtn't to be," remarked Martin. "Your brother's making a bloody mess of things—you can't sit back and say that's outside your sphere, can you?"

"I can and I do," said Roger. "You know Paul pretty well—or you ought to by this time—and you know that if I, or anyone else, interferes with him there'll be trouble."

"If I'd known he was going to be here," said Martin, a shade resentfully, "I don't think I'd have come down."

"I think you would," said Roger quietly.

Martin gave him an expressionless glance and remained silent for some time. When he spoke again, his voice had a touch of irritation.

"This damn silly attitude of his," he said, "all this

polite determination to throw Felicity and myself together as much as possible—is purely a pose. I presume
his idea is to get me on edge? "

" I wouldn't know," said Roger.

" Well, look, Roger "—Martin spoke with a sudden
explosive impatience—" it's no use our sitting here
having a sparring match. I'm not an unreasonable man.
I don't say I like some of Paul's qualities particularly,
but he's your brother and I hate to see him chucking
away a fine career. He's a good actor—some say a great
actor—and he's got a good chance of coming out on top.
Why can't you make him see what a damned idiot he's
making of himself? He walked out of a first-class con-
tract because I was getting on with Felicity better than
he was, and——"

" He didn't," interrupted Roger, " and you know
it."

" Oh, it wasn't a reason he could admit to," said
Martin, " but it was his real reason. All that talk
about——"

" Paul left your show," broke in Roger, " because
you gave Liss a part she couldn't play. I don't know
the ins and outs and I don't care about them anyway.
He maintains that you behaved like a wealthy backer
whose lady friend had stage ambitions, and that you
wrapped up the entire production and handed it to
Liss, just to amuse her. He says that sort of thing was
all right in the naughty nineties, but it isn't the way
he thinks a serious company ought to be run. I don't
know——"

" But I tell you," began Martin.

" I don't know anything about the technicalities, as
I said before," went on Roger, " but I take it that the
core and pith of the matter lies in the one question—
can the girl act, or can't the girl act? If she can, then
Paul's the bloody fool everybody takes him for, and
more conceited than even I thought he was. If she
can't—well then I'm on his side and we needn't go
further into the thing."

" The whole point is——" began Martin again.

" Can the girl act? " asked Roger.

" My dear fellow——"

" Can she or can't she? " repeated Roger.

" Oh, my God! " protested Martin, " I——"

" Yes or no? " persisted Roger.

Martin was silent, his brows drawn together and a look of dark anger on his face. Roger watched him with an unreadable expression. At last Martin looked up and met the eyes of the other man, his look of anger fading and an unwilling, twisted smile taking its place.

" All right," he said. " She can't act."

CHAPTER X

BRENDA'S room on the ground floor was known to be an office and strictly private, but it was also realized that this meant, in Brenda's interpretation, that it was forbidden territory to those she disliked and a pleasant meeting-place for her friends in leisure hours.

Goosey knocked on the door one evening and found that nobody was in. He hesitated on the threshold and then entered, beckoning Felix after him.

" Nobody here," he announced, " but Miss Mallard'll be along soon, I suppose. Let's take a seat."

They settled themselves on the two most comfortable chairs and smoked in silence until the sound of the door opening disturbed them. They turned their heads to find Roger and Paul Mallard entering.

" What're you doing here? " enquired Roger.

" I," said Goosey, " am waiting for Miss Mallard. Now state your business."

" You push off," directed Roger briefly. " Why the hell can't you keep to your own part of the house? "

" Because Brenda likes me to come and see her some-times," said Goosey. " Take a chair," he invited kindly.

"Are you trespassing too?" he asked, looking at Paul, "or are you here on business?"

Paul's reply was interrupted by a further addition to the party. Ruth and Felicity opened the door, looked in and hesitated. Ruth looked at her companion and wrinkled her nose.

"Three men and Roger," she said. "Let's go up to my room."

Goosey went to the door and led them inside ceremoniously.

"The two best chairs," he said generously. "Get out, you two," he added threateningly to Roger and Paul, who had installed themselves in the vacant places. "Go on—get out. There!" he said, settling the two women and beaming with satisfaction. "Now we're a nice cosy party."

"What were you looking for?" Roger asked his wife. "A place in which to pour out a mutual flow of girlish confidences?"

"I wouldn't go as far as that," said Ruth. "We just wanted to talk."

"You haven't time to talk," said Roger. "We're running a business."

"There you go again," said Goosey in a tone of disgust. "This life's going to sour you—more than you were soured before, I mean. Take me, now," he offered. "I came here to see Ruth after who knows how many years, and I haven't had more than ten minutes' conversation with her. Every time I run into her she's got her arms full of sheets and blankets. I don't like it," he complained. "In the old days you used to be able to talk to people, and now all they do is pant and explain that they can't stop because they're up to the eyes in this and that. Nobody's got any time any more—and nobody sits still and wastes any, any more. Nobody enjoys anything any more. It's all," he ended morosely, "too bally serious."

"What's wrong with being serious?" asked Roger.

"Nothing's wrong with being serious," said Goosey,

"when and if there's anything to be serious about. But why," he asked, leaning forward and looking belligerently round the assembly, "why should being weighty and serious be looked on as more—well—respectable— than being happy-go-lucky? A fellow who won't take things seriously gets put down as a bally ass, and very often he isn't a bally ass at all."

"And very often he is," said Roger.

"All right—I pass," said Goosey. "But I've got an old uncle who used to say that everybody can be happy when they're getting all they want. You mistake some of them for really happy-natured people. But meet them when their circumstances change for the worse, and you find they've gone sour—like Roger."

"Roger hasn't gone sour," said Ruth, "but I see what you mean. Like that—what was her name?—Amanda something——"

"That's exactly it," said Goosey. "You couldn't have hit on a better example. Amanda Foster. D'you remember—when Ted Foster was doing well she was no end of a roysterer—full of life and spirits and as gay as a—as a——"

"Lark," offered Ruth.

"Cricket," said Goosey. "Then Ted lost a bit of money and they went down and started a fruit farm— or was it chickens or something?—down in Hampshire or Warwickshire or one of those, and the last time I saw her, she had a face as long as a horse, hadn't smiled since Leap Year and chewed your ear off every time you tried to say something cheerful. So you see what I mean?"

"No," said Roger. "Explain."

"Well, I can only talk English," said Goosey. "If that doesn't drive it home——"

"I know what you mean," said Felicity soothingly. "You mean that if people are really sunny-tempered they'll be happy under most conditions, and that being serious——"

"Exactly," said Goosey gratefully, "is an over-rated

virtue. I believe that people should smile, whatever happens to wipe the smile off. That's what I believe."

At this, everyone in the room immediately assumed the widest smiles of which their muscles were capable. Even Felix Lenner did his best to produce something that might be called a pleasant expression. Goosey looked round the grimacing party with open dislike, and at the same moment the door opened and Brenda appeared. She stopped on the threshold, regarding with extreme astonishment the fixed grins on the faces of all but two of the party.

"Nice to see you so happy," she remarked. "But I don't see anything to look happy about." The men rose to their feet and the faces of the party assumed their normal expressions. Brenda looked at Roger.

"I've got trouble," she said.

Roger raised his eyebrows.

"What kind?" he asked.

"Do you want us to go away?" asked Felicity.

"No—it's nothing private," said Brenda. "Or it won't be soon—there's enough shouting going on to keep everybody within a radius of miles in touch with the affair."

"Well, what's the affair?" asked Roger, his brows drawn together.

"Well, that young man who calls for his girl friend —you know, our green overall—every evening to take her home, has arrived as usual in his van," said Brenda, "but instead of going off again and taking her with him, as he always does, he's standing outside that garden-room door—she always goes out that way—shouting his head off and using the most appalling language."

"Well, didn't you go out and ask him what the hell he meant by it?" asked Roger impatiently.

"I did," replied Brenda, "and it took some courage, I can tell you. But I couldn't get far without actually shouting him down—he wants you and when he gets you he's going to have your blood. He's waving a paper and saying he'll produce it in court and have the law on you and you'll go to prison for not knowing the right way to treat girls who work for you."

" Fellow's mad," said Roger.

" He's mad all right, but not in the way you mean," said Brenda. " I think you'd better go out and see what you can do."

Roger went to the door.

" No other clues? " he asked.

"None," replied Brenda, "except that the green overall keeps holding out her hand and wailing ' Oh Bob, give it to me and don't make such a carry-on over a drawing!'"

A startled sound came from Ruth.

" A drawing!" she exclaimed. Her eyes widening in dismay, she put out her hand to detain her husband. "Wait a minute, Roger," she said. She turned to Brenda. " Was it a mauve-coloured paper? " she asked.

" Yes, it was," said Brenda. " Do you know what it is? "

"Well"—Ruth hesitated—" I'm not sure, but perhaps Goosey——"

Roger's frown became black and threatening as he faced the bewildered-looking Goosey.

" My God! " he said furiously, " don't tell me you've been writing notes to——"

Goosey stopped him with a snort of indignation.

" I don't know what the devil you're talking about," he said, his voice almost squeaky with indignation. " I haven't done anything at all and I've never seen a piece of mauve paper in my——"

He came to an abrupt stop, his face paling. Roger watched him with tight lips.

" Well, go on," he said after waiting for him to continue. " For God's sake get it out before that fellow breaks in and does some real damage."

Goosey and Ruth were both looking at Felix. The latter obviously remembered nothing concerning mauve paper, and gave a slight, helpless shrug of his shoulders. Ruth prompted him.

"Yesterday," she said, "the girl came and showed me a sketch you'd done of her——"

"It wasn't of her at all," broke in Goosey defensively. "She came up and asked if Felix would draw a mermaid for her—everybody always does come up and ask him to do just one mermaid for them—and Felix didn't happen to have any paper on him, so the girl went away and came back with a pale purple-coloured bit, and Felix—in a couple of seconds—drew a mermaid on it and gave it back to her, and she said thank you with a bit of gush and went away. That's all, I swear," he ended.

"That's not quite all," said Ruth, a little hesitation in her voice. "She showed me the sketch and—well—it wasn't just any mermaid—I mean Mr. Lenner had sketched the girl's face and so it looked——"

"Oh, God," groaned Goosey. "So that's it!"

There was a short pause and then Goosey moved to the door.

"Where d'you think you're going?" demanded Roger.

"It's no use your going out there," said Goosey. "You're the one he'd like to get hold of—so you'd better keep out of his way. I'm the only one who can explain that Felix didn't draw his girl friend at all, but merely reproduced—for the millionth time—the same lines and the same mermaid. I didn't know he'd made it look like a drawing from life, but I can fix the bellowing swain."

Paul spoke for the first time.

"You stay here," he said in slow, lazy tones. "I'm going."

"What for?" asked Brenda. "It's nothing to do with you at all."

"That's why I'm going," said Paul. "I'm the only disinterested party. I'll go out with an air of interest and sympathy and invite him to pour out his troubles. He'll blow off steam and feel a lot better."

"There's something in that," said Roger. "If you want help, call me."

A peculiar sound from Mr. Lenner caused every pair of eyes in the room to fix themselves on him. There was a deep, expectant hush as the watchers waited for him to utter something further. Nothing more, however, was heard. Only by a look of more than ordinary melancholy and a move towards Paul did he indicate that he considered it his duty to take part in the proceedings. Brenda put out a hand and seized his coat tails.

" Not you," she said firmly. " Certainly not you. Let Paul go—you can have a fight some other time."

Paul went out, and the rest looked a little blankly at one another. Goosey noticed that Felicity's face was white, and attributed her paleness to a becoming girlish sensitiveness.

Though everybody appeared restless, no word was spoken for some time. At last a little cry from Ruth brought all eyes to her face. She stared at Roger for a moment and then spoke eagerly.

" Oh, Roger," she said, " I know—Paul's bathroom window. It overlooks that bit of——"

The last words were lost as the entire party, going through the door in a confused and tangled mass, stampeded up the stairs, took the bend at the top in fine style, spread into line and sprinted down the corridor, jamming badly at Paul's door and emerging singly from the scrum to arrive, panting, in the bathroom and take up a stand at the window.

Goosey, holding Felicity firmly by the hand, came first, followed by Brenda and Ruth, who had used the privilege of their sex to dig an elbow into Roger's ribs and pin Mr. Lenner against the bathroom door in the last lap. After some final shuffling and adjustments, a reasonable view was obtained by all, Mr. Lenner standing on the side of the bath and surveying events from on high.

" No blood," announced Brenda, a trace of disappointment in her voice.

" Ssh! " hissed Ruth sharply from the right.

"What's the matter?" asked Brenda in surprise. "They can't hear us."

"Ssh!" repeated Ruth, her forefinger upheld. "Listen to that language."

"My word," said Goosey, after a long pause spent in listening. "It's juicy, isn't it?"

"I hope," said Roger suddenly, "that Paul won't offer him money."

"How could he?" asked Brenda reasonably.

"Do look at that girl," said Felicity after a pause. "She's—I honestly believe she's making eyes at Paul."

It was true. Standing behind her raging and distraught swain, the maiden's glance rested on Paul with a look calculated to take all the sting out of her lover's oaths.

"By golly, she *is* making eyes," confirmed Goosey. He made a little sound of regret. "Perhaps I should have gone and given Paul a hand," he said. "My affair, after all——"

"Why's Paul asking for the paper?" asked Brenda, intent on the scene below.

"Trying to get the evidence away from the fellow," guessed Roger.

"No—I think he's trying to explain that Felix did it and that if there's a signature on it, it's worth money," said Ruth. "Yes—look—he's pointing it out. Now wait and see if that works."

There appeared, indeed, to be a lull in the violence hitherto shown by the outraged man. The girl behind him, realizing that the crisis had passed, climbed into her place on the van and, taking a pencil from her bag, wrote briefly and folded the tiny slip of paper.

"You don't think——" began Felicity.

"She's written him a billet-doux," said Brenda in an awed voice. "Right in the middle of the fight—to sit there and write a——"

"It needn't be a billet-doux, exactly," said Goosey. "It might just be a note saying don't mind him he's always like this and it doesn't mean a thing."

"Don't be so stupid," said Brenda contemptuously. "Look at her fluttering those eyelids. She's waiting—there! I told you—she's waiting until that man comes round the van to get into the driving seat. Ah! now watch—he's out of sight and—what did I tell you?—she's dropped the note."

Goosey gave a long, low, envious whistle.

"Crumbs!" he ejaculated. "Did you see that look she threw him, too . . . ?"

"The van's moving," said Roger warningly. The watchers stirred, but were unwilling to leave before the curtain fell. They gazed downwards as the van drove away. All eyes were on Paul, who stood below, looking down at the little paper. After a moment's hesitation, he took a few steps forward and stooped. . . .

The return journey was accomplished with even more speed than the upward move. Goosey gained an unfair advantage by poising gracefully at the top of the banisters and sliding down with arms outstretched in a manner reminiscent of a flying ballet. When the others reached the office he was once more in possession of the best chair.

Paul entered a moment later and all eyes were turned on him with looks of innocent expectancy.

"Well?" asked Roger.

"Nothing out of the way," said Paul. "He believed me when I told him it was just another mermaid, and I convinced him it was an outstanding honour to have his girl-friend's face attached to it. When he heard the thing was worth something, he took a less mean view."

There was a pause.

"And the girl," asked Brenda. "Was she—well, shaken?"

"Not particularly," said Paul. "Bit upsetting for her, of course."

"Oh, quite," said Goosey. "I mean to say, quite. She didn't, I suppose, speak to you or—or anything?"

"What on earth for?" enquired Paul in astonishment. "She merely stood there and then—well, they drove off and that's that."

"Ah," said Brenda. "No blood."

"The girl," said Felicity reflectively, "might have thanked you in some way, don't you think?"

"Quite," agreed Goosey. "Didn't she even look—as it were—grateful?"

"I wouldn't say that she looked grateful at all," said Paul. "Now if that excitement's over, perhaps I can go up and change. Any more questions?" he asked, from the door.

"Only one," said Roger. "What was in the note?"

Paul stared at him for a moment blankly, and then turned a look of withering contempt on the questioners.

"Well, my God!" he ejaculated slowly. "Of all the——" He stopped and continued in a tone of scorn. "Snooping," he said. "A pack of low, peeping, peering snoopers. Where," he enquired, "did you snoop from?"

"Dress circle," said Brenda. "What did she write?"

"What," countered Paul, "did who write?"

"The girl," said Felicity. "We watched her eye-lashes."

"It was a pretty sight," said Goosey with relish. "Come on, Paul," he urged, "where's the assignation?"

Paul pulled his face into a hideous mask and spoke in a low hiss.

"I'm to meet her," he said, addressing the absorbed Goosey, "as the hour strikes."

"Which hour?" asked Goosey.

"The midnight hour," said Paul, in his normal tones. "At the blasted oak. Alone. Now if you've quite finished, I'm going."

The door closed behind him, and Goosey went to it and opened it.

"He's a mean chap," he observed, preparing to follow him. "You'd think he'd let a friend in on a thing like this. I'm going to pursue the matter further."

He closed the door and hurried up the stairs after Paul, addressing him in a tone of dejection.

"You're not going to keep it to yourself, are you?" he asked.

"Certainly," said Paul. "Next time you go to a show, take a strong pair of glasses and you'll be able to read the correspondence too."

He stopped at the door of his room.

"Don't look so depressed," he said. "Lots of beautiful women left." He took his cigarette-case from his pocket, opened it and held it out. Goosey, after a glance at it, shook his head.

"No thanks," he said. "I'm trying a new kind—why don't you——"

His voice died suddenly. With his mouth dropping open and his eyes starting from his head, he stared speechlessly at Paul.,

"What the devil's gone wrong with you?" enquired Paul irritably. "You haven't remembered some more trouble, have you? I never," he went on, "met such a mud-stirrer in all my life. Roger's quite right—you really——"

Goosey shut his mouth, gave a gulp and appeared to pull himself together.

"Your case," he began falteringly, "that cigarette-case you just took out——"

"It isn't the one your uncle lost in '99, if that's what you're driving at," said Paul. "I came by it honestly."

"Inside," went on Goosey, haltingly. "Inside it—there's that time again—I saw it."

Paul, opening his mouth to say "What time?" shut it again, and remained silent.

"One p.m.," said Goosey slowly. "That's funny, wouldn't you say?" He frowned suddenly and spoke firmly. "You know, Paul," he said. "I'm not a fool."

"No?" said Paul. "Well, that's reassuring."

"You wouldn't, I suppose," went on Goosey, peering at him with half-shut eyes, "have another name before Paul, and it wouldn't begin with an I, would it?"

Paul opened the door of his room and went inside,

leaving the door open. Goosey followed him in and closed it behind him.

" It wouldn't be Ivan or Isaac, would it? " he continued.

" No, it wouldn't," said Paul. " Look," he continued impatiently, beginning to undress, "couldn't we go on with this some other time? "

" You're I.P.M.," went on Goosey, pursuing his line of investigation steadily. " And that lighter—the one she got so snatchy about—that's either yours, or it's one you gave her, and——"

He stopped speaking, concluded his investigations mentally, and sinking on to Paul's bed, took a deep breath.

" My God, what a fool I am! " he said slowly.

" Make your mind up," said Paul, sitting on a chair and removing his shoes. " First you are and then you're not and——"

" I most definitely am," Goosey decided. " If I'd had the least bit of nose I'd have smelt through all that throwing them together and all that——"

" Well, this discussion's over," said Paul abruptly, getting to his feet. " You can either get out now or you can stay in and talk about something else."

" Don't be a howling chimpanzee," implored Goosey. " I've known——"

" I know—you've known Roger for an unlimited period of years and you saw him through his meeting with Ruth, and his courtship and his marriage," said Paul in the tone of one indulging a troublesome child. " And so you feel qualified to butt into my affairs and knock the whole blasted show sideways." He came closer, and, standing over Goosey, glared at him venomously. " Well, let me tell you something," he said between his teeth. " If you so much as open your mouth on this subject again, I'll plug you full of dyna-mite and then light the fuse. Try and believe that, will you? "

Goosey made no answer. He sat on the bed watching

Paul perform the last stages of his undressing, his expression slightly amused.

"You're an odd chap," he said at last, "but then so's Roger. You're both sensible fellows until you get angry, and then it seems to me you stop using your heads altogether. Now me—I don't say I'm a model of brightness normally, but the moment I get angry, my brain starts working. It starts working because I don't believe that sitting down and going broody ever solved anybody's problems. Like a tooth—if it gives you trouble, I mean. You have to do something——"

He stopped, realizing that Paul's bath water was running and the sound rendered his little homily inaudible. He sat and meditated until Paul got the water to the right temperature and turned off both taps. Goosey half turned and called an anxious question.

"I say, Paul," he said, "you're not afraid of the chap, are you?"

Both taps were immediately turned on again. As if to make the hint a little more marked, the door of the bathroom was banged with an ear-shattering crash.

Goosey removed himself from the bed and went out, his steps turned towards his own bedroom, his expression glum.

"Damn touchy feller . . ." he muttered as he went.

CHAPTER XI

THE following day brought the end of the fine weather. The rain, beginning to fall as the first breakfasters entered the dining-room, increased steadily; low and heavy clouds hid the sun and gave a depressing, greenish tinge to the light. Occasional gusts of wind sent scurries of rain drumming on window-panes.

It was clearly a day to be spent indoors, but the dampness, the darkness and gloom were having their effect on more than one normally cheerful person.

Brenda, breakfasting as usual with Ruth and Roger, stirred her third cup of coffee wearing a frown of irritation not often seen on her placid countenance. Even the entrance of Paul to pay a morning visit failed to give her the usual pleasure.

"Good morning," said Paul. "Nice day."

"It's going misty," said Ruth, looking out of the window. "It's probably going to be one of those beastly foggy days ending up with visibility nil. And I've got to go into the town." She looked hopefully at her husband. "I suppose you wouldn't go in for me, would you, darling?" she asked.

"Correct," replied Roger.

"Why can't you go?" demanded Ruth indignantly. "It's mostly your shopping, and two pairs of your shoes from the mender's, and you can't have much to do in the house because you were going to do that garden hose with old Hyde and nobody could stand in the middle of a soaking lawn talking about hoses in this downpour."

She paused for breath and watched her husband as he finished his coffee, wiped his mouth on his table napkin and pushed back his chair.

"Do you mean you absolutely won't go?" she asked at last.

"Correct again," said Roger.

"Well then, you're a pig," said Ruth.

Roger rose from his chair, rested a hand on the back and addressed his wife.

"The last time you sent me into Petsham to do your errands," he reminded her, "you told me you had just —I think the expression you used was 'one or two little things.' I left the house at ten-thirty, waited twenty minutes in the cleaner's while they hunted for a suit which it then appeared you'd already collected——"

"Well, I forgot the ticket and they let me have it and I——"

"I then," proceeded Roger, "went into that stinking

little wool shop and waited while four women took their time matching little bits of this or that. At the first opportunity, I approached the old harridan at the counter, tendered your message and your parcel and said you had rung up about what you wanted. Not only had you not rung up, but the wool in the parcel had not been bought at that shop and therefore couldn't be changed there. I then——"

"But I——" said Ruth.

"I then," went on Roger, "staggered into the saddler's with an enormous trunk which you'd asked him to mend, only to find that it didn't require mending and that you'd got mixed up between the brown cabin trunk that had got battered and the small wardrobe trunk that hadn't. I then—it being lunch time——"

"You then came home in the most appalling temper and you've never stopped talking about it since," said Ruth. "Well, thank you. I'll drive myself in."

"Correct for the third time," said Roger, going out and shutting the door firmly behind him.

Brenda looked reflectively at the table-cloth.

"There are times," she said musingly, "when I'm more glad than I am at other times that I'm a spinster. This is one of the times."

Ruth looked at Paul, hope rising once again.

"Paul," she said, "I suppose you wouldn't——"

"No, I wouldn't," said Paul. "I love you, Ruth, but I didn't come down here to potter about a lot of rotten little shops."

"Oh, you didn't?" said Brenda. "Well, nobody's discovered yet what you did come down here for, but if you can't be decent for once and drive a few miles to save poor, wretched, overworked women, then you're even more of a pig than Roger is."

Paul seated himself on a chair, tilted it back as far as it would go with safety and looked across at her coolly.

"I take it," he said, "that this heated tirade isn't only sympathy for Ruth. You, yourself, have shopping to do—yes?"

"Yes," admitted Brenda, "I have. And if you were half a man, you'd go in and do it. And when you've finished ruining that chair, you can go away and do your lounging somewhere else."

Paul brought the chair to the ground and stood up, his expression half-mocking.

"I'm glad I came in," he drawled, on his way out. "Nice friendly atmosphere. Nice pleasant women— gentle, tender—with an old-world——"

"Oh—get out," said Brenda in disgust.

The door closed behind him, and Brenda put her elbows on the table and looked gloomily at Ruth.

"I hate women who spit and then say ' Men,' " she said, "but honestly I feel like doing it at this moment."

"I love my husband," said Ruth, slowly and carefully.

"That's right," said Brenda. "Keep on saying it and before the day's out you'll believe it. What," she enquired, "have you got to do in what is called the town?"

"Well, the chief thing," said Ruth without enthusiasm, "is that I've arranged to take Aunt Emmie in. She gave poor Uncle George a bad day yesterday and——"

"Oh, rubbish," said Brenda. "The old darling couldn't give anybody a bad anything."

"Well, she thought she'd brought all the wool she'd need," said Ruth, "and when she got to the second arm of Uncle George's fortieth warm waistcoat, she found she'd run out. She moped and drooped until he walked all the way into Petsham to get her some more—he's so sweet that he wouldn't come and ask for the car. He brought back the wool—it was exactly the colour but he'd never heard anything about ply, so she came to me and begged me to take her in so's she could change it without letting him know he'd brought the wrong thing."

"I see," said Brenda.

"You can't refuse a request like that," said Ruth.

" But the idea of puddling about on a day like this——"

" It's the dirtiest possible, certainly," said Brenda, taking another look at it. " I don't call myself a bad-tempered woman, but on a day like this I feel like chewing everybody into small pieces."

She was not the only one affected by the day. Martin West finished his breakfast and sat moodily at the table, staring absently out of the window. He was beginning to realize that this week, which he had hoped would be one of close companionship with Felicity, was proving quite the reverse.

They had been here for four days. Felicity's manner had not, he thought, changed, but she looked pale, and more than half her time was spent looking after her twin nephews. Martin told himself that he liked children, but not at the stage at which they expected him to get down on the floor and give them camel or elephant rides.

A sudden wave of irritation seized him as he stood irresolutely in the hall after leaving the dining-room. There was a pleasant fire in the library—if Felicity were not tied to somebody else's children, she would be free to enjoy a comfortable morning reading or talking. There was a good deal that Martin wanted to talk about —matters which concerned him more deeply than he cared to admit.

He swung on his heel and with angry, impatient strides walked into the children's room. It was empty. He hesitated for a moment and then made his way to the drawing-room. Lady Warne was in her usual chair and Rameses was on his favourite part of the hearthrug. On one of the sofas, curled up comfortably with a book, sat Mrs. Hellier. The sight of her, at leisure and at ease while Felicity amused her children, roused Martin to fury.

" I'm so sorry to interrupt you," he said icily. " I wonder if you can tell me where Felicity is? "

Mrs. Hellier raised her eyes reluctantly from her book and looked at him.

"Liss? Oh—she's in the children's room, I expect," she said.

"She isn't," said Martin. "I've just come from there."

"Oh. Well, she'll be somewhere about, I expect," said Mrs. Hellier, preparing to resume her reading. "Perhaps she took the twins upstairs."

Martin made an attempt to choke down his rage.

"Don't think me too interfering," he said with as much politeness as he could get into his voice, " but wouldn't it be a good idea if you got off that sofa and looked after your own children for a change? "

Mrs. Hellier gave him one of her wide, almost idiotic stares.

"But, my dear Martin," she protested, "you do talk the most awful bosh. Why—Liss *loves* looking after the twins. She simply does, and that's all. If she didn't she wouldn't, and so. Nobody else likes looking after them, and so nobody else does, don't you see? And I can't have them the entire time, can I?—I mean it isn't reasonable."

"I think," put in Lady Warne, who had forgotten to bring her own book down and was anxious to give vent to her irritation—" I think you ought to look after your own children."

Mrs. Hellier transferred her gaze to the new adversary with something of insolence added to her cold stare.

"Oh? " she said.

"Yes," said Lady Warne. " Certainly."

"Well, I know it isn't the popular attitude for mothers to adopt," said Mrs. Hellier, " but I, personally, don't like looking after children. I never did like it, and I never was any good at it, and why people who know nothing whatever about it should imagine that just because a woman happens to have children she has to be wildly enthusiastic about them and staggeringly good at looking after them, I really don't know. Having babies, as far as I can see," she went on, " doesn't change anything but your figure. The rest of you remains exactly as it was before."

"You're talking utter nonsense," said Lady Warne with contempt. "If you can't cope with your own children, why should you have the impertinence to expect strangers to help you?"

Mrs. Hellier closed her book.

"As a matter of fact," she said, "it just depends on the strangers. There are strangers and strangers. Sometimes they turn out quite possible people who adore looking after children—even other people's. Sometimes"—she leaned back, her head on one side, studying Lady Warne—"sometimes they're frightful outsiders who know nothing whatsoever about the whole thing and who not only don't like children any more than I do, but who actually prefer dogs."

"You'd better come and look for Felicity," said Martin. "I——"

"At least," said Lady Warne, her face an unbecoming mauve, "I look after my own dog."

Mrs. Hellier gave a brief glance at the swollen and snoring Rameses.

"I can quite see that," she said insolently.

"Will you come and look for Felicity?" asked Martin savagely.

"It's a very funny thing," said Mrs. Hellier, ignoring him and looking at Lady Warne. "People pretend to be staggeringly keen on children, so they insist on their being kept out of the way in a special room, so that their disgusting dogs can come into all the best rooms and climb over all the best furniture without interruption."

"Rameses," said Lady Warne in a choking voice, "has never——"

"—climbed into a chair," finished Mrs. Hellier. "Obviously not. It'd take two strong men to lift him into one."

Martin West turned abruptly and went out, banging the door behind him. Trying the children's room once more, he saw a sight not at all calculated to soothe his ill-humour.

Paul Mallard had just finished fitting a swing into a frame. He tested it with a pull and then hoisted one eager twin into it. Felicity lifted the other and after a little adjustment it was found that both children could fit. Paul pushed the swing gently to and fro.

" Isn't it time," said Martin, without preamble, "that Nan came and took over? "

Felicity gave an amused little laugh.

" Good morning, Martin," she said. " When did Nan do things because she ought to or because it was time to do them? Besides," she added. " I like looking after the twins."

" Why," asked Paul smoothly, addressing Martin, " don't you tell Nan to come? "

Martin realized, helplessly and with dismay, that his anger was getting out of control. The accumulated irritations of the past few days, added to his grievance against Mrs. Hellier and the jealousy which the scene before him had aroused, combined to stir him to an unaccustomed fury.

" Mrs. Hellier," he said in slow, careful tones, " is in the drawing-room. I suggested her coming and looking after her own children, and so did Lady Warne, who was in there. There is now a brawl in progress."

" You mean they're—they're quarrelling? " said Felicity, aghast.

" I don't know what you call quarrelling," said Martin. " They're sitting down exchanging insults."

Felicity gave a little cry of dismay.

" Oh, dear," she said, " I'll have to go in."

" You stay here," said Paul. " I'll go. I can deal with Lady Warne better than you can."

" You can't deal with Nan," said Felicity, as she moved away.

Paul put out a hand and caught her arm.

" You stay here," he said again. Something in his

tone—gentle and intimate, made the remnants of Martin's control snap.

"Suppose," he said, "you let Felicity do as she pleases."

Paul gave him a brief, amused glance.

"Surely," he said. "If she wants to go, she shall. I'll go too."

"You keep out of this," said Martin. "It's purely Felicity's affair and nothing whatsoever to do with you."

"Oh, Martin, there's nothing to get cross about," protested Felicity. "It's nothing new—Nan never does look after the children. I'm used to it. When I knew she was coming I divided my free time in half because I knew the twins would require at least that much of it."

"I see," said Martin. "Well, I didn't come here to watch you looking after Nan's children."

He stopped, too late. Felicity's manner became as cool as his own was heated.

"I'll be back in a moment—I'm going to get Nan out of the drawing-room," she said. "Will one of you please look after the twins for a moment?"

She went out, and Paul looked at Martin, his eyebrows raised.

"Shall we toss for the job?" he asked lightly.

Martin turned on his heel without a word, and went out. Paul's lips curved into a slow, rather contemptuous smile. After a moment he turned and gave his attention to the children.

A few minutes later, slow footsteps sounded in the hall. Mrs. Hellier entered the playroom, her expression disconsolate.

"Where's Liss?" enquired Paul.

"I don't know," replied Mrs. Hellier. "She's gone off in a temper. Everybody's in a temper. Martin's in a temper, and Liss, and that enormous woman with the fat dog in the drawing-room. It's a crushing day and I shall never go anywhere again until I've got an absolute guarantee that somebody'll look after the twins all

the time. Are you going off, too? " she asked, as Paul
turned to the door. " Can't you——"

" Sorry," said Paul firmly.

" What's become of Major Horder and Mr. Lenner? "
enquired Mrs. Hellier.

" They came down late—they're still in the dining-
room," said Paul as he went out. " Why don't you try
them? "

" I will," said Mrs. Hellier, on a note of hope. . . .

.   .   .   .

Felicity went upstairs and knocked on the door of
Ruth's room.

" Can I come in, Ruth? " she called.

Ruth's voice answered, and Felicity went inside.

" I came up to say——" she began, and stopped in
surprise at the sight of Ruth in outdoor garments. " You
don't mean to say you're going out on a day like this? "
she asked. " It's simply pelting."

" I know," said Ruth. " Don't rub it in. But I've
got to go—Brenda and I both loathe shopping—at least
this sort of shopping—and we always leave it until the
last possible moment. And besides," she ended, " I've
promised to take my aunt in."

" You ready? " enquired Brenda, appearing at the
door in a large mackintosh, an unbecoming waterproof
hood, and rubber goloshes.

" Well, you are, at any rate," commented Ruth,
looking her up and down. " You won't get wet, I
trust? "

" If I had a deep-sea diving suit," declared Brenda,
" I'd wear it. Where's your aunt? "

" There wouldn't be room for me, would there? "
asked Felicity.

Ruth and Brenda regarded her in astonishment.

" We're not going out because we want to," explained
Brenda. " We're doing it because we've got to."

" I'd like to come—if you wouldn't mind," said
Felicity. " On a day like this, I always think it's just
as gloomy indoors as out, and everybody seems to be in

a bad temper. Oh! that reminds me," she exclaimed. "I came up to say that Nan was rather rude to Lady Warne this morning—I went in and didn't exactly have to separate them, and I can't tell you exactly what Nan said, but Lady Warne was a rather alarming colour. I wondered whether somebody ought to go down and—well, look at her."

"I don't think so," said Brenda. "We've got enough to bear as it is. Let Roger go and look at her. Or Paul. I hope they enjoy it. Go and get your oilskins on," she went on, pushing Felicity towards the door. "Meet you in the hall."

Ruth and Brenda went downstairs to find Mr. and Mrs. Beddington waiting. Mrs. Beddington, by a series of nods, winks and signals over her husband's shoulder, made it clear that she regarded her little deception as a major conspiracy.

"I can't think," said Mr. Beddington in a tone of anxiety, "why Lena wants to go out on a shocking day like this. But she insists—she insists——"

"Of course she insists," said Brenda. "She's coming out on an all-girls-together party, and no husbands—in fact, no men of any kind," she added sourly, "are invited. Here's Felicity," she ended, as the latter came down the stairs. "She's coming too."

"Well, keep warm, Lena my dear," urged Mr. Beddington. "Keep her warm, Ruth. I've made her wrap up very well."

This was scarcely an overstatement. Mrs. Beddington, normally a slight, if not a thin woman, had grown to a bulk which made Brenda wonder whether anybody would fit beside her on the seat.

The four women arranged themselves in the car, Brenda at the wheel. She started the engine, and then, twisting in her seat with some difficulty, turned and addressed Ruth, who was sitting at the back beside Mrs. Beddington.

"I say, Ruth," she said. "Now that we're going, what's the use of rushing everything? We're a nice cosy party—let's do the shopping without hurrying, and then we'll drive out to that nice place—what's its name?—the Man o' War—and have a decent lunch, and then we'll find a cinema and finish up there this afternoon. How about it? "

Ruth looked at her aunt and smiled, and Mrs. Beddington, with a little nervous nod, smiled back.

" How about it? " said Ruth.

" Well, my dear, it sounds a nice change—a very nice change," answered Mrs. Beddington. " But you must tell your uncle—he's so anxious——"

" I will," said Felicity, opening the door at her side and running into the house once more. She found Mr. Beddington inside the door, shaking some drops from his coat, and repeated the details of the new arrangements to him, ending with a smile which was meant to be merely reassuring but which so bewitched Mr. Beddington that he was unable to find the handle of the door to open it for her as she went out. She opened it herself and threw him a parting look.

" Now don't worry," she said gently.

" Ah—yes, quite," faltered poor Mr. Beddington. " Good-bye. Yes."

CHAPTER XII

THE interior of the Man o' War looked extremely attractive at one o'clock that afternoon as Brenda, after parking the car, led her damp companions through the hall.

The four women took off their wet mackintoshes and hung them round the cloakroom to dry, leaving them in charge of the pleasant attendant, who had been watching Mrs. Beddington shedding layer after layer of protective garments, her eyes growing bigger as Mrs. Beddington became smaller.

" Now we're ready," said Brenda. " I could eat an ox."

" Does anybody feel like a glass of sherry? " enquired Ruth, pausing at the door of the lounge.

" No, nobody at all," said Brenda, proceeding without a halt to the dining-room. " Food is what we're here for, and food we're—ah! good morning, Robert. I haven't been here for ages."

The head waiter bowed.

" Good morning, Miss Mallard," he said. " It's nice to see you again."

" Thank you, Robert," said Brenda. " What about a nice table for four? "

Robert bowed once more.

" For six, madam?—this way," he said, leading the party past hurrying waitresses and leisurely lunchers.

" No—four, please," corrected Brenda.

The man, without pausing, made a movement that was half turn and half bow.

" Ah," he said. " For six, madam."

" What is this—an auction? " enquired Brenda. " I've got a party of——"

The head waiter reached a table, stopped, flourished his arm and bowed.

" For six, madam," he repeated.

The table was laid for six. Beside it stood two figures. The four women stood staring at them, their expressions an interesting study in emotions ranging from surprise and pleasure to disgust.

" Hello, dear," said Roger to his wife. " Had a nice morning? "

" I've had a beastly morning," said Ruth, " and you know it. What," she asked as the party settled themselves, " did you come here for? "

Roger looked across at Paul with a grin.

" Oh, just for fun," he said. " I heard old Goosey borrowing an umbrella off one of the maids, and—well—here I am."

" Don't talk rubbish," said Brenda. " And don't tell

half a story and wait to have the rest of it coaxed out of you bit by bit. What happened between the umbrella and the exquisite moment of our seeing you with us? "

" We suspected Goosey of wanting to join you," explained Paul. " He was very anxious to put us off— said he was going out to look at his car because it was giving trouble." He broke off and looked at the hovering waitress. " What's everybody going to eat? " he asked.

" Hot soup, hot roast meat, hot vegetables and the heaviest of puddings for me," said Brenda instantly.

Paul nodded at the waitress.

" That goes for everybody, I think," he said. " On a day like this," he observed, looking round the table, " one requires fuel rather than food."

" Go on about Goosey's engine," said Felicity, who was sitting on his right.

" I offered to help him," said Roger, from across the table. " I told Paul to wait at the house—then I tinkered a bit, got in and said I'd try it. I'm still trying it."

" You mean you took his car? " cried Felicity.

" Oh, dear, oh, dear," twittered Mrs. Beddington anxiously. " Won't he be cross? "

" I should think the garage air is purple," said Roger. " He'll get over it."

Ruth helped herself to a crusty roll and looked at her husband.

" If you couldn't come in for shopping——" she began.

" Too exhausting," said Roger. " It's all right for you because you haven't anything else to do, but Paul and I——"

" Acting," observed Paul, " is a most exacting profession."

" Exacting? What's exacting about it? " asked Brenda. " I can understand the fellow who lifts weights saying it's exacting—or a woman who has to stand

E

quivering while an enormous man climbs up and stands on his head on her head, but just walking on and reciting a lot of lines—what's exacting about that?"

Paul looked at Felicity.

"I'm a bit out of touch," he said. "You tell her."

"Oh, I know," said Brenda. "Up stage, down stage, cross over and walk off. I've done theatricals. All this business of coming off after a performance and fainting away—well—it makes a nice paragraph for the Sunday rags."

"You can't," said Paul, "talk about a noble profession like——"

"Well, I won't," said Brenda, "but it confuses the layman, I must say. It's surely on the same principle as any other bargain, isn't it?—you sell, I buy. I pay seven-and-six, or even fifteen shillings for a theatre seat, sit down, clap my hands and say ' Perform,' and the performer performs—you see?"

"Don't reduce it to a draper's shop level," begged Felicity. "You're one of The Theatre-going Public— with three capitals. I can't have you sitting there and saying that buying a yard of tape and watching a marionette show and—and *Hamlet*—all come under the same heading."

"Well, perhaps not *Hamlet*," conceded Brenda. "I wasn't really talking about heavy pieces of work like that. But I do get puzzled when I meet actresses—not that I do, very often—but I've never got used to the way they make a favour out of performing. One would think all the seats were given away." She turned to Roger. "Look at that frightful creature you used to take out before you met Ruth—don't you remember?"

"No," said Roger. "I don't."

"Don't be silly—of course you do," said Brenda. "I can still smell that appalling perfume myself. Well, take her—she called herself a singer. All she did was wait until the band had crashed out several verses and choruses, and then she held a little hankie between her clasped hands, moaned four lines without a recognizable tune and looked like a sick hen while she was doing it."

"They paid her——" began Roger.

"I know—a fabulous salary, which proves that the public liked her," said Brenda. "What I want to know is, who really does like some of this so-called popular entertainment? "

"Countless millions of——"

"Rubbish," said Brenda. "It's like that Emperor's Clothes story—they told the people what wonderful clothes they were, and the people said 'Yes, they are,' and applauded, when in reality the poor fellow didn't have a stitch on."

"Perhaps that accounted for the applause," suggested Roger.

Brenda, realizing that the others were getting ahead of her, applied herself to her meal. Felicity turned to Paul.

"Don't look now," she said, "but——"

"I know. I saw him as I came in," said Paul.

"Saw who? " asked Ruth.

"Whom," corrected Paul. "Oscar Tenby."

"Tenby? " repeated Roger. "That's that fellow, isn't it—that——"

"That's the man," said Paul.

A little sound came from Mrs. Beddington, and she was understood to say she knew a Mrs. Tenby, whose husband was a stockbroker.

"This one hasn't got a Mrs.," Roger told her. "He isn't a stockbroker either—he's one of those important London stage fellows—like Martin West."

"Who is? " enquired Brenda, looking up with interest.

On the matter being explained to her, she craned her neck and waved her nose exploringly from side to side in an endeavour to discover the person under discussion.

"You mean that enormous man over there? " she asked.

"He's a mere sixteen stone," said Paul.

Brenda continued her survey and Mr. Tenby, pleased

by her interest, raised a fat hand and made a pretty little movement as if he were plucking imaginary strings in the air.

"He's waving at me," said Brenda indignantly. "I don't know him."

"You were looking as if you'd like to," said Paul. "You can wave back if you like—it's years since he had a wife."

"Did he have one?" asked Ruth.

"At least one," said Paul. "He's an American citizen —he made a mild sensation by getting his divorce on the grounds that his wife was too house-proud."

Mrs. Beddington made another sound, and with an air remarkably like indignation was understood to ask what was wrong with being house-proud.

"Well, I gather she overdid it," said Paul. "It was the House Beautiful and she wasn't going to have Oscar dropping ash on the carpets."

"He's got all my sympathy," said Brenda. "I only once tried sharing a flat with a woman like that—I'm moderately clean and tidy, but this woman had hospital standards. She used to follow me about like a one-man posse to see whether I'd smirched anything. Then she started covering things up—covers on the chairs, cloths on every polished table, and finally she got cheap rugs to put over the good rugs in case anybody stood on them. I packed up and left—I was convinced she was going to buy spittoons and put them round the place."

Everybody was surprised to hear a little chuckle of laughter from Mrs. Beddington. Roger looked at her with mock severity.

"You mustn't encourage Brenda, Aunt Emmie," he said. "We always pretend we haven't heard her less delicate stories. Tell me," he went on, looking at Paul, "didn't Felix Lenner do one of his sketches with Oscar Tenby in it?"

Felicity broke into a little peal of laughter and several nearby lunchers paused in the business of eating and looked at her with interest and appreciation.

" He did a lovely one," she said. " Didn't you see it, Paul? "

" I did," said Paul. " It was just after Suzette Rayner's marriage."

" She's that dancer, isn't she? " asked Ruth.

" Yes—Oscar used to take her about a lot before she got engaged," said Paul, " and when she married, he enjoyed himself no end acting the part of a broken-hearted man. It was good publicity for Susie, and it amused Oscar. Finally he told the reporters he was going big-game hunting——"

" And he actually went," put in Felicity.

" Yes, but he didn't go alone," said Paul. " So Felix did a jungle picture with a mermaid seeing him off on his first trip—she had her tail curled round a bit of tropical foliage——"

" And a darling little solar topee on her curls," said Felicity.

" And she was waving Oscar off and telling him to keep his howdah dry," ended Paul.

Everybody enjoyed this recital except Aunt Emmie, who had some difficulty in remembering what a howdah was. Roger gave her a description and illustrated his remarks by going through the motions of a gentleman sitting in one. Ruth called his attention to the fact that the eyes of everyone in the room were upon him, and the performance came to a rather sheepish end.

Felicity put a quiet question to Paul.

" Have you seen Oscar lately? " she asked. " I mean in London."

" No," said Paul. " I rang him up once. Asked him to give me a part."

Felicity's eyes searched his face eagerly.

" Oh, Paul," she asked, " which part? "

" The part he gave Gavin Blake," said Paul lightly.

" Oh! " said Felicity in a smothered tone. " I—I didn't know. I'm—I'm sorry."

" Not for me, I hope," said Paul. " For Oscar, yes. Gavin won't do it half as well."

" That's what I like about actors," said Brenda. " You don't need to bolster them up—they're all self-bolstering."

Mrs. Beddington, summoning her courage, gave it as her opinion that Paul was a very good actor indeed.

" But, Aunt Emmie," protested Ruth, " you've never seen him act!"

" I will refrain," said Roger, " from pointing out that that's why she thinks he's good."

" I'm very grateful to you," said Paul, addressing the pink and flustered Mrs. Beddington. " You'll have to come back to Town with me and talk to some of these unappreciative high-ups. Oscar Tenby, for example—now he——"

He paused, seeing on the faces of the listeners looks of amusement caused by something more than his remarks. A slight rustle at his right shoulder made him look up. A stout figure stood by his side.

" Well, go on," said Oscar Tenby, with interest. " Don't stop—you were about to say——?"

" Well, if you'd waited a bit longer you'd have known," said Paul, getting to his feet. " Hello, Oscar."

" So this is where he gets to," said Mr. Tenby, holding out a hand to Felicity. " I've been ringing him up without result for the past five days."

" Bring up a chair, won't you?" invited Paul. He performed a laconic introduction. " My brother," he said, with a wave of his hand, " his cousin, his wife, her aunt, Mrs. Beddington—and, of course, Miss Grant."

Mr. Tenby made a series of charming bows but declined the chair.

" I want," he told Paul, " to talk to you on business."

Paul looked at him with an inscrutable expression.

" I'm not," he replied, " here on business."

Mr. Tenby gazed round at the company, his hands outspread in a gesture of despair.

" The fellow's mad," he announced.

" That's not news," commented Brenda.

Mr. Tenby turned once more to Paul and laid a persuasive hand on his shoulder.

"Oh, come, Paul," he said. "I've got a proposition for you. You're not getting choosey, are you?"

Paul made no reply, and Oscar Tenby, taking his hand off his shoulder, spoke in a tone in which there was noticeably less warmth.

"Gavin Blake's in hospital with three broken ribs," he said, "and one leg done up in plaster and hitched to the ceiling. If you want——"

"Thanks for coming and telling me," said Paul coolly.

Oscar Tenby stared at him for a moment, and Felicity, putting up a hand, laid it on his arm and spoke appealingly.

"Please—Oscar—will you leave it to me?" she begged.

"You tame bears?" Oscar asked, looking down at her. "All right—see what you can do with this one. Get an answer out of him if you can," he went on, "but "—his tone became serious—"get it pronto, will you? It's pretty urgent—I've already wasted five days and worn out my fingers dialling his number. Make him give me a ring to-night, will you? I leave him to you," he ended.

Felicity gave his arm a grateful little squeeze.

"Thank you, Oscar," she said.

Mr. Tenby looked at Roger.

"Did you ever punch his head when he was a little shaver?" he asked.

"It looks as if I punched all the sense out of it," said Roger. "I'm sorry."

Mr. Tenby took an easy and charming leave, and left. Roger and Paul resumed their seats, and Roger looked at his brother.

"One of us," he said, "has to look at the waitress and call for the bill."

"I thought," returned Paul, "that we were lunching with the girls."

Mrs. Beddington gave a series of little gasps, and,

clutching her purse tightly, brought it above the table to indicate that she was desirous of paying the bill and had plenty of money with which to do so. Ruth pushed the bag gently and firmly back on to the old lady's lap.

"Oh, no," she said. "He isn't going to get off so easily. Nobody asked him to come."

"Oh, but, Ruth"—Mrs. Beddington's face was pink with agitation—"so much spending this morning—those shoes—that bag—I feel——"

"What shoes and what bag?" demanded Roger, alarm on his countenance.

"Oh—just shoes and a bag," said Ruth carelessly.

"It wasn't her fault," said Brenda defensively. "It was all that"—she pointed a finger at Felicity—"that creature. She egged Ruth on."

"Oh, I didn't egg," protested Felicity. "I only said they were absolute bargains. Besides, she really needed the powder and cream—I didn't have to do any egging. I didn't dream," she ended, "you could get those Anna-Raymonde preparations in a funny little place like Petsham."

"Anna-Raymonde," said Roger in a dazed voice. "Have you," he asked his wife, "had an orgy or something?"

"Don't be silly," said Ruth. "I simply got a nice sensible pair of brogues—they were——"

"Dirt cheap," put in Brenda. "Only eighty-two shillings."

Roger looked relieved. He gave a deep sigh.

"Gosh!" he said. "I thought for a moment you were serious."

"Of course I'm serious," said Ruth. "I've been looking for brogues for a long time. They're——"

"They're ducky," said Felicity.

"You couldn't," stated Roger with certainty, "pay eighty-two shillings for a pair of shoes in Petsham."

"You could and I did," replied Ruth. "What are you making such a fuss about? They're a bargain. I don't think," she went on, her face falling, "the bag was worth as much as six pounds."

"Six pounds?" squeaked Roger. "Six pounds? You've paid six pounds for a bag? Why—you've got a black bag and a blue bag and a brown bag and the bag Paul gave you and the one——"

"Oh, Roger, this is a *travelling* bag," said Felicity. "It's a ducky one."

"Stop saying ducky at me," requested Roger. "My wife goes out for two hours and spends nearly twenty pounds——"

There was a cry from the four women.

"Oh, no!" said Mrs. Beddington.

"Bosh," said Brenda.

"Nothing like," said Felicity.

Roger looked at his wife.

"Fourteen pounds, eight and fourpence," said Ruth.

There was a long silence. Paul poured out some water and pushed it across to his stricken brother.

"I've got," he said, after investigation, "two pounds and a few sixpences. I shall pay for the lunch——"

"Thanks, Paul," said Roger.

"—and you can take it off my account," finished Paul. He took the bill from the waitress, glanced at it and gave the girl the money.

"Wait for us in the hall," said Ruth. "We've got piles of coats and things. Does anybody feel like a cinema?"

Nobody did. The women declared that they had had excitement enough, and Roger announced that his lunch had turned sour through shock.

Ruth helped her aunt into her succession of garments and then took her own off the peg. Brenda, arrayed once more in her storm-suit, searched for the key of the car and, having taken off her heavy mackintosh once more in order to go through the pockets of her suit, saw Ruth regarding her with amusement and holding the key in her hand. "You asked me to mind it," she said sweetly.

Brenda snatched it from her and attired herself once more for the road.

"We'll go together," she said to Mrs. Beddington. "You can warm yourself by the hall fire while I bring the car round."

Ruth and Felicity went to the entrance and found Roger and Paul awaiting them.

"Here you are," said Roger. "Where are the others?"

"Bringing round the car," said Ruth. "How are we going back?"

"Well, driving Goosey's machine isn't much of an entertainment," said Roger. "Every time you see a large stone, you have to drive round it. Paul can drive it back and you can toss who goes with him."

Brenda drove up, and Roger went forward to take her place at the wheel. Brenda alighted and addressed Ruth.

"I've got an idea," she said. "We'll send Aunt Emmie home with the men and we'll squeeze into Major Horder's car and drive it home."

"I'll drive it," offered Felicity.

"Don't be silly," said Roger. "The thing's not a car at all—it's a converted sleigh—it drags you over the bumps."

"Well, it'll be fun," said Felicity. "Come on."

The three women went over to the car park, and Roger called after them.

"Where's Aunt Emmie?" he asked.

"In the hall, by the fire," called Brenda. "Don't go in until we've seen whether this thing starts or not."

After some tuneful effects on the self-starter, Goosey's car coughed once or twice, burst into a roar of pain and shook with a terrible ague.

"They're off," said Paul, watching the vehicle perform a series of jerks and disappear down the road. "Now, how about Auntie?"

"I'll fetch her," said Roger, going into the building.

Paul waited for what he thought an unnecessarily long time and then went in search of his brother. Roger was standing in the hall, his eyes on a distant door marked "Ladies" and his brows drawn together in a terrible frown.

"What the hell do you think she's doing in there?" he enquired savagely of Paul, as the latter came up.

"Well, it's no use champing," said Paul. "We can't very well go in and fetch her out. We'll give her another few minutes."

After giving her another twenty minutes, Roger had reached a state of mind bordering on frenzy. He rose from the seat on which he had fidgeted so long.

"How long do we have to sit here?" he demanded furiously. "She's had time to powder forty blasted noses. What in God's name," he asked, "do you think she can be doing in there?"

Paul looked round for a few moments and then approached a severe-looking young woman who appeared to be in a position of authority in the dining-room.

"I'm so sorry to trouble you," he said, "but we're waiting for an old lady and we think we may have missed her. I wonder if you'd very kindly look in the cloak-room and see if she's there?"

The young woman went into the cloakroom, and emerging, announced that no old lady was in there.

Paul stared at the speaker.

"Are you—are you quite sure?" he asked blankly.

There was, it appeared, no doubt. Roger and Paul looked at one another in stupefied silence for some moments.

"Well, it's damn silly," said Roger at last. "She must be somewhere. I suppose she couldn't have gone off with the others in Goosey's car, could she?"

"She couldn't possibly have fitted," said Paul, "and besides, they would have let us know. Anyhow, we saw them go and she obviously wasn't ambling along the road waiting to be picked up."

"Well, we'll have to search," he said. "After all, she can't just disappear—the thing's impossible."

They searched the building, at first unaided and then with the help of the management and the entire staff. No trace of Mrs. Beddington, however, could be found. At the end of half an hour's search, the brothers looked at one another with white faces.

"Well, now what?" asked Paul slowly.

Roger made no reply. The thing was not, after all, impossible.

Aunt Emmie had vanished.

CHAPTER XIII

FELICITY drove Goosey's car to the door of River Lodge and came to a stop. The rain had ceased, but the afternoon was dull and depressing.

"Go on into the garage," said Brenda. "We'll all disembark there."

Felicity put the car away, and the three women walked slowly back to the house.

"I suppose," said Ruth, "Goosey'll be walking up and down the hall raging."

Felicity gave a little laugh.

"Poor Major Horder," she said. "It was a mean trick."

"Serves him right," said Brenda.

They entered the house, but there was no sign of a resentful man pacing the hall. The house seemed quiet, but from the direction of the children's room could be heard strange sounds. Ruth puckered her brows.

"That sounds like Uncle George," she said. "You don't think Nan's abandoned the twins again, do you?"

They hurried to the door of the room, opened it, and stood aghast.

"Holy Moses!" ejaculated Brenda. "An earthquake."

The room undoubtedly had a devastated look. Chairs were overturned, newspapers lay about—some in the shape of boats, some as paper hats, some merely crumpled sheets. A confusion of toys and games lay about the floor and articles of the twins' clothing were spread here and there.

In the midst of the confusion sat the twins, as stolid and as interested as ever. Their eyes were on Mr. Beddington who, hot and dishevelled, was on all fours before them, emitting a series of woof-woofs and pretending to be a large and ferocious dog. At the sound of Brenda's exclamation, he looked extremely shamefaced and began to struggle to his feet.

"This," said Felicity angrily, "is too much! Where's Nan?"

"Oh, no, no," protested Mr. Beddington, pulling his coat into position and speaking in anxious, hurried tones. "You mustn't blame her—it's perfectly all right. Yes. You see," he ended, "she's gone."

"Gone!" echoed all three women together, and Felicity added an incredulous, "But it's impossible—how can she have gone?"

"Well, you see——" Mr. Beddington paused, looking pink and flustered, and Ruth realized that the sight of three women facing him and hanging on his words was making him nervous. She drew him to a sofa and settled him on it, sitting by him and holding his hand.

"Where did Mrs. Hellier go, Uncle darling?" she asked gently.

"Well, it's been an extraordinary morning—a most extraordinary morning, really," said Mr. Beddington. "I don't know when I've—well I must tell you properly. You see," he went on, looking round at his interested listeners, "we had just had lunch—Mrs. Hellier had hers with the children—and suddenly she came into the drawing-room where we were having coffee, and said she had that moment had a telephone call from her husband."

"You mean Tippy's home?" cried Felicity.

"Well, I don't know what his name is," said Mr. Beddington. "She said he had telephoned and asked her to meet him in London—he had, I understand, gone to your mother's house and she had told him where his wife was."

"And so she went," said Felicity. "Did she say when she's coming back?"

"Well—no," said Mr. Beddington. "It was all—well, it was a little upsetting after she had told us the news, because she said she would go up and—well, she didn't think it would be worth while returning, as she only had two more days here. She asked Mr. West to drive her to the station, and Mr. West——"

Mr. Beddington paused, his eyes growing round over the memory of the scene. A low "Dear me!" escaped him, whetting the curiosity of the listeners.

"Go on, darling," said Ruth. "What did Mr. West say?"

Mr. Beddington gave a little start.

"Mr. West? Oh, Mr. West! Yes," he answered. "Well, he was a little harsh, I think. He didn't seem himself this morning—the weather, perhaps. He was definitely out of sorts and I think perhaps he wasn't feeling very well. He asked Mrs. Hellier what she intended to do with the children, and Mrs. Hellier replied a little too flippantly, perhaps. They had an argument—one had to listen, because one's coffee was there—but it was very embarrassing. Very, indeed."

"Did he take her to the station?" asked Felicity.

"No—he refused quite definitely," said Mr. Beddington. "He said it was one thing for her to go up to meet her husband—that was a natural and reasonable thing to do—but he would not be a party to her packing all her things and leaving without making any arrangements for her children or even "—Mr. Beddington hesitated and looked apologetically at Ruth—"paying her bill. Mrs. Hellier said that of course Miss—Miss Felicity would see to everything, and Mr. West seemed to become quite infuriated and broke into quite a—quite an harangue."

"Well, how did she go?" asked Brenda.

"That's the most painful part," said Mr. Beddington. "When Mrs. Hellier saw that he was really not going to take her, she thought for a little while and then said —with great good nature, I thought—that she could wait until you all returned and catch a later train. Then she turned to Lady Warne and said she supposed there was no chance of Lady Warne's looking after the twins for a day or two. I don't think," continued Mr. Beddington, with a shake of his head, "that she really meant it—I think it was said in a spirit of—of jest, but Lady Warne seemed very much offended and I'm sorry to say that there was a——"

"Another shindy," said Brenda. "Poor Mr. Beddington!"

"Oh, not at all, not at all," said Mr. Beddington. "I'm only sorry——"

"How did Nan go?" asked Felicity, unable to help interrupting.

"Well, she left the drawing-room and went upstairs," said Mr. Beddington, "and we all tried to settle down and forget the rather painful scenes, when suddenly Mr. West got out of his chair and went to the window and seemed very much upset and said he was sure he had heard the sound of an engine. I soothed him by telling him it would no doubt be all of you returning, but he didn't seem satisfied, so he went out to make investigations and when he came back he was really in a very angry state indeed, and told Lady Warne that—that Mrs. Hellier had sent for her chauffeur and informed him that his mistress had given orders that she was to be driven to the station."

Felicity gave a little cry of anger and dismay. Her face pale, she looked at Ruth.

"I'm sorry, Ruth," she said unsteadily. "I'm—oh well, it's no use saying anything. The beast," she murmured to herself. "The little beast."

"Don't worry, Liss," said Ruth. "It's nothing to do with you. And I don't suppose Nan would have done it if she hadn't been over-excited. What with hearing from—what did you say his name was? "

" Tippy," said Felicity.

" Tippy, and then being browbeaten by Martin and snubbed by Au—by Lady Warne," went on Ruth, " I honestly feel I might have been driven to it myself."

Felicity looked at Mr. Beddington.

" It was sweet of you to take on the twins," she said earnestly. " I hope you're not exhausted."

" Not at all," said Mr. Beddington. " I enjoyed it very much." He glanced round the room and then looked ruefully at his niece. " Such a mess——" he murmured.

" I'll see to it," said Brenda. " You must go up and rest. And you haven't," she went on, " enquired where your wife is."

Mr. Beddington smiled.

" That's easy to guess," he said. " She's with Roger."

" She is," said Ruth, " and she'll be home soon. There! I think that's the car," she went on, " so she'll be here in a moment. I'll take one twin, Liss, and you take the other and bring them upstairs for their sleep."

" I'll go up and take these things off and then see about the room," said Brenda.

" And I," said Mr. Beddington, " shall go and meet Lena. I must tell her what she missed. Such upsets . . . such excitements . . ."

He watched the three women and the placid twins going upstairs and stood in the hall, his eyes on the front door, waiting for his wife.

.   .   .   .

Roger and Paul walked slowly to their car and stood irresolutely beside it. The faces of both men were pale. Roger's brows were drawn in anxiety.

" Well, what do we do? " he asked at last. " Go to the police? "

" God knows," said Paul. " What do we tell them, anyhow? An old lady's left in front of a fire for roughly ten minutes and in that time vanishes completely.

But then," he pointed out, "she's always vanishing."

"Do you know what I think?" said Roger. "I think she stood in front of the fire dreaming comfortably for about three minutes, then roused herself, thought she'd been there for a devil of a long time, and got into one of her nervous fits and thought we'd gone off without her. Perhaps she even looked out and saw the three of them driving off in Goosey's car and thought they'd forgotten her. So what would she do?—she'd rush out in a panic and start paddling down the road in a hell of a state, and then somebody would stop and pick her up and find out where she was trying to get to and take her there. What d'you think?"

"Sounds all right," said Paul, "except that you and I were standing in the entrance after they drove off, and she couldn't have got by us without our seeing her."

"Oh—well," said Roger impatiently, "I'm going home to find out. We'll go in carefully," he went on. "The thing to do is fend off old Uncle George until we've more news to give him. Somehow—I don't know why—I feel she must be all right. Who'd want to harm a—a harmless old lady who obviously isn't wealthy?"

"Well—let's go," said Paul. "It's better than standing here."

Roger drove the car homewards, coming to a stop at a part of the drive which was not overlooked from the house.

"I'll park here," he said. "We might need the car again—and nobody can look out of a window and see there are only two of us——"

They walked to the front door and stood for a moment outside it.

"I can't hear anyone," said Roger, listening intently. "I think it's clear. Let's hope Uncle George——"

He opened the door quietly and stepped in, followed by Paul. A murmur of dismay escaped both men as they entered.

Before them, in the hall, a smile of welcome on his face at the sight of them, stood Mr. Beddington. Paul, after a glance at his brother's blank expression, stepped forward and took the situation in hand.

" Ah," he said.

" Ah," beamed Mr. Beddington. " So you're back."

" Yes," said Paul.

" That's right," said Roger.

There was a pause. Now was the dreadful moment when Mr. Beddington would look round and enquire fearfully for his wife.

" It's been a shocking day," said Mr. Beddington, " hasn't it? "

" Yes," said Roger. " It has."

" Taking one thing with another," said Mr. Beddington.

" Yes," said Paul.

" You mustn't stand there," said Mr. Beddington. " You're no doubt very damp, even though the rain has stopped. You must get into dry things and then I'm afraid we shall have some rather upsetting news to tell you."

Roger and Paul, their mouths open, their expressions stunned, stared at him speechlessly.

" But we won't upset you now," went on Mr. Beddington. " Ah! here's Ruth," he said, as his niece came downstairs. " Here they are, my dear. I've been telling them we won't upset them with that worrying news until they've changed."

" Oh, I don't think they're wet," said Ruth. " And anyhow "—she smiled at her uncle—" it isn't so terrible."

Mr. Beddington looked disappointed.

" I don't know about that," he argued gently. " After all—she's gone."

" Yes, she's gone," agreed Ruth.

She turned to her husband and brother-in-law and was astounded to find them regarding her with expressions resembling those of men who had seen a ghost.

" What on earth——? " she began.

A patter of light footsteps sounded from the direction

of the drawing-room and a small figure came into view. At the sight of it Ruth's mouth opened and her expression became an exact copy of those on the faces of Roger and Paul. Together the three stared at the newcomer.

"Here they are, George dear," twittered Mrs. Beddington. "Have you told them yet?"

Ruth shut her mouth, swallowed and spoke.

"Aunt Emmie . . ." she said.

"Yes, dear," said Mrs. Beddington. "George told me when I came in—what a morning! Such a——"

Roger found his voice.

"When," he enquired, a touch of hoarseness in his voice, "did you come in?"

Mrs. Beddington pursed her lips, put her head on one side and looked at her husband.

"Half—three-quarters——?" she calculated.

"Oh, hardly," said her husband. "I should say about —well, let me see—I think forty minutes would be exact."

"And how—I mean, did you get back all right?" asked Paul.

"Oh, thank you, yes," said Mrs. Beddington. "So comfortable. I've never been in one of those nice little vans before—like a shooting brake—so comfortable."

Ruth looked at her uncomprehendingly.

"You came back in our van, forty minutes ago?" she asked in a dazed voice.

"Yes, dear—oh! perhaps you didn't know," said Mrs. Beddington. "You had driven away, I think. And Roger sent such a kind message to say that this would be a good opportunity for me to have a little drive in the van. Thank you, Roger dear."

"I didn't," said Roger, speaking slowly and carefully, "see the van drive away——"

"Well, no," said Mrs. Beddington, "it wasn't at that entrance—it was standing at the side entrance because Major Horder said——"

"Goosey," breathed Ruth.

"Goosey," said Roger, in a deep, vibrant bass.

"Goosey," said Paul, with no expression at all in his voice.

"I wonder," went on Roger casually to Mrs. Beddington, "where Major Horder is now—do you know?"

"Oh, he said he wouldn't be in to tea," said Mrs. Beddington. "He said he needed a little exercise—he asked me to tell you that he'd been feeling—what did he say now?—cooped up all day."

"Ah," said Roger. He took a deep breath, put his shoulders back and looked at his brother. Paul looked back, his expression calm.

"I suppose," he said, "we should have known."

"We know now," Roger told him grimly.

"Yes," agreed Paul, a look of happy anticipation appearing on his face. "We know now."

CHAPTER XIV

NOTHING was seen of Major Horder at tea. Mr. Lenner, who had gone out for a walk immediately after lunch, returned about two hours later and looked more melancholy than ever at his friend's absence.

When dinner was over and Goosey had still not put in an appearance, Roger sought out Brenda. He found her with Felicity in the children's room, picking up toys and putting them away. She returned Roger's look of suspicion with calmness.

"You needn't say it," she said. "And the answer is, no, I haven't. After a rotten trick like that I wouldn't hide the little brute from you."

"Have you looked under your bed?" asked Roger.

"I overlooked that," said Brenda. "But I——"

She paused as the sound of arrivals was heard in the hall. All three moved to the door and looked into the hall. Felicity gave an incredulous exclamation.

"Tippy!" she cried, running forward with hands

outstretched in welcome. "Oh, Tippy, how nice to see you!"

The pleasant-looking young man standing beside Mrs. Hellier took Felicity's hands and kissed her lightly and then, appearing to enjoy it, drew her to him and pressed his lips warmly on hers.

"So there!" observed his wife, who was looking extremely sulky. "It was to do that, obviously. I knew it wasn't the twins that made you drag me back here."

Lieutenant-Commander Hellier released his sister-in-law reluctantly.

"I enjoyed that," he said simply. "But I didn't," he asserted, "come back specially to collect it."

"He says," announced Mrs. Hellier with obvious disbelief and contempt, "that he wants to see the twins. Can you imagine? He wouldn't stay in Town—he wouldn't stay even one tiny night—he wouldn't even take me to a show."

"Where," enquired Tippy, looking round, "are my children?"

"They're asleep and you're not to disturb them," said Felicity. "Nan'll take you up."

"Leave the suit-cases," said Roger. "I'll have them sent up and see about fixing you up. Have you had any dinner?"

"We didn't have anything," said Mrs. Hellier. "I don't know what's the matter with him—he wouldn't stop for anything. He could have had at least a night or two having some fun and going to some places and—oh!" she ended on a note of exasperation, "I can't make him out."

"Nor can I," said Felicity, linking her arm in her brother-in-law's and looking at him affectionately. "Tippy, you never showed this enthusiasm for your sons before," she said. "Have you lost your youthful zest?"

"Gone paternal," explained Tippy. "Let's go up."

"This way," said his wife in gloomy accents, going up the stairs. "The Brahmaputrid. They wake at half-past six and sing two different tunes, one about a hen and one about I can't tell what. You'll be terribly, terribly amused. And they throw biscuits at you and they . . ."

Her voice died away as the three turned the corner at the top of the stairs. Brenda looked at Roger.

" Well, thank goodness the twins have got a mother at last," she commented. " What d'you suppose made a sensible young man like that look at a girl like that one? "

" Takes all sorts," said Roger vaguely. " I'll see about their meal. Send me a signal, will you, if you see that human seal flapping about anywhere? "

" With pleasure," said Brenda. She looked after his retreating form for a moment and then glanced up at the sound of footsteps. Felicity ran lightly down the stairs and stopped beside her.

" He's sweet," she said. " Hanging over them without saying a word, and looking ecstatic. Can people turn into fathers all of a sudden like that? "

" When was he last with them? " asked Brenda.

" About eighteen months ago," said Felicity. " He was rather like Nan then—he used to fasten them to the nearest prop and rush madly about to shows and parties and things."

" Well, there isn't much in those early stages to interest fathers," observed Brenda. " All washing and baby powder. It smells nice, but it isn't an atmosphere I care for myself—I'd much rather wait a bit until they're adorable mites like the twins, wearing real clothes instead of merely protective layers. A baby's a baby," she went on, " but, much as I like them, I'm always glad when they get to the stage when you don't have to keep on answering your own questions all the time. This Tippy, as you call him, is going to enjoy himself taking a couple of very young men about with him—so different to pushing them round in a perambulator."

" That's true," said Felicity. " But what'll Nan do? "

"Well, it doesn't matter very much, does it?" asked Brenda. "I mean, she did nothing before, so what's the difference? I imagine she'll leave father to mind the twins and——"

"Oh, but she adores Tippy," said Felicity. "If he's going to stay with the twins all the time——"

She paused, her brows knitted. Brenda smiled.

"It's a nice little situation," she observed. "I'm sorry I'm not going to see the way it works out. You must write and let me know how your sister goes on."

"Here they are," said Felicity, as the Helliers descended the stairs. Mrs. Hellier's expression was bewildered and her stare more in evidence than ever, but one small hand rested firmly under her husband's arm.

"I'll take you into the dining-room," said Brenda. "You must be starving. How do you think your family looked?"

"Magnificent," said the proud father. "They both sleep with their mouths shut."

"And their eyes, too," added their mother. "They're phenomenal."

Her husband gave a pleasant grin and followed her into the dining-room.

"Jealous," he remarked to Brenda. "Dog-in-the-mangerish, too. Doesn't want to play with them herself, and won't let anybody else play with them either."

"Anybody," Mrs. Hellier informed him, "except you. Oh, Tippy darling," she begged, "do be human!"

Brenda, having seen to their needs, left them together and went back to Felicity. She was just in time to see her entering the children's room once more. Martin West followed her, closing the door behind him.

Brenda stood still for a moment, and then went on her way. The look on Martin's face interested, but did not surprise her. The man had, she reflected, been warming up for the past three days and she judged he must now be on the point of boiling over. Felicity had been out all day and, when she returned, had taken tea with Brenda in her office and dinner with the Mallards in their own dining-room. It was no wonder that Martin West's face wore a look of bleak anger.

"If I know anything," said Brenda to herself, going upstairs, "he's going to stage a proposal. I hope," she added charitably, "it chokes him."

.   .   .   .

There was certainly some constriction in Martin West's throat as he faced Felicity. She had crossed the room and was sitting in a big, deep chair upholstered in a striking shade of royal blue. Against it her lovely head leaned carelessly—on the sides lay her long white hands. Her eyes were on Martin and there was interest in them, but it was a casual interest. It was evident that there were other things in her mind—other things as important and as absorbing as anything he might be about to say. It was only a few days, Martin reflected, since she had stepped out of the train and smiled at him —there had been a bond between them, a link of friendship and companionship. Now she sat in the chair, charming and attentive—and remote.

"It was a mistake," he said suddenly, "to come down here."

Felicity frowned a little, as if considering the reasons for his remark. After a while her brow cleared and she shook her head.

"I don't think so," she said. "From my point of view——"

Martin sat on the edge of the table in the middle of the room and gazed at a neat pile of gaily-coloured bricks near his hand. He moved them absently, picking them up and setting them down in fresh places.

"It was a mistake," he said again, as if he had not heard Felicity's words. "Last week we were—well, friends, and now something's happened." He raised his head and looked at her. "Do you feel that too?" he asked.

Felicity looked at him, feeling a little at a loss. He had, she knew, been neglected during the past few days, and she was moved by a feeling of sympathy. Roger and Ruth, she knew, liked him, but were much occupied and had little time to spare. Brenda disliked him; Paul —Felicity went hastily on. She had not been conscious of avoiding the man before her, but she realized that the week had been a bitter disappointment for him. He had come down expecting a great deal of her companionship, and she had left him alone.

"Martin," she said, "I'm so sorry—I mean, about this week. I do see that perhaps it hasn't been much fun —for you."

Martin West regarded her expressionlessly.

"And have you," he enquired, "had fun?"

Felicity considered.

"Well, perhaps not fun," she said after a while. "But something much more than fun. Ruth and Roger, for instance—I'd almost forgotten how nice they are. I didn't know it could be so nice to talk over silly school things with Ruth. And I hardly knew Brenda at all . . . and that funny Goosey. I'm sorry if I've been a pig and let you come down here for—for——"

She paused in embarrassment. Martin, watching her, gave her no help.

"When I came here," began Felicity again, "I thought it would be like coming to an ordinary hotel and just knowing the people who ran it. I didn't see that I'd get such a—a family feeling, but I can't help it —I have got it, and it's been lovely. But not," she ended lamely, "for you."

"No," agreed Martin evenly, "not for me."

"Well," repeated Felicity, "I'm sorry. I wish you hadn't been so——" She stopped, unable to use the words "out of things." It was quite impossible to acknowledge that he had counted for so little during the past week. She had never seen him anywhere but in London and then only in a circle in which he played an all-important part. He could make reputations—he had made hers. He was an outstanding personality, well known and respected. She could not point out that here, in what had turned out so unexpectedly to be a happy family atmosphere, he had no place.

"The past week," began Martin slowly, his eyes on the bricks, "isn't important. But the future's important, and it's only the future I'm worried about. Why didn't you tell me," he went on abruptly, "that Ted had sent you that script?"

He raised his eyes as he spoke and sent her a keen look. In spite of herself, Felicity felt her cheeks grow warm.

"You got it two days ago, didn't you?" pursued Martin.

"Yes," said Felicity. "I was going to——"

She paused, and Martin waited.

"You were going to what?" he asked presently, with a noticeable hardening in his tones.

"I was going to tell you about it," said Felicity, "some time soon."

"I see," said Martin. He got off the table, pushed his hands into the pockets of his trousers and walked to the fireplace. He stared absently before him for a moment, and then swung round and looked down at the girl in the chair.

"Now look, Felicity," he said, a little grimly, "you're not a good liar and you're not even the kind of girl who can beat about the bush. You're intelligent and you're —you're fair-minded. So listen to me. A fortnight ago," he went on slowly, "we discussed Ted's play in Town. You were eager, you were keen and impatient to see it, you were more than disappointed when the script didn't reach you before it was time for you to come down here. You—you almost worked yourself up about it. That's right, isn't it?"

Felicity, her face now a little pale, nodded without speaking.

"So," said Martin, "you came down here. A few days later the script reached you. I don't know what you did with it—I don't know whether you even opened it and looked at it. All I know is that you didn't so much as mention it to me. I wouldn't have known Ted had sent it if he hadn't written to me at the same time."

He took his hands out of his pockets and took a few slow steps across the room. He turned at last and faced her. "Between the frenzy about wanting to see the script," he continued, "and the apathy on getting the script, something happened. Have you," he asked quietly, "any idea what?"

Felicity made an impatient movement.

"Yes, I have," she said. "A perfectly normal thing happened. I came here to have a change, and the change did me good. There's no point in having changes if your mind's going to stay full of the same interests and the same ideas—you can only get a rest when they become less important for the time being, and slip into the background. Then when you've had your change, you go back and—and take them up again and——"

To her dismay, Felicity found herself faltering. A weight, inexplicable and crushing, came out of nowhere and settled on her tongue, on her mind and spirits. She sat silent, staring ahead of her unseeingly. Martin West watched her, a look of pain and fear on his face.

After what seemed a long time, Felicity turned her head and met his eyes.

"Martin——" she began.

Martin West's face contracted suddenly.

"I was afraid of it," he said. "It wasn't only the script—it was—oh, a lot of things. Every time I mentioned—certain things—you shied." He came close to her and, standing by her, stared down at her beseechingly. "Look, Felicity," he said, "if there's anything wrong, you must tell me. I've worked for you—worked with you—it was all going so well. Since you came here——"

Felicity looked up at him and spoke quickly.

"No, Martin," she said. "It—it's really been there for a long time, but I pushed it away and wouldn't think about it. I promise it wasn't until I was talking to you a few minutes ago that I—that I really knew what I'd been feeling."

Martin West put out a hand and pressed her shoulder reassuringly. He gave her a smile of encouragement.

"Look, don't let's get too serious about this," he said. "I ought to be angry with you. Couldn't you," he asked, "have come to me, instead of bottling it up and worrying and getting all mixed up in your mind? We could have put it right at the start and you wouldn't have built it up into a major scare like this." He took his hand from her shoulder and gave a short, pleasant laugh. "Everybody," he said, "feels the job going stale on them at times. If they're wise, they recognize the symptoms at once and give themselves a break. A holiday. A vay-cation. Then they come back fresh and fit and get into things again. Why," he ended, "didn't you have the sense to treat the thing that way?"

Felicity sat silent, her hands lying loosely on her lap.

"Come on," urged Martin, "and stop worrying about nothing. We've diagnosed the trouble and we can cure it. Now smile."

Felicity could not smile. She rose slowly to her feet and faced him, her face white.

"Martin," she began.

Martin West took both her hands and held them warmly.

"Don't talk now, Felicity," he said. "I always think it's a bad thing to discuss symptoms. You'll say a lot of things you'll have forgotten in a week or two when you've got back into the swing and seen the lights again."

"No, Martin," said Felicity, more firmly now. "It's something that won't pass off—I know it won't. For a long time I've known that things weren't the same, but I couldn't understand what was the matter with me. Now I know. I don't want to——"

"Don't say it, Felicity," warned Martin.

"But it's true," said Felicity. "I don't want to—I don't want to act any more."

There was a heavy silence. Then Martin dropped her hands and, taking her shoulders in a firm grasp, gave her a little shake.

"Stop being a little fool, Felicity," he said roughly. "You don't know what you're talking about."

"I do," said Felicity, with calmness and decision. "I'm sorry, Martin, but I'm sure now and I—I've been unhappy for months. I'm terribly sorry," she added slowly, "but I'm going to leave the stage."

Martin West stared at her for a few moments and then gave a short, incredulous laugh.

"My God!" he said. "Just like that. Quite simply and with no complications of any sort. ' I'm so sorry, so terribly sorry, and I'm walking out, good-bye.' " He stopped, his face darkening with rage. "After all I've done," he said chokingly. "After all the risk and the time and the patience and the hopes and the training and the build-ups and the——" He laughed again, and it was an ugly sound. "After all that—a frown, a puzzled look, a deep sigh, a simper and an ' Oh—I'm terribly sorry, good-bye.' Why, you—you incredible— you incredibly *young* little fool," he ended savagely, "you don't know what you're saying. You're—you're out of your mind!"

Felicity turned away from the crimson, distorted face before her. Martin grasped her arm and swung her round to face him once more. He stared at her, watching the tears rolling down her cheeks. In a few moments he spoke, a little gratingly, but with a steadiness which showed that he had himself once more under control.

"Hold on, Felicity darling," he said. "I'm an—an unqualified swine. But the thing popped up and hit me, and when I'm hit—I hit back and hurt. This thing," he went on, "isn't important and we're not going to stand here and get into a state over it. Other things are far more serious—like telling a girl you love her and want to marry her." He took out his hand-kerchief, unfolded it and continued to speak gently, as he wiped her tears. "Only you can't do that when she's crying. When we get back to Town," he said, "we'll take hold of your little trouble, lay it all out, study the whole thing and remove its fangs." He put the handkerchief back, studied her face critically and, putting up his hand, touched her hair and put a straying curl back into place.

"Martin," said Felicity suddenly.

Martin West bent and put his lips gently on hers.

"They tell me that's the quickest way to stop a woman talking," he said. "Funny I never tried it with you before."

His hands on her shoulders, he looked down at her with a smile. Felicity looked back at him, her mind in confusion, her head aching.

"Smile, please," begged Martin.

Felicity, with an effort, put from her mind every thought but that of the kindness she had received from the man facing her. She owed him a great deal—he had been unfailingly good to her. She looked up at him and smiled.

At the same moment the door opened and Paul Mallard appeared on the threshold. For a brief instant his eyes rested on the scene before him, and the next moment Martin and Felicity had moved apart. Paul, standing aside, made way for Brenda and Ruth. The latter paused at the sight of Martin and Felicity.

"Oh—we didn't know there was anybody in here," she said. "We came in to play bridge. But don't move," she added quickly, "you stay in here and talk if you want to, and we'll go to Brenda's office."

Felicity shook her head. "I'm going, thank you," she said. "I've got a most frightful head——"

"Oh, my dear," said Ruth sympathetically. "Shall I bring you up a hot drink?"

"No, thanks," said Felicity. "I'll take an aspirin and go straight to bed."

She said a brief good night and went out.

"Bridge, Martin?" asked Ruth.

"I'm not keen, thanks, to-night—unless you're stumped for a fourth," said Martin.

"No—Roger said he'd come," said Ruth, "but we can cut in."

"No, thanks," said Martin again. "I'll go and get a drink and then turn in."

The door closed behind him, and for a few minutes nobody spoke. Brenda, glancing at Paul's face, looked away hastily and, going to a drawer, opened it and took out two packs of cards. With her back to the others, she waited a moment to subdue the wave of hatred flowing over her. She looked down at her neat finger-nails and wondered how it would feel to embed them deeply in Martin West's face. She had never scratched anybody's face . . . but there always had to be a first time. . . .

She turned, the packs of cards in her hand. Paul was unfolding the card-table, his face calm, his expression a little bored.

"Did Goosey ever turn up?" he asked casually.

"No sign of him," said Ruth. "Roger's been prowling all the evening. I think——"

She stopped as Paul's hand came up in a peremptory gesture. There was a silence, and each of the three in the room listened intently. Presently Paul looked at the others and nodded.

The door opened to admit Roger, and Paul, looking across the room, made a warning sign to his brother.

"Here it comes," he said softly, pointing towards the window.

Roger raised his hand to the light switch and a second later the room was in darkness. In silence the four waited as the sound of stealthy footsteps drew nearer and passed the window. Still the listeners waited, and soon the sound of the garden door being cautiously opened came to their ears.

Paul moved quietly across the dark room and waited beside his brother at the door. A stealthy tread sounded in the hall.

"Now," said Roger suddenly.

With a war-whoop that came simultaneously from both throats and swept Brenda back twenty years to the days when the same yell had struck terror into her heart, the brothers charged. There was a roar from Goosey, a chase and a scuffle and the sound of heavy falls. Ruth and Brenda moved into ringside seats in the hall. From the dining-room came the Helliers, watching the progress of events from the door. Mr. Lenner, making no attempt to rescue his friend, watched from the foot of the staircase.

In a few minutes Goosey, fighting gamely and uttering loud protests against the heavy odds, was overpowered and carried, kicking vigorously, towards the door through which he had lately entered. One foot, eluding the efforts of Paul and Roger to confine it, waved dangerously. Tippy, his eyes shining, moved forward and grasped it firmly. Goosey's shoe fell off in the struggle and Tippy, stepping over it, assisted Roger and Paul with their burden towards the fountain. Mr. Lenner picked up the shoe and, holding it, walked to the door and stood watching the procession moving into the darkness.

The three women listened unmoved to the piteous cries and gurgles which proceeded from outside.

"Funny things men do," commented Brenda, listening to the sound of splashing. "Imagine three women carrying another woman out and putting her—clothes and all—into some water."

"It might be fun sometimes," observed Ruth. "But cold——"

She stopped and, looking towards Mr. Lenner, spoke in a low tone. "I think he must be cold, too," she said. "He's shaking all over."

"It's probably fright," murmured Brenda. "He didn't seem anxious to join in."

Ruth was still staring at the artist.

"You don't think he's upset or anything, do you?"

she asked in an anxious whisper. "He's—he's got his mouth wide open——"

"And—look, he's showing all his teeth," said Brenda. "He looks awfully peculiar——"

They stared for a few moments longer, and suddenly the reason for Mr. Lenner's unusual appearance burst upon them with unnerving force. Only one thing could account for the half-shut, streaming eyes, the wide mouth and the shuddering form. . . .

Mr. Lenner was laughing.

CHAPTER XV

ALREADY the first signs of departure were in the air.

The Helliers were leaving first. Tippy had a grand-mother in Newton Stewart who wished to see her grand-children, and to Newton Stewart, therefore, the twins were being taken. Mrs. Hellier's loud and bewildered complaints had no effect at all upon her husband, who listened to them wearing the expression he wore when the twins pulled his hair—a look of patience and indulgence.

The little family provided a good deal of amusement for the onlookers. Tippy displayed an astonishing aptitude for his joint role as father and nurse, handling the children quietly and competently and contriving to keep his wife under control at the same time. He reminded Ruth of a busy young mother looking after her children and keeping an eye on a troublesome puppy.

To Brenda, he was another example of the magnifi-cent training which was undergone by those in what she secretly considered the finest of the Services. She had always been convinced that it turned out the finest men; she was now able to point out that it also turned out the finest mothers.

F

Felicity watched the situation with a feeling of deep relief. She had been worried about her sister, but her brother-in-law's easy, assured handling of his family left no doubt of his being able to solve his problems without any outside help or interference.

Goosey and Felix sat in the children's room and looked on the scene admiringly. Goosey's comments on the change in the situation were more frank than tactful.

" I used to be afraid to come in here," he said. "Before you knew where you were, you'd got twins."

" No use taking it on if you haven't the knack," observed Tippy. " Kind of flair."

" I see what you mean," said Goosey. " What's that you're building? "

Tippy studied the instructions on the lid of the box of bricks.

" It says a country cottage," he replied. " Looks like a ship to me."

" It certainly does," agreed Goosey, looking at the edifice critically. " You couldn't have read it right."

" Yes, I did," said Tippy. " I——"

" Gimme the lid," said Goosey, coming across and studying it. " Four cubes," he read, " sixteen uprights —yes, you've got all those right—eight squares——"

His head close to Tippy's, he pored over the figures in the instructions. While the others were thus engaged, Mr. Lenner took two steps forward and, putting his head on one side, gazed at the bricks with a melancholy expression. After a moment he put out a hand, made some neat, unhesitating changes in several bricks, and studied the new form with half-closed eyes.

" I see what you've done," went on Goosey to the interested Tippy. " You've treated the whole thing this way—sort of North to South—instead of round the other way. I'll show you what I mean." They turned back to the bricks. " Now, this——"

He stopped. The ship was a perfect country cottage.

"Gosh!" exclaimed Tippy. "Did you do that?" he enquired of Mr. Lenner.

Felix, still regarding the cottage earnestly, nodded.

"There you are, you see," said Goosey. "That's what I was going to tell you."

"You're the fellow who does those mermaids, aren't you?" asked Tippy, regarding Felix with interest.

Felix nodded once more.

"How much would it cost," asked Tippy, moving the brick-box swiftly from the path of the twins just as they were about to trip over it, "how much would it cost to do me one absolutely ravishing mermaid all to myself?"

Mr. Lenner looked at him and shook his head slowly and sadly.

"He says," elucidated Goosey, "that it wouldn't cost anything."

"How d'you know?" asked Tippy. "Perhaps he said he wouldn't do it at all."

"Rot," said Goosey. "What's one little mermaid? What," he enquired, "do you want to do with it?"

"Oh—just look at it," said Tippy. "Just a mermaid," he went on, turning to Mr. Lenner. "No public personalities, no jokes, no setting and no topee—just a simple little mermaid."

"Well, give him something to draw it on," said Goosey. "He can't do it on air."

Tippy, after looking round for a few moments, felt in his pocket and produced a wallet. Opening it, he disclosed a charming photograph of his wife. He drew this out and, turning it over, handed the blank side to Mr. Lenner.

"Do it on that," he said. "That'll do."

Felix drew his pencil from his pocket, adjusted it, and began to draw. The heads of the other two men were close to his as they watched the pencil moving swiftly over the thick sheet. From time to time Tippy raised his head and sent a keen glance round the room to assure himself of the twins' well-being.

"Make it as big as you can," he requested.

There was silence in the room for a few minutes, broken only by occasional thumps as the twins, who were practising somersaults, descended on the cushions their father had placed for their reception.

Mr. Lenner drew a last flourish and handed the paper to Goosey.

"Not bad," commented that gentleman. "Not bad at all."

He passed the picture on to Tippy and the latter looked at it and gave two low, long-drawn whistles.

"Holy Mike, she's a beauty," he exclaimed gleefully. "She's a real wonder. She's a—here," he said, handing the paper back to Mr. Lenner and pointing—"could you put just one more curl over here—just on that shoulder, like that."

Mr. Lenner added the curl, and Tippy took back his treasure and gazed at it ecstatically.

"Wait till they see that," he said. "Just wait. They'll——"

He looked at Mr. Lenner with deep gratitude. "Thanks," he said. "You're——"

The door opened and Mrs. Hellier entered, her voice no longer loud and confident, but low and complaining.

"I've packed everything," she announced. "At least," she amended, "I've packed everything that'll go in and the rest'll have to stay behind, that's all." She came a step closer and stared curiously. "What's that you've got?" she enquired.

Her husband went on with his task without answering. Looking more closely, she saw that he was sliding a photograph of herself into its place in his wallet.

"Goodness—that old thing!" she exclaimed, "don't you want a new one?"

Tippy put his wallet into his pocket and patted it. "This'll do me," he said.

"Oh," said Nan. "Well," she went on, reverting to her theme, "could you go up and sit on the cases or do something?"

"No use sitting on them," pointed out her husband, "if the things aren't all in."

"Well, perhaps not," agreed Nan. "But it's perhaps because I didn't fold anything much. What do creases matter," she asked, "when you're only going to a grandmother's? What time are we leaving?"

"Five-thirty," said Tippy. He glanced at his wrist watch. "Nearly time for the young gents' lunches," he remarked. "I'll take them up and wash them."

He picked up the twins expertly, settled one under each arm and waited for Goosey to open the door. He nodded to Felix and gave Goosey a wink on the way out.

"Thanks," he said, "for everything."

.   .   .   .

Ruth offered to take the Helliers down to the station, and Felicity was grateful to be spared the necessity of accepting the offer she knew Martin West would make.

"Are you sure it's no bother?" she asked.

"None at all," Ruth assured her. "I've got something to do in town after the train goes—could you look at the shops while you're waiting? I don't think I'll be long."

"I don't mind how long you are," said Felicity.

Ruth brought the car round shortly before five o'clock, left it at the door and ran upstairs to get ready. She changed her dress for a coat and skirt and put on a becoming little hat. Studying her reflection earnestly for a few moments she smiled happily, humming under her breath.

Another hour or two, and she could tell Roger . . . She stood pondering on the various ways in which she could break the news. There was the old way—Ruth cast her eyes down and tried the effect of fluttering her eyelashes. There was the new way . . . casual, matter-of-fact . . .

It would, after all, have to be her own way—any way. Just the way it happened. And then Roger wouldn't look away quickly when he saw men like Tippy Hellier playing happily with their children. He wouldn't have

to avoid the topic of a family.   He wouldn't look
hungrily at the room which they had set aside . . .
in case . . .

Ruth changed the humming to a merry tra-la-la of
sheer excitement and happiness.   This was a wonderful
day—the sun was shining and the birds were singing
and everybody——

She glanced out of her window as she prepared to go
downstairs, and stopped singing.

Everybody, after all, didn't feel too happy.   On a
little bench in the garden sat a thin, lonely little figure.
Even from the window it looked forlorn and drooping.
Ruth's full heart was touched.   She gave a little look
of tenderness and affection at her aunt's pathetic form,
and ran lightly downstairs and out into the garden.

Mrs. Beddington looked up at her niece's approach
and gave her a little smile of appreciation.

"You're looking very nice, Ruth dear," she said.
"Are you going out?"

"Not for long, Aunt Emmie, darling," said Ruth,
sitting beside her.   "I'm taking the Helliers to the
station and then I'm—then I've just got to go into Petsham, but I shan't be long."

"No, dear," said Mrs. Beddington. She patted Ruth's
hand and gave a sad, breathless little sigh.   Ruth looked
at her with a trace of anxiety.

"Aunt Emmie, you're tired," she said.   "You've been
walking too much, or something, and you've worn
yourself out."

"Oh, no—no!" protested Mrs. Beddington earnestly.
"Indeed, I've done very little—very little indeed."

"Well, if you're not tired," said Ruth, "then you're
sad, and you can't be sad in my house.   What's the
matter, silly little Aunt Emmie?" she ended tenderly.

To her dismay, two large tears welled up from the
faded blue eyes and rolled down Mrs. Beddington's
cheeks.   Ruth took her aunt's hands and held them
firmly.

"What's the matter, darling?" she said.   "Tell

me. Aren't you well? Is Uncle George all right?"

"Oh, yes, yes," said Mrs. Beddington hastily. "He's very well. I'm only being very foolish—you mustn't take any notice."

"You couldn't be foolish," declared Ruth. "Tell me, Aunt Emmie."

Mrs. Beddington turned a little on the bench and faced her niece, looking earnestly into Ruth's eyes.

"Ruth, my dear," she began, and stopped. She took out a little handkerchief smelling faintly of lavender and wiped her eyes. She looked up again, this time with a firmness and decision not often seen on her timid little face.

"It was that nice Commander Hellier," she said. "Seeing him with his lovely little children . . . Oh, Ruth, my dear," she went on with almost desperate earnestness, "don't think me an interfering old woman, but I beg of you—I do beg of you not to—to wait too long—not to—— That is," she went on painfully, "while you're young, if you can have children and—and——"

Ruth pressed the hands she held, and Mrs. Beddington, a faint flush appearing on her cheeks, spoke again.

"Your uncle and I——" she said. "I've often thought that if only we—if only I could have had children, we shouldn't have become the odd couple we are. There would have been something—but you and Roger—I've prayed so often for you both. I prayed for myself, too, all those years ago, but God didn't will it. I don't understand young people very well, but I know that sometimes they feel—like Mrs. Hellier—that children are a trouble—a—a nuisance. Dear Ruth," she ended tremulously, "if you—if you——"

Ruth felt the tears running down her own cheeks, but she was reluctant to release the trembling old hands she held in order to wipe her eyes. She spoke in a low, hurried voice.

"Oh, Aunt Emmie," she said, "you shouldn't have worried, because—oh, there was nothing to worry about.

It's all absolutely all right and—oh, everything's going to be as you want it to, and—and soon——"

She stopped, her eyes shining through her tears. Mrs. Beddington gazed at her with an expression of incredulous happiness.

" Oh, Ruth darling," she cried. " Oh, how wonderful. Oh—and I've been sitting here like a silly old woman, wasting this lovely evening worrying about nothing at all! " She leaned forward and placed a soft little kiss on her niece's cheek, and then, leaning back, studied her with a look of anxiety.

" You'll take care of yourself, won't you? " she said.

" Yes, darling," said Ruth.

" That's right," said Mrs. Beddington. " You mustn't "—she searched her mind for the kind of advice she had heard given to young mothers—" you mustn't hang curtains."

Ruth shook her head.

" And ladders," went on Mrs. Beddington thoughtfully. " They're so dangerous. You mustn't fall off ladders."

" No, Aunt Emmie," promised Ruth.

" Mrs. Stellar-Smith," remembered Mrs. Beddington, " fell off a ladder——"

" Oh, dear! " sympathized Ruth.

"—but of course," went on Mrs. Beddington, " she wasn't—it wasn't at the time when she was having a baby. And put up your feet, dear," she went on dreamily, " and milk—lots of milk——"

Ruth got to her feet and smiled down at the happy little figure on the bench.

" I've got to go," she said. " You stay here in the nice sun." She turned and took a step or two, when her aunt's remark brought her to an abrupt halt.

" Roger," cooed Mrs. Beddington in the same dreamy tones, " will make a wonderful father."

Ruth's eyes became wide and startled. She swung round quickly and stared down at her aunt.

" Aunt Emmie," she said.

"He'll make a wonderful father," repeated Mrs. Beddington with conviction.

"Yes," agreed Ruth, "but——"

"I don't think it matters in the least," said Mrs. Beddington, "whether it's a boy or a girl."

"No," said Ruth. "But——"

Mrs. Beddington's mind was far away. Ruth bit her lip and considered the situation. She would be gone, perhaps, an hour. If Roger came out——

It was not a likely event. Roger was busy indoors. She could attempt to persuade her aunt to say nothing, but she was late, and she knew that if she made the request, she would become involved in lengthy and difficult explanations. She began to wish she had not mentioned the matter at all, but a glance at her aunt's tearful, happy countenance made her feel that the communication had had a tonic effect which she could not bring herself to regret.

She stooped and patted her aunt's hand in farewell, and ran along the path into the drive, where Brenda waited beside the Helliers and their luggage. Tippy handed his wife in and lifted the twins into their places.

"Well, if it's a choice between Brahmaputrid and grandmother," observed Mrs. Hellier to Brenda, by way of farewell, "I'll take the river every time."

"Enjoy yourself," said Brenda, handing in the last package. "Good-bye, twins. Good-bye, Commander Hellier—it's been nice to meet you."

"Good-bye," said Tippy. "Nan'll bring the twins to see you in their midshipmen outfit soon."

"Midshipmen!" screamed Nan. "All that time ahead? Why," she said, "by that time I'll be a desiccated old hag of thirty heavens knows what."

"You must try and wear well, like me," said Brenda, closing the car door. "Good-bye!"

Ruth drove to the station and waited until the family had been settled in their carriage. She and Felicity watched the train as it went out, and then turned to walk out to the car. Ruth looked at the girl beside her and thought she was looking pale and tired.

"How's the head, Liss?" she asked.

"The head? Oh, it's all right, thanks," said Felicity.

A certain listlessness in her tone made Ruth look at her again, but she closed her lips determinedly. She had promised Roger to keep out of that business . . . She had, moreover, just talked too much to her aunt—she would keep a firmer guard on her tongue.

"Ruth "—Felicity spoke as they got into the car and turned towards the town—" do you know whether Paul —has he said anything about Oscar Tenby and that offer? "

"Not to me," replied Ruth. "And not to Roger. We wanted to ask him about it, but—well, Roger——"

"I know—Roger decided to keep out of it," said Felicity wearily. "Well, it doesn't matter—Paul will have to take it."

"Why'll he have to? " asked Ruth.

"Because—oh," said Felicity with an impatience which Ruth thought had a strained, nervous sound, " because if he doesn't take it, nobody'll ever offer him a part again, that's all."

"Well, in that case," said Ruth, " I suppose he'll take it."

"Yes," said Felicity, with an intensity which puzzled Ruth. "But of course," she went on with a sarcastic inflexion in her tone, " people like Oscar Tenby don't mind being kept waiting—they're used to rising young actors behaving as if—as if good parts fell off trees. Oscar won't mind at all if Paul drifts on thinking of —of other things for weeks and then wakes up and remembers about his career."

Ruth drew the car up to the kerb and stopped.

"I'll put you down here," she said, " and call for you in about half an hour. Will that be all right? "

"Yes, thank you," said Felicity quietly. She got out of the car, held the door open and stared at Ruth oddly.

"Oscar had to know quickly," she said. "And it was

a good part. And Paul must have wanted it badly, or he would never have gone to the length of actually ringing Oscar up and asking for it. And so—and so you've *got* to do something about it, Ruth. He ought to have told him last night—I was going to talk to him but—oh, I was upset. And this morning when I tried to say something about it he wouldn't listen—he——"

She stopped and looked at Ruth with desperate urgency.

"You'll make him tell Oscar soon, won't you—please?" she begged.

"I'll do my best, Liss," answered Ruth. "But you know what Paul is——"

"Yes," said Felicity bitterly. "I know."

She shut the door quietly and Ruth drove on.

CHAPTER XVI

BRENDA waited until the car bearing the Helliers was out of sight, and then walked up the steps and into the house. She went into her office and worked busily for some time, only pausing when the door opened and Roger came in.

"Sorry to interrupt," he said, seeing her absorption. "I only wanted to know the name of those people we got that length of hose from. Old Hyde wants to order some more."

Brenda got up and found the receipted bill form and handed it to him. Roger studied it and handed it back with a nod of thanks.

"There's Ruth back," said Brenda, looking towards the window as the car went by.

Roger nodded. "How did the Helliers go off?" he asked.

"I hardly noticed," said Brenda. "I was so excited over actually getting our first receipts that I could

hardly make my polite farewells. Real banknotes,"
she went on. " It made me realize that I shan't really
enjoy taking money until it comes to Aunt Ella's turn.
Then I'll simply revel. I've done my best to pile on
the extras on her bill, but of course she'll put it to her
nose, smell her way down it and sniff out all the ones
she didn't have."

" Poor old girl," said Roger reflectively.

" Still feeling sorry for her? " asked Brenda. " Well,
I'm beginning to have a curious sort of leaning that
way, too. Her incognito was a bit embarrassing in some
ways—people could tell you what they thought about
her without realizing they were slurring the family
honour. Martin West always refers to her as Lady
Badly-Warne and when Goosey Horder saw Mr. Lenner
with Rameses yesterday he asked what he'd done with
the other Waddling Wonder. I found myself getting
quite stirred up about it."

" Well, it was her own fault for not coming out into
the open," said Roger. " Damn," he said. " What was
the name of those people again? "

" Bird and Tennant," said Brenda. " Think of linnet
and lodger."

" Now you've bally well put me off," said Roger
disgustedly. " Bird and——? "

" Lodger," said Brenda.

Roger went into the garden and found the old
gardener waiting for him. They went into the details
of lengths and prices of hose pipes and then, the business
finished, Roger went back to the house with thoughts
of a bath and change.

He walked across the grass and along the path, passing his wife's aunt, who was sitting on the bench gazing
straight in front of her. Roger was about to walk on,
when he noticed signs of tears on her face. He hesitated.
It was not, he told himself, his business. If Ruth's aunt
wanted to sit out on the bench in the garden and cry,
the matter was one to be dealt with by her husband or
by her niece.

Having decided this point, he turned back and walked up to Mrs. Beddington. She looked up at him a little shamefacedly and wiped her eyes.

"Is there anything I can do?" asked Roger gently. "Are you—are you feeling ill?"

"Oh—no," replied Mrs. Beddington hastily. "Oh, no. I never," she went on, shakily and surprisingly, "felt better in my life."

It was so unexpected that Roger could not help laughing. He sat on the bench beside her and looked at her with a smile.

"Well, that's all right," he said. "I only worry when people feel ill. The other troubles aren't worth crying over, surely?"

"I wasn't crying—not in the way you mean," Mrs. Beddington assured him in a steadier voice. "I was only—just thinking."

"Well, don't think any more," advised Roger. "You can see it doesn't agree with you."

Mrs. Beddington smiled at his little joke, and then put out a timid hand and rested it on his knee.

"I was crying about you—and Ruth," she said. "I felt so happy that I didn't feel like going inside—I thought I'd just sit out here for a little while."

Roger looked at her more closely.

"You're sure," he said anxiously, "you wouldn't like me to bring you something? If you'll stay here quietly——"

"Oh, no, I don't want anything, thank you," said Mrs. Beddington gratefully. "I've got over it now—at first I couldn't realize it."

"No, of course not," said Roger soothingly. "How could you? Now let me get you a tiny little drink, and then you'll feel fine."

"I do feel fine," said Mrs. Beddington in gentle earnestness. "And you must be feeling fine, too," she added affectionately.

"Me? Oh, yes, I'm fine, thanks," said Roger. He glanced anxiously towards the house in the hope of seeing Mr. Beddington or Ruth. He looked back at the patient and was alarmed to find her looking agitated.

"Oh, Roger dear," she said. "So many things I wanted to tell Ruth—but she went off in such a hurry. You must look after her, you know."

Roger stared at her in astonishment. Mrs. Beddington clasped her hands in a little gesture of appeal and went on speaking.

"You mustn't mind me, Roger," she said. "But it means so much to me. I've prayed so earnestly all these years, ever since you and Ruth were married, and it's wonderful to feel that you're to be blessed. Oh, my dear boy," she went on, her eyes fixed on him with deep affection, "please do allow me to say that I think you'll make—you'll be a wonderful father!"

There was a long silence. Roger, his mouth open, sat staring at his wife's aunt. She wiped some more tears from her eyes and looked back at him with a smile of sympathetic understanding.

"It *is* a difficult thought to get used to," she said. "You must still feel dazed. I know I do."

Roger closed his mouth, swallowed, and opened it again. There was another long silence. At last his eyes left her face. He looked slowly round the garden, noting carefully the familiar sweep of lawn and the flagged paths. Everything was still there, and everything appeared to be in order. He brought his eyes back to Mrs. Beddington's face once more, closed his mouth and cleared his throat once or twice.

"I thought I heard you say," he said, speaking slowly and clearly, "that I would be a—a——"

"A wonderful father," she repeated firmly. "I do say so. When Ruth told me, I said, 'Well, dear, Roger will be a good father.' And Ruth agreed with me."

"She did?" asked the dazed Roger.

"Yes. And I told her she must look after herself and she promised she would," continued Mrs. Beddington.

"Oh—she did?" said Roger, again.

"I told her she mustn't do too much and she must

leave more to you, and she promised," went on Mrs. Beddington.

" Oh, she did? " said Roger, his lips closing in a grim line. He raised his head and, looking over the old lady's head, fixed his eyes on the windows of his own rooms. The little white curtains fluttered prettily through the open casements.

" I do so wish you could name it after us," said Mrs. Beddington dreamily. " Ruth said it didn't matter whether it was a boy or a girl."

" Oh, she did? " said Roger once more. At the tone of his voice, Mrs. Beddington looked at him in faint surprise. Roger was still staring at a point over her head. If the circumstances had not been what they were, she would have said that he looked—perhaps it was the light—almost angry.

He rose abruptly to his feet and turned towards the house.

" If you're going in," said Mrs. Beddington, " tell Ruth——"

" I'll tell her," said Roger, stepping across the grass with long firm strides.

He entered the house through the library, leaving the long window wide open behind him and seriously annoying Lady Warne, who sat reading in a chair close by. Unheeding, or not hearing her protest, he flung open the door into the hall and, walking through, left it yawning wide. He crossed the hall, his mouth tight and grim, and brushed past Goosey and Felix, who had just come downstairs. He took the stairs in four bounds and, at the top, came up against his brother, who was on his way down. Paul glanced at his brother's face of fury and uttered a questioning exclamation.

" Out of my way," gritted Roger furiously.

Paul stepped aside and Roger swept on. Paul, looking after him, saw him kick aside an empty coal scuttle, go up three more steps in a bound and turn into the corridor leading to his own rooms.

Paul hesitated. His brother looked dangerous, but

he supposed Ruth knew how to handle him. He went downstairs, paused at the bottom and then went across to his cousin's office and entered.

Roger reached the door of his bedroom, flung open the door and went in. His wife, in a long robe, was seated before her dressing-table, one arm upraised in the act of passing a comb through her loosened hair.

"Hello, Roger," she said, without looking at him. "Shut the door, darling—I'm not dressed for visitors."

There was no reply from Roger, but the door was shut with a crash which made Ruth's heart give a jump. She gave an exclamation of protest and looked up, her voice fading into silence as she saw her husband's face. She lowered her arm slowly and, without taking her eyes from his, felt for the dressing-table and laid the comb down.

"What's the matter, Roger?" she asked quietly. "Has anything happened?"

Roger moved forward two or three steps and stood staring down at her.

"Nothing's happened," he said thickly. "Nothing at all. I just happened to run into your aunt, that's all, and she—we——"

Ruth made a little sound of dismay. Roger continued without pause.

"We had a little chat," he went on. "She gave me a lot of news. All the latest family gossip—brought me up to date in all——"

"Please, Roger," said Ruth.

"In all the intimate details and titbits," went on Roger, his voice rising steadily. "Told me one or two quite interesting bits about my own wife. She told me my wife was—doing very nicely and——"

"Roger—please don't shout," begged Ruth.

"I'm not shouting," shouted Roger. "I'm not shouting. I'm merely telling you what your aunt told me— what my wife's aunt—not my wife, take note, but what my wife's aunt told me. D'you know what she told me? She said——"

"Roger, I——" began Ruth.

"She told me I was going to be a wonderful father," shouted Roger. "That's what she told me. Out there——" he flung out an arm and his voice came down to a sardonic snarl—"out there in the garden, just as you'd say 'Isn't it a lovely day,' or 'Aren't the flowers doing well,' or some other bloody ordinary remark. And you sit here "—his arm came down to indicate his wife—"you sit here and comb your hair and——"

He stopped abruptly. His glance, having fallen on the mirror, showed him the reflection of his wife's white and tear-stained face.

There was silence in the room. Roger, his fists clenched and plunged deep into his pockets, stood staring down at the back of his wife's head. Ruth gave a little sob and, opening a little drawer, took out a handkerchief and wiped her eyes.

"Well?" asked Roger after a while.

Ruth blew her nose and, twisting round on the little seat, looked up at her husband.

"I'm sorry, Roger," she said, her tears beginning to fall as she spoke. "I'm terribly, terribly sorry. You'll never understand how it came about. She was so upset about—about her own married life, and said it would have been different if only they'd had children and wanted us to have them, and it was so heart-rending— she upset me, and before I could stop myself I told her that——"

Tears overcame her and she stopped. Roger opened the little drawer, took another clean handkerchief and handed it to her. He waited until she had wiped her eyes and gained some measure of self-command. She could not read his expression.

"You told her——" he prompted after a time.

"I told her that I hoped—I hoped there would be a baby," said Ruth, looking up at him appealingly. "I only said I hoped there would be. There wasn't any harm in just saying that, just to—to comfort her, was there?"

Roger made no reply. Ruth looked at his sombre face and, putting out a hand, took one of his.

" Oh," she said. " I know it was a terrible thing to do, but I swear—I swear I couldn't help it. Oh, Roger—do forgive me."

Roger released his hand and, turning, walked across the room and sat on his bed, staring moodily at the floor. Ruth looked at him in despair and rose to her feet to go over to him, but as she stood up, a slight feeling of giddiness swept over her and she gave a little cry. Roger sprang to his feet and, reaching her in a single stride, took her into his arms.

" Oh, Roger——" she began.

" No—don't say anything," broke in Roger, speaking in a low, quick tone. " I'm a swine, Ruth, and I'm sorry." He rested his cheek on her hair and rocked her to and fro. " Don't let's say any more about it, my sweet—we'll forget it and——"

" But, Roger," said Ruth, raising her head from its comfortable resting place and looking at him, " I——"

" Let's forget it, darling," repeated Roger, pressing her head on to his chest once more. " And don't worry. One of these days we'll have babies just as—as other couples have them. I'm sorry I lost my temper and made a beast of myself. It was——"

" But, Roger," tried Ruth once more.

" It was only," went on Roger, " that—well, you see, darling, when you do know you're going to have a baby, you won't go and tell your relations about it first, will you? I——"

" No, Roger," promised Ruth. " I only——"

" What I'd like you to do," said Roger, beginning to rock her gently back and forth once more, " what I'd really like you to do is to come up to me one day and take my face in your hands like this "—he placed his wife's hands on his cheeks—" I always like it when you do that—and then say ' Roger darling, I've got something to tell you—something that only you and I are concerned in—just you and I, and no aunts or anybody at all.' Just say, 'Roger, I'm going to be the mother of your child.' "

He bent and kissed his wife lingeringly and then led her to the dressing-table and placed her once more on the little chair. Stooping, he dropped a light kiss on her hair.

"There," he said. "Now you can get on with your dressing and I can go and have a bath and wash my filthy temper off."

"But, Roger," said Ruth.

Her husband went towards his dressing-room.

"We're late," he warned her. "Tell me when I come out of my bath."

He opened his door and heard his wife's voice once more.

"Just a moment, Roger."

Something in her voice made him turn and look at her in surprise. Ruth sat still for a moment and then, rising, came up to him and, putting up her hands, placed them gently on his cheeks.

"Roger darling," she said, "I've something to tell you."

Her husband caught her wrists in a rough grasp.

"Look, Ruth——" he said.

"Something," went on Ruth, "that only you and I —and the doctor—are concerned in." She gave a sound between a sob and a laugh, and Roger looked anxiously towards the bathroom. She clung to him, crying and laughing in turn.

"Oh, Roger," she hiccoughed, "I'm not hysterical— at least, I don't think I am. But you wouldn't listen——"

"But you said——" broke in Roger.

"Oh, I said I only hoped," said Ruth, "but that was when I was telling you what I'd told Aunt Emmie. When I told her this afternoon, I wasn't sure—well, I was pretty sure, but it was only a hope. Then when I took the car in this afternoon I went to see Doctor Mills and he said—oh, Roger—he said you're going to be a father, and you wouldn't listen"—Ruth gave a little laugh which ended in a sob—" and you said "—she gave an unsteady giggle—" you said tell me when you come out of the bath, and—oh, Roger——"

She put her head back and burst into a peal of laughter. Roger looked at her aghast, watching the tears running down her face. He picked her up and, carrying her to her bed, laid her down gently and bent over her in alarm. At the sight of his expression, Ruth gave a little shriek of laughter.

Without pausing further, Roger rushed out of the room and passed like a tornado through the corridor, tripped over the coal scuttle, rushed down the stairs and into his cousin's office. He flung the door open and stood looking at the faces of Paul and Brenda, turned in surprise and alarm to his.

" Come quickly, can you, Brenda? " he said urgently. "Ruth's—I think she's hysterical—for God's sake come and do something."

"What's she hysterical about? " asked Brenda, getting hastily to her feet.

" Oh—it's a baby," said the distracted Roger. " We're having one. For God's sake come."

After a pause of blank surprise, Brenda hurried through the door and up the stairs, followed closely by Roger and Paul. They entered the room to find Ruth sitting on the bed, her handkerchief pressed to her eyes and her form shaking. Brenda took a seat by her side and the two men watched anxiously.

" Ruth darling," began Brenda.

Ruth lifted a face down which tears rained and looked from the anxious face of her cousin to the alarmed countenances of her husband and brother-in-law.

" Oh, I can't bear it! " she cried, breaking into a peal of helpless laughter once more. " Look at their faces! "

Brenda looked at her in astonishment. There was nothing hysterical in the laughter. Ruth made an attempt to speak, but, overcome by mirth once more, spread her hands in a gesture of helplessness and looked at her cousin through her tears.

"I can't bear it, Brenda," she sobbed. "He looked so funny—first he was mad with rage and shouted, and then he said it didn't matter, and then he said, 'Well, tell me after my bath,' and then he went for help—oh!" She stopped to wipe her eyes and Brenda found herself laughing in sympathy.

"Well, before I get hysterical myself," she said, turning to Roger, "perhaps you can tell me what's wrong."

"I tell you," said Ruth, "there's nothing wrong. It was because——" She paused and looked at her husband. "Can I tell them, Roger?" she asked.

"If you mean about having a baby," said Brenda, "Roger told us."

Ruth's eyes widened to their fullest extent, and she stared at her cousin.

"You mean he told you—you mean he actually—oh!" she said, breaking into an irresistible peal of mirth. "Oh! that's too much!"

Roger began to laugh, unwillingly at first and then helplessly.

Paul and Brenda looked at one another.

"What's so funny about having a baby?" enquired Paul.

"You'll know one day," said Roger, "when your wife's aunt—when your wife's aunt says you're going to be a—be a——"

He relapsed once more into helpless laughter. Paul watched him with a grin and then opened the door and signed to Brenda.

"Let's go," he said. "There's nothing we can do until they've adjusted themselves to the idea."

"Well, of course," said Brenda, going out, "I suppose it is exciting to produce a baby."

"Baby?" repeated Paul derisively. "They won't produce a baby. All they'll produce," he stated with conviction, "will be an infant hyena!"

CHAPTER XVII

IT was obvious that the evening called for some form
of celebration. Ruth and Roger, after some discussion, decided to invite Major Horder and Felicity to
dinner.

"Won't that make Mr. Lenner feel rather left out?"
asked Ruth.

"He won't feel any more left out than Martin will,"
Roger pointed out unfeelingly. "They can keep each
other company. This is a special occasion for very old
friends."

"What about Uncle George and Aunt Emmie,
then?" said Ruth.

"Well, no—not as old as that," said Roger. "Besides,
your aunt's only got one topic now, and it isn't one for
a dinner party."

"No," agreed Ruth. "What'll I wear?"

"The green," said Roger promptly.

Ruth gave a little sigh.

"It's depressing, don't you think," she said, "when
one's wardrobe is so limited that one's husband can
make up his mind in a flash between the green and the
blue."

"Well, what do you want me to do?" asked Roger.
"Go to the mirrored sliding door, push it aside and
finger a dozen models to decide which of them'll suit
your mood—or my mood?"

"Something like that," said Ruth. "I saw a film
once——"

"Ah!" said Roger. "And he fingered the filmy
fabrics, did he?"

"No," said Ruth. "He took one out—a gorgeous
one—and held it against her and buried his face in her
neck——"

"My God," said Roger. "And you sat through it?"

"Of course," said Ruth. "What d'you think wives

go for if not to see what life could be like if only husbands had a little more——"

"Technique," finished Roger, coming across the room, taking his wife in his arms and demonstrating a very sound technique. "Now," he asked at its conclusion, "how does that feel?"

"Lovely," cooed Ruth, nestling against him. "You always smell so nice when you've had a bath."

"I always," Roger informed her, "smell nice. Now I'm going to finish dressing and get hold of Goosey and that girl."

"Felicity?" asked Ruth. "Why do you say 'that girl' in that tone?"

"Because she wants turning up and slapping," said Roger. "I do hate to see a girl with so much in the way of looks and so little in the way of sense."

"She's got a lot of sense," said Ruth.

"Well, why doesn't she use it?" asked Roger. "She's done nothing but hang round for a week looking paler and paler, while Paul looks a wreck and Martin West's losing all his stiffening. She ought to be ashamed—only two men on her hands and she makes an absolute muck of the whole thing. Why the hell," he enquired from the door of his dressing-room, "can't she say Eeny, meeny, miney, mo, if she can't make up her mind, and settle it that way?"

"Of course, you manage Paul pretty well yourself, don't you?" said his wife sweetly.

"That's different," said Roger. "But before I knew you, when all those beautiful women were after me, did I ever have any of them cluttering up the place looking sick? No. I carried it all off extremely well, and when I saw you, I said at once 'That's the one,' and settled it at once. You didn't see me shillyshallying, did you?" he asked in conclusion.

"You were the wonder," said Ruth admiringly. "Do hurry and go down."

By the time Ruth finished dressing and went downstairs, a merry party was gathered in the family dining-room. It was at once obvious that Goosey had been let into the great secret, for he came towards her with his hands outstretched and his eyes shining with joy and affection.

"I say," he exclaimed, seizing her hands and patting them in a fatherly way, "this is magnificent! I thought you were never going to make me a godfather, but I was just telling old Roger that I was always sure he could bring it off—I mean——"

He stopped in some confusion, and Roger rescued him with a drink.

Ruth found Felicity beside her, and thought the girl looked better than she had done for some days. There was a steady, calm look in her eyes which Ruth was glad to see.

"Isn't it a shame—this is Goosey's last night," she said.

"Is it, Goosey?" asked Ruth. "I thought you weren't going until the day after to-morrow."

"Papa needs me," said Goosey simply. "Or else," he added, "he's just found out what it costs to stay here, and he's snatching the brand before it gets entirely scorched. Did you," he asked Brenda, "remember to put all the drinks down under Laundry and Aft. Tea?"

"I did," said Brenda. "What time are you off?"

"Immejitly after breakfast," said Goosey. "Poor old Felix isn't at all keen on leaving. You wouldn't, I suppose," he suggested, "like to re-christen this place the Mermaid Tavern and let him make it famous for you?"

"No, thanks," said Roger. "We'll just worry along as we are. Come on," he ordered, "dinner."

The meal was a great success, Paul unexpectedly proving more gay and amusing than he had been since his arrival. Roger looked from his smiling, attractive face to Felicity's, and could read nothing in her eyes but the same calm, almost placid look which Ruth had observed.

There was a general movement when dinner was

over. Roger had work to do and a word to say to Paul —he beckoned him at the close of the meal and the two men went out together. Brenda announced her intention of completing Goosey's bill, adding it up and multiplying it by six. Ruth, feeling a little tired after the excitement of the day, went up to read quietly in bed.

Roger stopped outside the door and faced his brother.

"Look—I don't want to interfere in your affairs or anything of that sort," he said quickly, "but oughtn't you to ring up that fellow—what's his name?"

"Tenby?" hazarded Paul.

"That's the chap," said Roger. "I heard him say he was in a hurry. I think you've left it a bit late— that is, if you haven't done it already."

"What do you want me to do?" asked Paul, a gleam of amusement in his eyes. "Turn it down?"

Roger gave him an answering grin.

"Well, you'd be fool enough for anything," he said, "but I don't think even you could let a chance like this go."

"As a matter of fact," said Paul. "I'd already rung up. I meant to do it last night, but"—his eyes darkened as he thought of what he had seen the night before— "well, I didn't. But I did ring up about half-past six this evening."

"Well, what happened?" asked Roger.

Paul frowned. "He wasn't there," he replied. "He'd left his place almost at that moment and they said he wouldn't be back for two days."

"That's bad luck," commented Roger. "What are you going to do?"

"I'll write," said Paul.

"Good," said Roger. "And by the way, Aunt Ella goes off to-morrow—you'd better say good-bye."

He went away and Paul turned in the direction of his aunt's room. If she was alone now, he could get his brief farewell over.

Goosey, meanwhile, found to his astonishment and

satisfaction that he was alone with Felicity. He looked across at her and spoke haltingly but with eagerness.

"I wonder," he said, "if you'd find it awfully cold outside? There isn't a bad moon and it's really quite warm. Couldn't I get you a wrap or a coat or something and then we could go out and—and talk in the moonlight." He gave a short laugh. "Sounds romantic," he went on, "but when I said that to a girl once she looked at me and said 'Captain Horder, let me warn you about something—don't ever use the word romance —it doesn't go well with that moustache.'"

Goosey laughed heartily at this memory, and Felicity rose.

"Wait for me near the fountain," she said.

He watched her coming across the grass, her pretty frock half hidden under a dark coat which she had draped over her shoulders, and greeted her with a half-regretful shake of his head.

"I wonder," he said, "if lovely girls ever know how lovely they can look?"

Felicity smiled.

"I think some of them have a rough idea," she said. "But they also know how little of it is girl and how much is dress, and shoes, and the things that come out of little jars . . ."

Goosey looked at her.

"Guess what I brought you out here for," he said.

"Proposal?" said Felicity teasingly.

"Ooh," said Goosey on a sharp breath. "I'd never dare."

Felicity laughed.

"Star-gazing," she hazarded.

Goosey shook his head. "I've been doing that all the week," he said neatly.

"Well—I give it up," said Felicity. "Unless it's a lecture."

"Well it is and it isn't," said Goosey. "Sit here," he invited, leading her to the bench.

Felicity sat down and Goosey took a seat by her side.

"Now the lecture," said Felicity.

"Yes. Well," began Goosey, "you may not have noticed it, but I'm a rather silly chap in some ways."

Felicity smiled, but said nothing.

"And one of the ways," said Goosey, "is the way I've got of poking my nose in where it isn't wanted. I do," he went on, "like helping my friends. Anybody'll tell you that of all the pernicious habits to let get hold of you, trying to help your friends is the worst. You don't get any thanks, you don't do any good and you probably knock the whole show to pieces."

"So what?" enquired Felicity.

"Don't hurry me," begged Goosey. "It's extraordinary how everybody tries to hustle you. 'Where's the point?' they're always saying. I find that once you've come to the point, people don't listen any more —they think it's their turn to talk. Besides," he went on, "there isn't any point in what I'm saying to you. I'm only trying to tell you that I think more of Roger Mallard than I do of—well, pretty well most people. And I'd do a lot to see him happy. And Ruth, too."

"Well," pointed out Felicity, "they are happy."

"They are—except in one matter," said Goosey, "and this is where you come in."

"Me?" said Felicity.

"You," said Goosey. "You can make them completely happy by——" He paused.

"By what?" enquired Felicity, who knew already.

Goosey took a deep breath.

"By being nice to Paul," he said.

"Ah," said Felicity softly. Then, as softly: "Dear Goosey," she said, "you're wasting your time."

Goosey put up a hand.

"Don't talk," he said. "Just keep quiet and listen to me. I don't know what goes on in girls' minds. But I know a good fellow when I see one. I've known Paul for years and I tell you—without any charge whatsoever—that even a young'n lovely like you won't do any better. No. Roger and Paul are both right up in the top class. Both a bit tricky, of course—they'd both bite you as soon as look at you, and wherever you tread they seem to have corns sticking out, but you won't—believe me—you won't find a finer fellow."

"I don't want to," said Felicity.

"Eh?" said Goosey, taken aback.

"I said I don't want to," said Felicity again.

"Don't want to what?" asked Goosey.

"Don't want to find a—a finer fellow," said Felicity.

There was a short silence. Goosey broke it on a note of slight irritation.

"I know I'm half-witted," he said, "but it seems to me that the affair's a bit tangled. I knew there was something going on when you dropped that lighter— I thought it had one p.m. on it—I thought it was a time, at the time, but afterwards I found it was the same as the I.P.M. on Paul's cigarette-case. I knew he was pretty miserable because there you were turning him down for somebody else, but now you say you like Paul —or isn't that what you meant?"

"I told you," said Felicity, "that you were wasting your time. If you really wanted to do some good, you'd invite Paul out into the moonlight and tell him he couldn't find a—a finer girl—and——"

"Did you ever," asked Goosey abruptly, "hear that song about the fellow who bought a hen?"

"No," said Felicity.

"Well, he did," said Goosey. "He bought a hen and took it home and it 'clucked and clucked again but never an egg did lay.' So he felt awfully let down. That's just how I feel now. I'm sitting before the loveliest girl I ever had the honour of having a tête-à-tête in the moonlight with, and she opens her mouth and admits—without penance and without shame— that she can't manage her own love affairs."

"I asked Ruth," said Felicity, "to talk to Paul, and she said Roger wouldn't let her and——"

"What the hell, pardon me for polluting this lovely

night," said Goosey, "has it got to do with Ruth or Roger or Uncle Tom Cobley?"

"Well, I——"

"I came out," said Goosey, "to try and make you see what a grand chap Paul was. You tell me you knew it all the time but hadn't got round to telling him you thought so. You've been here a week, haven't you?"

"Almost," admitted Felicity.

"And do you, if you'll also pardon my shoving my nose into your private affairs," said Goosey, "do you like Paul better than that other fellow?"

"Yes," said Felicity.

Goosey regarded her with wonder.

"My God," he said simply.

"What do you expect me to do?" asked Felicity mutinously. "Go up to him and throw myself at him?"

"If necessary, and if you can't think of a more dignified way—yes," said Goosey. "Certainly. But you can't be the girl I thought you were if you've sat here for a week making a poor devil miserable and doing nothing about it. Where's your—your initiative? Where's your womanly wit—your—— Instead of running round expecting everybody else to solve your simple problem," he went on, "why don't you get at it and do it yourself? It's your pigeon, isn't it?"

"It isn't so easy——" began Felicity.

"Look," said Goosey, taking one of her hands and patting it, "if I could stay a couple more days I'd manage the entire affair for you. I'd organize it. You've seen my genius, haven't you? Well, I'd use it on your behalf. But as I can't stay, will you promise me faithfully that before you leave here you'll go to Paul and say, 'Look, you dim-witted partridge, we love each other and if you don't want to marry me, say so and I'll start working down the list'—will you promise?" he asked.

Felicity looked at him for a moment and then nodded.

"I promise," she said. "And—thank you very much."

"For what?" asked Goosey in surprise. "I was shinning up the wrong pole."

"Everybody told me," said Felicity, "that it wasn't their business, but nobody went to the length of pointing out that it was—well, just mine. I was waiting and waiting for Paul to do something."

"Well, you'd have waited a long time," stated Goosey. "When Paul and Roger get hurt they go broody—they wrap themselves up in a—in a cloak of trouble and they can't see further than their own noses. They need a good kick in the—they need a good shaking up before it occurs to them that a little less brooding and a bit more straightforward action would cure most of their troubles. Don't you," he warned, "do any waiting for Paul to do something, or you'll grow into a white-haired old lady and still be no forrader."

Felicity rose and Goosey got reluctantly to his feet.

"I believe you're right," he said. "I have been wasting my time. I ought to have been down on the damp ground on one knee making an impassioned declaration. Shall I do it now?"

"No, thank you," said Felicity. "Having declared my love for another——"

"Well, yes, there's that," admitted Goosey. "Now go up to bed and think out a nice plan of campaign."

They walked to the garden door and parted.

"One p.m.," said Goosey, raising his clasped hands above his head like a boxer.

"One p.m.," replied Felicity.

Goosey turned back and walked round the garden idly and happily. He felt thoroughly contented. Roger had got his dearest wish. Ruth was going to have a series of delightful children; the hotel was going to prosper—and Paul's happiness was assured.

In a mood of beneficence, Goosey walked to the garden door and stood aside as Martin West came out.

"Going for a turn?" he enquired genially. "Lovely night."

Martin West appeared to be in no mood for exchang-

ing civilities. He gave Goosey a cold look and stepped
past him, tripping as he went over the form of Rameses,
who had waddled in Martin's wake towards the garden.
Martin uttered an imprecation.

"I wish to God," he said viciously, "that somebody
would shoot that foul animal."

He went out and Goosey entered the house, stopping
in dismay as he came face to face with the owner of
Rameses. It was obvious that she had heard Martin
West's remark. Her breath was coming in short gasps
and her small eyes were glaring at his retreating back
with a hatred and venom that startled Goosey.

"It's a—a lovely night," he faltered.

Lady Warne brought her eyes to his face. Goosey
was alarmed at her colour.

"He said——" she began. "He called Rameses——"

"You mustn't mind," said Goosey hastily. "Things
like that happen. People get tired and fall over something and don't know what they're saying. Come and
look at the beautiful night," he urged.

He offered his arm and after a moment's hesitation
Lady Warne took it and walked slowly along the path
outside. Presently she stopped and turned.

"I'll go inside and rest," she said.

Goosey led her into the little passage near the children's room. There were two chairs against the wall,
and Lady Warne moved towards them. Goosey had a
sudden inspiration, and good-naturedly embarked upon
a scheme for taking her mind off the recent unfortunate
incident.

"I shouldn't sit on those," he advised. "They're
—well—show pieces. Come on into the drawing-
room."

"These," said Lady Warne, sitting on one, "are
extremely comfortable chairs."

"They're interesting chairs," said Goosey. "They're
looked upon by the family as—well, not relics, exactly,
but—sort of curiosities."

Lady Warne fixed her eyes on his and Goosey congratulated himself on the success of his plan for diverting her mind.

"Curiosities," he repeated. "They represent the sole takings, as it were, of over thirty years. An ancient aunt——"

Lady Warne stood up so suddenly that Goosey thought the chair must have pinched her.

"That's right," he said. "Come into the drawing-room—it's much more comfortable."

He led her to the drawing-room, where Mr. Lenner, who was in there alone, rose at their entrance.

"Sit there," said Goosey, arranging the cushions on the sofa and lowering his charge on to them. He inspected her countenance and thought that it was still unhealthily flushed. Of course, she thought a great deal of that terrible dog——

"I was just telling Lady Warne about the chairs she was asking about," he told his friend a little inaccurately. "You see," he went on in a tone of commiseration, "poor old Roger's got an aunt and she threw those two chairs out for his wedding. I remembered 'em the moment I saw them here. They were on view with all the other presents at the wedding and I remember saying to Roger at the time 'What d'you want chairs for, old chap, when you're just off to foreign parts? Cheques, you want,' I said, 'not chairs.' And Miss Mallard— she was there too, naturally, being his cousin—she told me the whole story."

Brenda would have been surprised at Goosey's free translation of her simple comment. She had merely made a facetious remark to the effect that one cheque would have been better than two chairs, but Goosey was in the habit of grafting a twig of fact on to a whole tree of fancy. Something on Lady Warne's face told him that he had a good audience, and he made a kind effort to give of his best.

"Those chairs, as I told you," he went on, "represent the total takings of thirty years, of——"

"I don't know what you mean," broke in Lady Warne.

" Well, Roger's thirty—thirty-two, to be exact," said Goosey, " and he had an uncle and an aunt—both rolling. Absolutely rolling in it. The old boy died and left his pile to the aunt, so you see, the aunt got two piles."

An envious murmur came from Felix.

" Three piles," said Goosey, encouraged by this interest. " I think she had an original pile and then she married an old chap and he very soon shuffled off this mortal soil——"

Felix made another sound.

" All right—coil," said Goosey. " Sinister, in a way," he observed, " the old chap dying like that and——"

" Like what? " enquired Lady Warne in a choked voice.

" Well, I don't know exactly," confessed Goosey after a swift review of likely ends. " But she got his pile and then Roger's uncle suddenly popped off. Perhaps the aunt had something to do with that too," he mused, " but I shouldn't think so, because Miss Mallard was living here at the time to keep an eye on things."

He paused and looked at Lady Warne, who appeared to be having trouble with her breathing. He felt a tinge of remorse—he had made her walk in the garden after a heavy dinner and the poor thing was beginning to wheeze. He walked to the window and pulled out a chair. " Come and sit here," he said kindly. " We shouldn't have done all that exercise."

Lady Warne left the sofa and took the seat he held for her, looking at him with an expression which he found slightly puzzling.

" Thank you," she said.

" Now," said Goosey, " lean back and relax quietly and I'll tell you the rest of the story. I don't suppose you knew," he went on, addressing Felix, " that Roger had a rich aunt? "

Felix shook his head.

" That's the trouble," said Goosey. " Nobody knows it. Even Roger doesn't know it, because as far as the

G

odd cheque or present's concerned, she just doesn't exist."

"Perhaps," suggested Lady Warne, "she has her—her own charities."

"Oh, no," denied Goosey stoutly. "No husband, no children, and just two nephews struggling for existence."

"Struggling?" repeated Lady Warne.

"Well, not Roger, perhaps," admitted Goosey, "but take Paul. Now there," he went on, speaking to Felix, "there's a picture for you—one with a moral. Nothing in the mermaid line. Go on," he ordered. "Draw it."

Mr. Lenner felt in his pocket and produced a small pad and a pencil and prepared to illustrate the story.

"First you draw the aunt," instructed Goosey, leaning over him, "and then you do her money bags. Go on," he urged, "put in a few more—remember she had three piles. That's it. Now the moral. She's holding on to the bags, while beside her yawns an open grave——"

Felix looked up with a questioning glance.

"Why?—because that's the whole point of the story," said Goosey. "You draw her with outstretched arms, vainly trying to reach her wealth as the grave yawns wider." He took the sketch and examined it critically. "No—you've got it wrong," he said. " I thought you said you were an artist. How could an aunt that size get into a grave that size? Go on—open it up, open it up."

Mr. Lenner obligingly went to work opening it up and Goosey, looking at Lady Warne, was sorry to observe that the rest was doing her very little good.

"Here you are," he said comfortingly, taking the sketch from Felix and handing it to her, "you keep this —if you get Felix to sign it, it'll be an original Lenner and worth a packet. No—keep it," he urged kindly, as Lady Warne drew back. "There. Only don't leave it about where Roger can see it."

He put his hands in his pockets and walked slowly about the room.

"It's no joke," he said more seriously. "Not for Paul, I mean." He paused, gazing into the fire, and then spoke dreamily. "Think what he could do with five hundred quid," he said. "Leave that stinking room he lives in and go back to his decent flat. For a thousand, he could go about a bit. He's an actor and nobody ever sees him—where's the publicity? For two or three thousand," he went on, his excitement rising, "he could get into the swing again and entertain a few theatrical wire-pullers and"—he took his hands out of his pockets and waved them in the air—"and for five thousand"—he dropped his voice and stared at Lady Warne with a conspiratorial air—"for five thousand he could marry the girl and wipe Martin West right out of the picture——"

He stopped abruptly, aware that his excitement had carried him beyond the bounds of discretion. He found that Lady Warne was staring at him curiously.

"What picture?" she enquired.

"Picture? Oh, well, nothing really," said Goosey, regretting his loquacity.

"You mean that with—with money, he could——" went on Lady Warne.

"Put West's nose out of joint," finished Goosey.

Lady Warne rose, and the little sketch fluttered to the ground.

Goosey picked it up and handed it to her.

"Look after it," he said. "Pop it in your bag—that's it."

He opened the door for her and Lady Warne, with a brief nod to the two men, walked slowly out of the room. Goosey looked after her regretfully.

"Pity she couldn't have been Paul's aunt," he said. "Judging by all those blinding flashes coming off her corsage, she must have a pretty packet herself."

Lady Warne went slowly up the stairs and reached her room. Outside her door, Rameses waited. She looked down at him with a deep murmur of affection and then entered the room and closed the door.

She undressed slowly, her mind confused. She put out the central light and stood looking round the room in the dim, rosy glow of the bedside lamp. She went slowly across to the table on which she had placed her bag and, taking out the sketch Felix Lenner had drawn, looked at it for some minutes and then let it fall, her stout form shaking in an uncontrollable shudder.

She lay awake for some time, trying vainly to calm her disturbed mind. The gruesome picture rose again and again before her eyes, between other visions more gruesome . . . She attempted to think coolly, but Goosey's words went round in her brain until she felt her head bursting.

She slept at last, to wake from an appalling dream with her face damp with sweat and her heart pounding. She sat up stiffly in bed, one hand groping for the switch of her light. Before she found it, a swift flash of lightning gave a second's warning of the crash of thunder that followed. Lady Warne gave a cry of terror and at that moment her hand closed on the switch and the light came on.

She wiped her damp face and sat still, breathing heavily. She was not a woman who thought deeply, and she certainly never thought of others. She was scarcely interested in Paul or in Roger; she disliked Brenda intensely.

Goosey's story, however, had been told under peculiar circumstances. Lady Warne's emotions were sluggish, but Martin West's contemptuous reference to Rameses had roused her to a fury deeper than anything she had ever felt before. If the story had been related when she was in her normally torpid state, it is doubtful whether she would have been more than angry and offended. But she had been shaken and the story was told before she had had time to recover. It had been illustrated with a grim picture of a grave, and she feared death above all things. Her latent superstition was aroused, and the storm, seeming to her a symbol of the tumult in her mind, added the last blow to her shaken nerves.

She sat shivering in bed for some time and then, with a gesture of decision, put her feet to the ground, thrust them into her furry slippers and wrapped a dressing-gown about her. She went to her bag and drew out her cheque book.

It was difficult to see clearly. She moved nearer to the light, drew out her pen, and, sitting on a chair, began to write. She put down the date and the name —Paul Mallard. Then she wrote the figure five in a shaking hand and paused. . . .

Five hundred pounds was a great deal of money. It was, she knew, a mere fraction of what she could afford —but it was a large sum. But . . . if five hundred pounds would rob Martin West of one single moment of ease, it would be well spent. She put the pen to the paper, added two noughts and paused again, this time staring before her into the dimness of the room beyond the table. A picture grew out of the darkness—a scene so vivid that it was impossible to believe it was not actually taking place. A figure—Paul's—stood at the door. Rameses lay at his feet and as Paul turned to go out he paused and, stooping, placed a hand on the dog's head. . . .

With a hand that no longer shook, Lady Warne added one more nought and wrote a firm ' five thousand ' on the cheque. She signed it, folded it, took an envelope from a box on the table and, putting the cheque into it, sealed and addressed the outside.

She felt curiously calm. Rising, she put her cheque book away and got once more into bed. Her heart was beating quietly, her mind was clear.

She settled herself on her pillows, switched off the light and fell asleep.

CHAPTER XVIII

RUTH went out of the house with real regret on the following morning to say good-bye to Goosey and his friend. The suit-cases were in the car, the two men stood on the drive, Goosey looking almost as melancholy as Mr. Lenner.

" Who's having my room next? " he asked as Roger followed his wife.

" Miss Exell," said Roger.

" Exell—you mean that girl Nora or Dora Exell— the one with all that money? " asked Goosey.

" The same," said Roger.

" Well, she'll need it if she's staying here long," commented Goosey. " Ruth," he went on, turning to her and taking her hands. " I've had a magnificent time and thank you very much. I think your hotel will prosper, even without me to give you a hand."

" It won't feel the same without you, Goosey darling," said Ruth affectionately. " Come back soon. And give my love to all——"

" The back room boys," finished Goosey. " I will— they're always asking me about you both. 'Bye, Roger. Nice of you to have me."

" I didn't see you coming," explained Roger.

Mr. Lenner advanced a few paces and stood before Ruth. He gave her a brief handshake, made a low sound and held out a square, flat package. The wrapping was merely a loose sheet of paper and Ruth, removing it, looked at the picture in her hand and gave a cry of delight.

" Oh, Mr. Lenner—it's—it's——"

Unable to find words to express her feelings, she stopped, gazing at him in gratitude. Goosey and Roger walked up to her and looked over her shoulder.

Felix had drawn a faithful representation of the fountain in which Goosey had so lately been immersed.

Seated on the edge, one dimpled hand trailing in the water, was an adorable little baby mermaid, innocent and gleeful. Roger looked at it and then gave Goosey a long stare.

"News travels fast, doesn't it?" he said.

"Funny how these things get about," said Goosey blandly. "Where's Miss Mallard—isn't she coming to see us off?"

"Here I am," said Brenda, coming down the steps. She was followed by Felicity, who shook Goosey warmly by the hand.

"Good-bye," she said. "At least, not good-bye— we shall meet again heaps of times. Good-bye, Mr. Lenner."

Felix nodded sadly and climbed in beside Goosey. The car jerked, roared and started down the drive, the passengers waving until they were lost to sight.

"He's quite mad," said Ruth sadly, going into the house, "but I'll miss him."

Roger followed his cousin into the office.

"I'm not taking any chances with Uncle George and Aunt Emmie," he said. "Paul's taking the car and he's going to drive them up to King's Cross and see them into the train."

"That's a good idea," said Brenda. "We really can't spend another day being rung up by the police. What time are they going?"

"About eleven," said Roger. "Aunt Ella leaves after lunch."

"She told me," said Brenda. "She isn't looking very bright this morning—she said the storm last night woke her up and upset her. She looks a peculiar cheese colour."

Lady Warne certainly looked a little pale. She came into the office an hour later and sat on the chair Brenda placed for her.

"I should like to pay my bill," she said.

"Thank you—I've got it ready," said Brenda, handing it across. "Shall I make out a receipt?"

"One moment," said Lady Warne, studying the account. "This item—extra food——"

"Rameses," explained Brenda smoothly. "Three meals a day, you said——"

Lady Warne, reading on, gave an incredulous exclamation.

"You don't mean to tell me you charge—you actually charge for baths?" she enquired frigidly.

"We weren't going to," said Brenda. "As you see, there's no printed column—but we thought that with so many bathrooms it might become quite a—a source of income, so to speak. Roger says it's quite a good plan because people never like to admit they haven't had any, and——"

"I shall deduct the amount from the total," said Lady Warne. "I don't think," she added, "that I have ever met such exorbitant prices before."

"That's what Major Horder was saying," said Brenda in a friendly tone. "But he said it would keep out the purse-proud."

Lady Warne made her deductions and paid the remainder. Brenda opened the door for her and watched her as she walked slowly across the hall. Paul ran down the stairs and looked curiously at his cousin's serious countenance.

"I never thought you'd look like that with dear Aunt Ella on the point of departure," he said lightly. "What's the matter—did she try to tip you, or didn't she remember to—which was it?"

"I don't know how it is," said Brenda, walking slowly back to her desk, "but I feel about her now as I used to feel—towards the end—about Uncle Jake. He had so much wealth, and he grabbed it all so tightly and in the end it all had to be left behind. I remember the last time he got ready to travel," she went on dreamily. "There was all the usual fuss of finding out how much he'd save if he went by this or that route, and how many fewer servants would be needed while he was away. He was to leave early the next morning, poor fellow . . .

ut he went earlier than that . . . and he didn't go by
rain . . . and I stood by the bed looking at him and
ounting the pieces of luggage all ready by the door—
e died in Mr. Lenner's room, Hudson—that's why
Aunt Ella asked particularly for Ganges, because it was
ne other end of the house. And I looked at the
uggage," she ended slowly, " and I thought of all the fuss
nere'd been packing it all up and then . . . in the
nd, he had to go without it . . ."

She stopped, her look absent and dreamy. Paul's
oice recalled her to the present.

" Isn't this getting a little morbid? " he asked.
" You're not suggesting that Aunt Ella's going off with-
ut luggage, are you? "

" No, I'm not," said Brenda, " but she used to irritate
ne, and now I just feel sorry for her."

" Rubbish," said Paul. " You just tell yourself that
drown your longing for some of her shekels."

" Indeed I don't," said Brenda indignantly. " Can't
ou give me credit for any decent feelings? "

" No," said Paul. " I don't feel sorry for her at all
-I only feel sorry for the dog. Just think," he went on,
aning on the desk and looking earnestly at his cousin.
If you'd been a protégé of hers you'd have looked
actly like that wretched Rameses."

" It's a grim thought," admitted Brenda. She looked
ore closely at Paul. " You're looking better this
orning," she said. " The place must be doing you
od. If you stayed here another week——"

" Even my luggage wouldn't cover that," Paul told
r. " Look," he went on, " what I really came down
ask you was—will you go up and see that the old
uple really get off with all their stuff? I nearly went
azy in the train coming down—Aunt What'shername
ent the entire journey enumerating all the things
e'd probably never see again. If you could number
the suit-cases——"

" There won't be any fuss," promised Brenda.
I'll put them all in this end and you can just

unship them at King's Cross. I'll go up now."

Paul brought the car round and soon Mr. and Mr
Beddington were making their earnest, grateful speeche
of farewell.

"You'll look after yourself, Ruth my dear, won
you?" said Mrs. Beddington.

"Of course, Aunt Emmie," said Ruth. "You mu
come down often and see me."

The remark was unfortunate, as the prospect of
future journey, added to the terrors of the one ju
before her, had the effect of reducing the old lady to
state bordering on collapse.

"In you go," said Paul gently, handing her into th
car. "Close your eyes tight and next time you ope
them you'll be at home. Where's Roger?" he aske
turning to Ruth.

"He was in the office ten minutes ago," said Rut
"I can't think what's keeping him."

"I'll get him," said Paul.

He ran up the steps and into the house, taking
letter from his pocket as he went. He entered the offi
and looked in surprise at his brother, who was standi
by his cousin's desk staring down at a newspaper whi
lay upon it. He raised his head at Paul's entrance a
looked at him with an odd, almost vacant look.

"Don't day-dream," said Paul. "The car's full
Uncle Georges and Aunt Emmies all waiting to s
good-bye to you. Get a move on, will you?—I dor
want to drive too fast or they'll both jump out. Oh "
he held up the letter—" give me a stamp, will you
he asked. "I'll post this somewhere in Town."

Roger stood without moving for some seconds, l
eyes on the letter.

"Is that," he asked slowly, "the letter—I mean, th
wouldn't be the letter to Oscar Tenby, would it?"

"Why wouldn't it?" asked Paul. "It is. Put
stamp on it, will you?—I haven't got any."

Roger's eyes went to the newspaper. He picked
up, folded it once or twice and then spoke again.

"There's something here," he said, "I think you ought to look at—it's—it won't be a very good piece of news for you, but——"

"Well, what is it?" asked Paul impatiently.

"You can read it," said Roger, handing him the paper. "It says that Oscar Tenby has—doesn't it mean that the cast is now"—he spoke the word with difficulty—"complete?"

Paul stared at him for a moment, newspaper in hand, and then bent his head and read the lines swiftly.

There was a short silence as he finished reading and laid the paper carefully down on the desk. Roger searched his face in vain for any trace of feeling. Paul was pale, but calm.

"Well, that's—that," he said slowly. "He didn't wait long. I wonder who—got there first?"

Roger made no reply. The short paragraph had mentioned no name but that of Oscar Tenby.

"Come on out and say good-bye," said Paul suddenly, in the tone he had used when he came into the room. "Then I can get away."

Roger went out and Paul waited a moment, looking at the letter in his hand. He tore it across deliberately, crushed the pieces in his hand and dropped them into the waste-paper basket.

.   .   .   .   .   .

Lady Warne's departure was quiet and orderly. Her car was brought round and, with a brief word of farewell to Ruth and Roger and a nod to Brenda, she was assisted in and the large vehicle rolled smoothly away. Rameses, from the seat beside his mistress, turned his head for a parting look.

Lady Warne leaned against the comfortable cushions and looked absently through the window. She was glad to leave the house—she had come purely from curiosity, as her niece had surmised, but she had failed to take into consideration the associations the house held for her. Her brother's memory had, more than once, risen to disturb her, and she wished she had stayed away.

She was still feeling shaken from her night's alarm but as the house, with its inmates and memories, receded she found herself growing steadier. She opened her bag and took out the envelope into which she had put Paul's cheque, looking at it with a faint feeling of wonder at having so lost her sense of proportion. In the afternoon light, seated in her warm, comfortable car, the terrors of the night seemed childish and stupid. She had actually, she told herself, allowed her imagination to run away. She would destroy the cheque and forget the whole unpleasant experience.

She looked into her bag and, with a little tremor, brought out the picture which had done the mischief.

It was the first time she had seen it by daylight, and she found it grim indeed. The yawning grave—the money bags—the arms outstretched in a vain effort to reach the gold . . . Lady Warne found herself shuddering once more. She looked more closely at the face in the sketch, and stiffened as she thought she discerned in it some slight resemblance to her own.

Herself . . . in the cold, cold ground . . .

The car passed under a railway bridge, and a sudden shadow fell on the occupants. Lady Warne glanced up in terror, and in the same instant the face of Paul Mallard flashed by her.

Her heart pounding, she uttered a choking cry and putting out a hand, clutched the speaking-tube fixed to the side of the car. She held the mouthpiece and attempted to speak into it, but could utter no words.

She dropped the tube and, with a series of twists and pulls, shifted herself forward on the deeply-sprung seat and, leaning across, tapped on the glass partition. The chauffeur glanced round, saw his mistress's ashy face and brought the car to a stop. He turned and slid the partition open.

" Are you all right, m'lady? " he asked anxiously.

Lady Warne was far from all right, but she took no notice of the query. She was holding a letter in her hand and fumbling awkwardly to detach a stamp from a little booklet. Handing the stamp and the letter to the man, she spoke in a thick voice.

" Next pillar-box," she said. " Put it in."

The man opened his mouth to make a further anxious enquiry, but Lady Warne leaned back in her seat and, with a peremptory wave, motioned him on.

He drove slowly, passing through a village a little way ahead. Halting at its tiny post office, he got out of the car and looked questioningly at his mistress.

"Post it," she ordered.

The chauffeur dropped the letter into the box and took his place in the car, turning for one more glance behind him.

" May I get you a drink, m'lady? " he asked.

Lady Warne wanted nothing, but the man was relieved to see her colour returning. Her manner was almost normal as she settled herself in her seat and tidied the articles in her bag.

" Wait," she said suddenly.

She stooped and picked up a paper from the floor, tearing it and crushing it into a ball. She handed it to the man and indicated that he was to throw it into the road.

The crumpled paper fell, was caught by the wind and whirled against a wall. It lay there, mud-stained and torn. Nobody would have recognized it for an original Lenner. . . .

CHAPTER XIX

THE owners of River Lodge passed the rest of the day quietly but busily. It was odd to have the house full one moment and empty the next. To-morrow it would be full again—and so it would go on.

" Do you like the empty feeling? " Ruth asked her husband.

"Yes," replied Roger. "They go, but they leave their money behind."

"We didn't have any murders," commented Brenda in a disappointed tone. "Nothing at all."

"We had a kidnapped aunt," said Ruth. "That was exciting enough."

"No, it wasn't," denied Brenda. "We didn't know anything about it until it was all over—only Roger and Paul."

At the mention of Paul's name a sober silence fell on the party. The car was back, but nothing had been seen of its driver. Roger stood for a moment wondering whether he ought to go up and look for his brother, but decided there was little he could do to help.

"What's become of Martin West?" he asked.

"He went out after lunch," said Brenda. "Felicity's up in her room—she's been there practically all day—packing, I think."

It was not until almost time for dinner that Paul made his appearance. Ruth met him and put a question.

"You're dining in our room, aren't you, Paul? It's your last night," she said.

"Thanks," said Paul. "I'd like to."

His manner at dinner was pleasant and easy, with no sign of strain.

"I passed Aunt Ella's car," he said. "At least, I think I did. I was doing about seventy on the way back, so I didn't really get a chance of a good look."

"Any confusion getting Aunt Emmie off?" asked Roger.

"All plain sailing," replied Paul, "except at one point when she saw a policeman and thought he might be the one who'd been so kind to her at Paddington. She wanted to go and make sure, but I dragged her firmly on."

"Poor Aunt Emmie," said Ruth.

"Poor Uncle George," corrected Paul. "The old boy nearly goes off his head, and you can't blame him. She never gives any indication that she's going to move in a new direction—she's going along quite steadily and then she gets an idea and without saying a word to anybody she changes her direction slightly and when you look round, she's out of sight."

"Can you wonder," said Ruth, "that Uncle George doesn't often go travelling with her? It's like taking out a toddling child—you think it can't get far, but if you take your eyes off it for long, it manages to disappear."

"I made up a piece of poetry about her," said Roger with a modest air.

"Proceed," invited Brenda.

> "*I'm going to be a father*
> *And that is all I know,*
> *I'm going to be a father—*
> *Aunt Emmie told me so,*"

recited Roger.

"You're coming on," applauded Brenda. "D'you remember the Valentine you wrote at the age of fifteen?"

"I never wrote a Valentine in my life," denied Roger stoutly.

"Oh, yes, you did," said Brenda. "You showed it to your mother and she told me about it. It went something like——

> "*I'm awfully keen*
> *On Josephine*
> *I'd like to lean*
> *On Josephine.*"

"Who was Josephine?" asked Ruth.

"I remember Josephine," said Paul. "She was at the fat stage and they used to make her ride to try and get it down and she used to go slumping up and down like a sack—I can't imagine what Roger saw in her."

"That wasn't Josephine—that was Jean," corrected Roger. "Josephine was the one who took singing lessons—we used to wait until she passed and then——"

" My God, yes!" said Paul. "We used to say Mee-Mee-Mee-Mee-Mee in squeaky voices and then sing arpeggios. Didn't her father come and make a fuss about it? "

"'Fuss' doesn't quite cover it," said Roger. "I often wonder whether she took it up as a career."

There was a pause, and Roger looked at his brother.

"Speaking of careers," he said slowly. "Have you got any—plans? What are you going to do if you don't get—well—fixed? "

"Do? " said Paul lightly. "Oh—there're lots of openings, you know. Cooking, dress-making, road-mending . . ."

"Oh, don't joke, Paul, please," begged Ruth. "You see, we've been wondering——"

She stopped and looked at her husband. Roger continued.

"We've been wondering," he said, "whether you'd consider coming in with us—you know—cutting in and seeing what you could make out of it. What d'you think? "

Paul looked round, his eyes taking in the affectionate anxiety on the faces of those before him. He smiled suddenly, and the three watching him caught a glimpse of the old Paul—gay, affectionate, happy and extra-ordinarily attractive.

"Thanks," he said. "It's—well, thanks. But—don't think I don't appreciate the efforts of the rescue squad —I'm going to be all right."

"But if you don't—get anything? " asked Ruth.

"Don't be silly," said Paul. "Don't you know that all good actors have to starve? "

"I see," said Ruth.

Paul, looking round at the happier expressions on the faces of his relations, felt that he must be something of an actor, after all. He was a little doubtful about Roger, but Ruth and Brenda were certainly feeling reassured.

Roger rose to his feet and looked at his brother. "Come and have a cigarette in the garden," he invited. "It doesn't look too promising, but it's mild."

They went outside and paced slowly up and down the grass, talking between thoughtful pauses.

"I forgot to say I'm glad about being made an uncle," said Paul. "Nice going."

Roger agreed. The two walked for some minutes in silence. "It's a funny thing," observed Roger after some time. "When you came down here I was a bit worried in case you—well—stirred up mud. I thought you'd get hold of Liss and——"

He paused.

"Well?" prompted Paul.

"Well, now I'm feeling sorry that you didn't," said Roger. "I feel I might have done a bit more to—to patch things up," he ended awkwardly.

"There's nothing," said Paul, "to patch up."

"I see," said Roger, hoping to see still more.

"Liss," went on Paul obligingly, "told me a long time ago to—to—to keep off and I—kept off."

"I see," said Roger, this time with greater accuracy. "Well, you know your own business best, but I wish——"

He came to an abrupt stop. They had turned the corner of the house and were approaching the terrace. Before them, outlined in the darkness, stood Martin West and Felicity. They were close together, and Felicity was looking up and speaking in a low, urgent tone.

The two watchers turned and went back the way they had come. Neither spoke for some time. At last Roger turned towards the house.

"Coming in?" he asked.

Paul hesitated and then turned and followed his brother indoors. They walked into the library, and Paul, refusing the offer of a drink, sat down and stared into the fire. Roger sat in a chair opposite, trying to think of a subject which would rouse his brother from his abstraction and failing to find one.

Time passed as both men sat dreaming in their chairs. Roger felt almost ashamed of his own happiness—he was sitting here, he reflected, debating the merits of various preparatory schools while Paul brooded unhappily on the girl who was still out on the terrace with another man.

After some time, Roger rose.

"I'm going up," he said. "Will you change your mind about that drink?"

Paul shook his head.

"No, thanks," he said. "I'll stay here for a bit and then turn in."

Roger nodded and went out of the room, and Paul raised his head and looked bleakly in the direction of the terrace. He leaned forward with his elbows on his knees and, resting his head in his hand, remained motionless for some time.

The sound of light footsteps roused him. He rose and waited tensely for a few moments, expecting Felicity to come into the room. The footsteps passed, however, and he heard her go through the drawing-room and up the stairs.

Paul looked once more towards the terrace. She had come in alone . . . and Martin West was out there. . . .

He walked to the door leading on to the terrace and opened it. The light shone out and beyond its gleam he could see the figure of Martin West.

A few drops of rain began to fall.

Beyond, on the lawn, a prowling tom cat, stalking his love, gave a low and unmusical howl.

"Shut up," said Martin West in a low, fierce growl.

The cat responded with a repetition of the howl in a higher key and Martin, stooping, picked up a small clod of earth and hurled it at random. An offended mew proved that the missile had found its target.

Paul put his shoulders back and took a deep, lung-filling breath. The fellow, he thought savagely, had taken Felicity from him. He had blasted his hopes and ruined his career. He had strutted for the past week like a prize bull in the ring. He had done all this, and gone unpunished.

But when it came to shying stones at the cat . . .

Paul stepped on to the terrace and walked forward steadily . . .

.   .   .   .

Roger went upstairs to find his wife sitting before her dressing-table patting cream on to her face and talking to Brenda, who sat on the edge of a bed.

" Aren't you tired? " he enquired of his cousin.

" I'm not going yet, if that's what you mean," responded Brenda.

" You haven't done the lights yet, have you? " asked Ruth.

" No," said Roger. " Paul's still up, and Martin and Liss are out on the terrace having a prolonged discussion about—well about whatever people do talk about on moonlit terraces."

" There's not much moonlit about it," commented Brenda, " and if they don't want to get wet they'd better come in—it's going to rain."

" I don't suppose they'll notice," said Roger in a voice that sounded a little depressed and brought the eyes of both women to his face. " I don't know how it is," he went on morosely—" I think perhaps we're all a bit prejudiced, being closely related to Paul, but I'm damned if I don't honestly think he's a better partner for Liss than West is. I like Martin, but if I'd been a girl—and a girl of Liss's age—I don't think I could have overlooked Paul's appeal."

" I don't think she did," said Brenda. " I think if he'd lifted a finger during the past week, she'd have been round his neck and then all this silly mess would have been cleared up. I can't think what's got into them both," she mourned. " You hear a lot of talk about the young moderns—there's nothing, you gather, that they're afraid to talk about, and they've swept all the old reticences away and so on—but look at these two. Both in love, as far as I can see, and one of them going to marry someone else and the other——"

She stopped, and the three fell into a gloomy silence.

"I was hoping," said Ruth at last, "that Goosey might have done something."

"Goosey!" exclaimed Brenda and Roger together in the same tone of horror. "Goosey?" went on Roger. "Why, if he'd tried his fatheaded methods on this muddle, then the whole thing would have gone right up the chimney."

"I suppose so," agreed Ruth unwillingly. "But he did get as far as finding out that there was something between Paul and Liss, and I wouldn't have said he was a person to go away without trying to straighten things out."

"Well, thank God he didn't try," said Roger. "Things are bad enough this way. I don't want to seem inhospitable," he went on politely to his cousin, "but how about clearing out? I want to undress."

"Who's stopping you?" enquired Brenda. "You've got a perfectly good dressing-room, haven't you? Considering," she went on, "that I've undressed you myself scores of times when you were a tiddly little fellow——"

The door of the dressing-room shut with a crash, and Brenda grinned at Ruth.

"He used to be a sweet little thing," she told her. "Very serious and quite equal to kicking your shins if you annoyed him, but very sweet. And Paul was—oh, he was angelic," she said, getting to her feet with a heavy sigh. "And now look at him—miserable and unhappy——"

"I tell you what," said Ruth, turning round on the stool and facing her. "Let's get hold of Liss in the morning—you and I—and see if we can make her tell us anything. I told Roger I wouldn't, but——"

"Oh—Roger!" said Brenda contemptuously— "Why——"

She stopped, observing that her cousin, in shirt

sleeves, had opened the door of the dressing-room and stood waiting for her to finish her remark.

"You were saying——? " he asked.

"I was saying," Brenda informed him, "that if you'd been a decent brother instead of a selfish pig, the whole thing could have been straightened out in the last few days."

"Ah," said Roger.

"Ah, yourself," replied Brenda. "Good night, darling," she said to Ruth.

"Good night, darling," returned Roger, his head coming round the door to watch his cousin make a stormy exit.

"Nice woman," he observed sardonically as the bedroom door crashed behind her.

"Sometimes," said Ruth enigmatically, "she hits the nail on the head."

Her husband looked at her and completed his undressing in silence. He put on a dressing-gown and went downstairs to put off the lights, passing Felicity's room as he went and hearing sounds which told him she had come upstairs.

He looked into the library—it was empty, but the light was still burning. Roger switched it off and went round the rest of the rooms. There was nobody in them. Paul and Martin, he presumed, had gone up to bed.

He put his hand on the switch in the hall, when a sound from the direction of the garden door made him pause.

"Anybody there? " he asked.

There was no reply, and Roger went across the hall to investigate. He approached the door leading into the garden and came to a dead stop.

Martin West was standing in the open doorway. His hair was wet, his coat mud-stained and torn, his shirt disordered, and his tie hanging loosely. He put up a hand to his collar and Roger saw blood on the knuckles.

"Where's Paul? " asked Roger quietly.

Martin replied in a voice as steady as his own.

"He's outside," he answered. "On the bench. I told you," he ended expressionlessly, "that he was a bloody fool."

Roger, opening his mouth to ask how Martin was, shut it again. It was obvious that he was all right. Roger had seen him box many times—there was no need to wonder how he would fare against Paul, who had never been able to use his fists in his life.

"If I were you," went on Martin slowly, "I'd go and —and get him in."

Roger went to the door and Martin put out a hand to detain him.

"I'm sorry," he said. "He started it. He followed me out and I had to keep him off, but I didn't—do much." He looked round. "Is there—anybody about?" he asked.

"Nobody," replied Roger. "Can I get you anything?"

Martin shook his head. "See to—to that madman out there," he said. "I'm going up—I'm all right."

He went towards the stairs, and Roger went through the door and into the garden. The rain had stopped, but the grass soaked through his slippers. He went towards the bench but could see no figure on it. He stopped and called softly.

"Paul," he said.

There was a moment's pause, and he heard his brother's voice.

"Here," said Paul.

Roger moved across in the direction of the voice. Paul was standing beside the bench, one hand holding the back of it.

"I suppose," he said slowly, as Roger came up, "Martin sent you out?"

"Yes," said Roger. "What the hell," he asked, "did you have to do this for?"

"Is he—all right?" said Paul.

"Of course he's all right," said Roger savagely. "You

don't think you could do anything to a man of his weight
and skill that would stop him from being all right, do
you? "

" No," said Paul quietly. " I only wanted to—to
smash his face in. Did I do that? "

" His face," said Roger, " is dirty but undamaged.
Now for God's sake will you come inside? "

They turned towards the house and Roger, putting
out a hand, steadied his brother.

" You needn't do that," said Paul, " I can walk.
Just," he added grimly.

They neared the door which Roger had left open
and by the beam shining into the garden Roger could
see his brother's face. He suppressed an exclamation
and shut his mouth in a grim line.

They went into the house and upstairs, Paul pausing
at the door of his own room. Roger held his arm firmly
and led him on.

" I can——" began Paul.

" For God's sake shut up," said Roger, " and come
on."

He entered his dressing-room from the corridor and,
pulling out a chair for Paul, went through into the
bedroom. Ruth was lying in bed, reading.

" I've got Paul in there," said Roger quietly, jerking
his head towards the dressing-room. " He went out
and—and tackled Martin. He wants cleaning up—will
you come? "

Ruth, without a word, slipped out of bed and got
into the dressing-gown Roger held for her. She hurried
into the dressing-room and stood for a moment gazing
down at the mud-stained, bloody figure in the chair.
Then she went through the room and tried a door on
the other side. It was locked.

" Where's the key, Roger? " she asked.

" What are you——" began Roger.

" If you'll go through the other way and open this
door," said Ruth, " we'll put him in there for the
night."

" In where? " asked Paul.

"Oh, it's the room Uncle George and Aunt Emmie had," explained Ruth. "You're not going back to your room to-night in that state. Get his pyjamas, Roger," she went on.

"And get him a drink too," put in Paul.

Roger went out and Ruth, going to the medicine cupboard, began to take out cotton-wool and bandages.

" I'm sorry about this," said Paul.

" I'm sorry, too," said Ruth. " I mean, I'm sorry it isn't Martin West I'm patching up. But—thanks for trying."

There was the sound of a key turning and Roger entered through the inner door. He held a pair of pyjamas and a drink in his hand.

"Why," he asked, as he stood watching Ruth, " did it have to finish up like this? "

Paul frowned and then flinched as Ruth dabbed iodine on a cut.

" I don't know, quite," he said. " He was out there with Liss for a long time, and then she went upstairs and I went out and—well, we talked a bit and then I didn't think that was getting us anywhere and I hit him. After that . . . I don't remember much after that," he confessed. " Next thing I remember is being on the bench—I suppose he put me there."

" Well, I knew you were a bloody——" began Roger.

"Oh, for goodness' sake, Roger," interrupted Ruth, "please stop bullying and stop saying bloody all the time. Go and run the bath," she ordered, " and help Paul off with those filthy clothes."

Roger, with a cold glance, obeyed her, and before long Paul was settled comfortably in bed in the adjoining room.

"Good night, Ruth," he said, as his sister-in-law put out his light and prepared to leave. " And thanks."

"Thank *you*," said Ruth. " Better luck next time."

She went into her own room, got into bed and sat clasping her knees and brooding over the incident.

"I'm going down to put the hall light out," said Roger. "I might come up supporting another bloody —I mean bloody—warrior, so I'd keep awake for a bit if I were you."

He went downstairs, locked the garden door and put out the lower light. With one foot on the stairs to ascend, he stopped and gave a growl of impatience. On the landing above, Felicity stood looking down at him anxiously. She came down the stairs in a swift little run and stood beside him, and Roger studied her with a sour gaze.

"What're you walking about the house like that for?" he enquired.

Felicity glanced down at her attire. She wore wide-legged pyjamas of a material patterned with little Chinese pagodas, and a short, heavy Mandarin coat of brilliant blue. Her hair hung about her shoulders, and Roger understood with a pang what Paul was going through.

"I'm not walking about the house," said Felicity, answering his question. "I'm looking for Paul."

"I see," said Roger. "Well, while you're staying here I'd be glad if you wouldn't walk about at this time of night looking for Paul—or anybody else—in that—that rig-out."

"You're in pyjamas yourself," pointed out Felicity.

"Never mind me," said Roger coldly. "You go to bed."

"I can't," said Felicity. "I'm worried about Paul. He——"

"Well, go to bed and worry in the morning," ordered Roger.

Felicity looked at him with something like irritation on her lovely face.

"I'm serious, Roger, you don't seem to understand," she said. "I've got something to say to Paul and I came to find him but he wasn't in his room and——"

"Oh, he wasn't?" said Roger. "Well, you——"

"No, he wasn't," said Felicity, "and I waited for a

bit and then I looked out and I saw Martin and—oh, Roger," she went on, "I'm sure something's wrong because he looked—peculiar, and there was mud on him and I can't find Paul—— Oh! what do you think could have happened to him?"

"Why didn't you ask Martin?" said Roger.

"Because I—well, I couldn't," said Felicity lamely.

"Why not?" demanded Roger. "You've been chatting to him for a whole week without stopping— one more question wouldn't have mattered, surely?"

Felicity's face paled. She stared at him for a moment and then spoke coldly.

"Do you know where Paul is?" she asked.

"Yes, I do," said Roger. "He's in bed. Nicely and comfortably in bed. I'll tell him he missed the Chinese pyjamas and the little Chink coat. Now you'd better go to bed before Martin catches you having a tête-à-tête with me in that stir-up-the-boys attire."

Felicity turned without a word and went up the stairs. Half-way up, however, she paused, turned and came down again.

"Look," she said, "I think I know how you feel, but you're—you're—oh, Roger," she begged, "do help me. All I want is to see Paul for just a few minutes."

"I'm not stopping you," said Roger. "But nobody can get a fellow out of bed at this time of night. You can tell him the news in the morning. If it's what I think it is, you won't have to tell him—he's probably guessed it, poor devil."

Felicity came a step nearer and spoke in a low voice.

"You're a mean, selfish pig," she said slowly, "and any girl who—who loved Paul would think twice before she married him and got you for a—a brother-in-law."

"Oh, is that why you hesitated?" said Roger. "It wouldn't have been because Paul hasn't a job, for instance?"

"Paul," stated Felicity, "has got a job."

"Paul," said Roger, "has not got a job. He wrote to Oscar Whoever-he-was and before he posted the letter

I saw a bit in the paper saying the house was full and they'd closed the doors."

"You saw what?" asked Felicity in amazement.

"You heard me," said Roger.

"Didn't it give any names?" asked Felicity.

"None. We weren't very much interested in names, anyhow," said Roger. "We can take a hint. Paul didn't get the part."

"Paul," said Felicity, "did get the part."

"Did get what?" asked Roger blankly.

"You heard me," said Felicity.

"I tell you," said Roger, "that I read the paper myself. The cast was complete."

"Of course it was," said Felicity. "Paul completed it."

Roger stared at her.

"I can see you're Chinese," he said, "but I can't speak the language. Can't you talk plain English?"

"I rang up Oscar Tenby myself," said Felicity. "When I went in with Ruth into Petsham I told him that Paul would—would take the part."

"Oh," said Roger, "you did? And why couldn't Paul have been left to do a thing like that for himself?"

"Because Paul," said Felicity, "was in a moody state, and when he's in a moody state he doesn't think sensibly. And he's got people round him who won't lift a finger to help him or advise him and who go round doing nothing whatsoever and merely saying they won't do a thing about it because it isn't their business. Their business, obviously, is to sit by and do nothing while their brother makes a mess of his life, and of—of other people's lives. Their business is to snap and bully and say 'Go to bed,' when one bit of help would clear everything up and make everybody happy. Their business——"

"I've looked on for a week," said Roger, "watching you playing Martin West against Paul. I know those monkey-up-a-stick methods. It's a good thing," he went on grimly, "that Ruth didn't try to make a monkey out of me."

"She didn't have to try," said Felicity. "And I wasn't playing anybody against anybody. If you think that all men leave a girl alone and go away just because she asks them to when she's angry, then you're mistaken. Only people like Paul go on remembering things you never meant to say, and are—are sorry for——"

"You stood out on that terrace for an hour this evening——" began Roger.

"Telling Martin what I want to tell Paul, now," said Felicity. "That I can't act, and that Paul was right. That I'm not going to go on acting and that Paul is. That I can't cook but I can learn. That—that I can't marry Paul unless he asks me, but I'm willing to be asked. That even if it means having to have you as the uncle of my children—even then, I'm willing to be asked." She took a step forward, and Roger moved back involuntarily. "Where—is—Paul?" she demanded fiercely.

Roger hesitated. Paul had been beaten by his rival. He was in bed with his face half hidden by bandages. It was scarcely the moment to introduce a vision in Chinese pyjamas and a flaming temper.

"I'm sorry," he said. "In the morning——"

"I'll go to Paul's room," stated Felicity, "and wait there, if I have to wait all night."

Roger watched her go up the stairs.

"You will have to wait all night," he informed her.

. . . .

Ruth looked up from her snug, warm bed as her husband entered the room.

"Everything all right, darling?" she asked.

Roger sat wearily on his bed, shrugged himself out of his dressing-gown and yawned noisily.

"Lord!" he said. "I'm whacked. If this is a sample week of hotel-keeping, I'm not going to last long."

He got into bed, squirmed down between the bedclothes with a contented sigh, switched off his light and closed his eyes.

"Roger," said Ruth.

"Well, what?" answered Roger.

"Goosey said something about having told Aunt Ella a story—he said, 'I told Lady Warne the story of the two chairs.' Which story would he have meant?"

"Never heard of two chairs," grunted Roger.

"Well, but he said two chairs," persisted Ruth.

"Rot. Three bears," said Roger, giving the bed-clothes a final pull.

There was a long silence, and he felt himself wafted gently on waves of sleepiness.

"Roger," said Ruth.

Roger gave a wrathful exclamation.

"Well, what the hell now?" he enquired irritably.

"Well, you haven't drawn the curtains," said Ruth, "and you haven't kissed me good night."

"Well, can't you draw the curtains?" demanded Roger, "instead of waking me up to do it?"

"Of course I can draw the curtains," said Ruth gently, "but I can hardly kiss myself good night, can I?"

Overcome by this reasoning, Roger swore and, throwing back the bedclothes, went to the window and drew the curtains. He kissed his wife and climbed into bed once more, realizing as he did so the hollowness of her argument.

He had just dropped into a heavy sleep when a little cry from Ruth roused him. He sat up, his heart pounding, and felt for the light switch.

"What's the matter?" he asked, looking across at her anxiously and blinking in the light. "Are you all right? What is it?"

"I'm all right," said Ruth, sitting up and staring at him with round eyes. "I only——"

"What the hell is this?" ground out Roger, alarm giving way to anger. "I came up here to get some sleep. I——"

"Ssh!" said Ruth, holding up a hand. "I thought I heard something. In—in Aunt Emmie's room."

Roger sat up and listened intently. From the room next door came a low, continuous murmur, sometimes broken by a little laugh. With an unprintable oath, he flung back the clothes and strode through his dressing-room.

"Oh, Roger, do be careful," called Ruth anxiously, "they——"

Past all caution, Roger threw open the door of the adjacent room, and glared at the picture before him.

On her knees beside Paul was Felicity, her arms about his neck and her lips close to his. She looked up at Roger's entrance and then continued her murmuring in Paul's ear.

"Out," said Roger.

"He says out," said Felicity. "Shall I go out, darling?"

"He's quite capable of kicking you out," said Paul. "Perhaps you'd better."

"Out," repeated Roger in a higher key.

Felicity put her lips on Paul's in a lingering kiss, and rose to her feet. Roger strode to the farther door and opened it for her.

"You see, Roger——" she began.

"Out," roared Roger.

Felicity, with a little grimace, went out and Roger shut the door and locked it. He walked back and stood for a moment looking down at his brother.

"I'm very——" he began.

"Out," requested Paul.

Roger went back to his room and Ruth looked at him.

"What was all the shouting?" she asked.

"Oh, nothing," said Roger, getting into bed.

"Well, what were they doing?" asked Ruth.

"They weren't doing anything," said Roger. "She was kneeling by him and kissing all the parts of his face you hadn't wrapped up."

"I see," mused Ruth. "And what was Paul doing?"

Roger regarded her disgustedly.

"Paul," he said, "was embracing her fervently and —and he was burying his face in her neck. Does that satisfy your thirst for nauseating detail?"

"Not quite," said Ruth, "but I suppose it'll have to wait till the morning."

"You're sure I can go to sleep now?" asked Roger.

"Quite sure," said Ruth. "God bless."

"Mm, Mm," returned Roger.

He put out the light and turned over. From the other bed came a soft, seductive coo.

"Roger," said Ruth.

Roger clutched the bedclothes and drew them protectively about his neck.

"Not to-night," he muttered. "Some other——"

"About the baby's name——" said Ruth.

Roger relaxed with a grunt.

"I thought," she continued, "we could call him——"

"For the love of heaven," besought Roger, "go to sleep. That's all fixed up and settled. Ian, Roger, Beddington, Mallard. Now pipe down."

Ruth lay in the darkness, staring up at the ceiling.

"Ian, Roger," she murmured happily. "Ian . . . Roger . . . Beddington . . . Mallard. . . ."